WEB OF FEAR

GLENMORE PARK BOOK 3

MIKE OMER

WEB OF FEAR

All rights reserved.

© 2016 by Mike Omer
Cover art Copyright © 2016 by Deranged Doctor Design

This book is a work of fiction. Names, characters, and incidents are product of the author's imagination or are used fictitiously. Any resemblance to actual events, locales, living or dead, is coincidental.

All rights reserved. Except as permitted by the U.S. Copyright Act of 1976, no part of this publication may be reproduced, distributed, or transmitted in any form or by any means, or stored in a database or retrieval system, without prior written permission of the publisher/author.

Printed in the United States of America

ISBN-13: 978-1539360971 paperback

For Shira

ONE

The merry-go-round turned slowly in the chilly wind, emitting a high-pitched squeak in the dark playground. Gracie Durham stared at it, shivering in the cold, wishing she was home in her warm bed. Instead, she sat on the double-sided swing, Abby in front of her. The swingset was a bit rusty, its yellow paint peeling to reveal a blackened metallic tinge underneath. Gracie exhaled, her breath clouding in the crisp night air.

"I don't think he's coming, Abby," she said.

"He'll come," Abby said, biting her lip.

"Did he text you?"

Abby checked her phone. "No. But he'll come. I mean … it's only five past eight."

It was Saint Patrick's Day. The streets were rife with drunken grownups laughing and hollering. Gracie saw one man throwing up on the corner of a building. A few minutes later, a hugging couple zigzagged their way past her, the guy's hand in the girl's pants. Gracie hoped she'd never grow up to be so disgusting. She was relieved to leave the festivities behind them, as they turned toward the playground on Babel Lane, where Abby and Noel had agreed to meet.

Gracie wished they'd met during the afternoon, instead of the evening. Neither Gracie nor Abby were allowed to go out this late on a school night, and if Gracie's parents found out she wasn't home, they'd kill her. But she'd promised Abby, and … well, Abby had always been there for her. Abby had stood up to Tara and her friends when they bullied Gracie about her clothes. Last year, in fifth grade, she'd taken the blame when Mrs. Moreno caught them cheating, even though it was Gracie's fault. She was always supportive about Gracie's music.

Abby was an amazing friend. The least Gracie could do was come with her to meet Noel.

She looked around her, hugging herself; the swing rocked them both. Abby and Gracie had spent many afternoons in this playground. Abby claimed they'd met for the first time on the merry-go-round, though Gracie was pretty sure they'd actually met in school, during lunch. Regardless, they'd played here for hours when they were smaller, swinging on the swings, sliding down and climbing up the slide, even though you were supposed to use the ladder. When they grew up, they'd still hang out there, talking about school, music, boys, books, whatever. Just talking and talking. Sometimes sharing Skittles, or Reese's, or (once Abby's mother forbade her to eat candy every day) apples.

Seeing the playground at night was a whole different story. There were only two street lights, and the playground equipment cast eerie, long shadows. The only sound was the occasional squeak from the merry-go-round. During the day, the squeaking was kinda funny, and kids turned the thing faster and faster to get the pitch even higher. But now it was unpleasant, making Gracie's skin prickle. Patches of snow dotted the ground, white-blue in the shadowy darkness.

The swingset's metal frame was cold beyond belief, and it froze Gracie's ass through the thick pants she wore. She fidgeted, trying to sit on her coat as much as she could.

"Anything?" she finally asked.

Abby checked the screen again, her face momentarily lit by it. "No," she said, her voice subdued.

"We need to go, Abby. He probably couldn't make it."

Abby was shivering slightly as well. "Yeah," she said, the disappointment in her voice palpable. "Let's go."

Gracie had a feeling Abby was about to cry. She'd talked about this evening for the past three days, so excited to finally meet Noel. Gracie would console her friend later, but now they had to walk home before they froze. She leaped down from the swing and held out a hand for Abby, facing the adjacent park as she did so. The dark trees hid the city lights beyond them.

When a tall figure appeared, walking toward them on the path from the park, Gracie was startled. He moved strangely, his pacing careful, and she tensed, a foreign thought blinking in her consciousness: *He doesn't want us to hear him.* It took her another second to realize she couldn't see his face—not because of the darkness, but because he wore a ski mask.

By that point he was already moving much faster.

"Abby ... Run!" Gracie shrieked.

Abby hesitated in confusion. Gracie, still holding her hand, pulled her and ran toward the street. When she glanced backward, the man was much closer than before, his feet a blur. Her mind registered an assortment of little details. A small object in his hand, a glimpse of white. His eyes, narrowing as he chased them, flickering in the darkness. Their long shadows, cast on the path, holding hands. A larger shadow looming over them, getting closer and closer.

Abby's speed picked up. She'd always been the athletic one, quicker and stronger than Gracie. Now she was the one pulling Gracie, not the other way around.

They neared the exit to the street. From there, it was just a short dash to the open gas station across the road, and they'd be safe.

A dark van came hurtling down the road in front of them, its engine roaring. Its front wheels thumped as it hit the sidewalk; its brakes screeched and it came to a halt, blocking the exit. The door swung open, and another figure got out. A ski mask hid his face as well.

Gracie screamed in fear as the man in front of them rushed forward. Behind them, she could hear the thudding steps of their pursuer, intermingling with the thudding of her own heart. Abby almost didn't hesitate, veering right, getting off the path, running through the icy frozen ground of the park. She didn't let go of Gracie, yanking her along behind. They were both stumbling, panting. Gracie tried to talk, couldn't, her lungs burning, fear clenching her throat. There was nothing to do but run.

The ground became muddy, slippery, uneven. Gracie's foot twisted; she faltered, losing her grip on Abby's hand, and then they were running apart. Gracie, lagging behind, found her voice. "Help!" she screamed. "Somebody help us!"

A crazy idea materialized in her brain. Perhaps she could climb a tree before they caught her. She was a good climber.

There was a large tree not far from her and she pivoted right, ran toward it. She could see that both pursuers were still going after Abby, but one of them glanced in her direction, predatory eyes following her movement. Gracie's eyes frantically looked for a low branch to grab, but it was too dark to see anything, let alone climb a tree.

Despair overtook her.

The ground was sleek, a mix of mud and sludgy ice. She slipped, stumbled, fell, trying to protect her head, but she was slow, her hands failing to move in time, and she crashed head first into the tree, the blinding pain consuming her.

Detective Hannah Shor had swiped right earlier that evening, and now found herself in the midst of a date with an unemployed twenty-five-year old man in a leprechaun hat. She wasn't sure what was more upsetting: that Bob Mills thought it would be cute to show up to the date with the hat, or that she hadn't terminated the date as soon as she saw it. It was fraud, pure and simple. He hadn't had a leprechaun hat in his photo, nor had he mentioned it anywhere in his bio or tagline. He'd just said he was friendly and fun, and liked dogs.

To be fair, below the hat he was the perfect eye candy. He was six years younger than her, with carelessly shaggy blond hair and wide shoulders. When he went to the bathroom, she verified that he had a cute ass as well. She was willing to forgive and forget the whole leprechaun hat thing. He *had* removed it immediately after sitting down, after all.

He smiled at her with perfect teeth, and she smiled back, brushing aside a strand of her frazzled brown hair. She hoped she looked as if she was just casual and easygoing, and not as if she hadn't had time to shower, put on makeup, or even take a good look in the mirror—which was the case.

Then he began to speak.

Bob Mills was suffering from what Hannah called Owl syndrome. Named after the owl in *Winnie the Pooh*, Owl syndrome inflicted people with the feeling they knew everything, and that their knowledge had to be shared with everyone. It was a dreary disease, but almost never lethal, except for extreme cases.

Bob was getting less and less attractive by the minute.

He knew things about Saint Patrick's Day, which he shared. He asked her why she hadn't dressed for the holiday. She avoided the obvious answer—she thought St. Patrick's

Day was dumb—and said instead that she was Jewish. It turned out that Bob knew things about Judaism. And about Israel. There was a whole monologue about the Middle East situation, during which her mind detached as she sailed down memory lane, comparing this date with other terrible dates. It ranked a seven-point-five on the David Ferguson Meter, a scale based on her worst date ever, which had included bad sex, a ruined shirt, and a lot of sobbing … on his part.

She looked around her in despair. The people in the bar were clearly enjoying themselves, almost as if they didn't care she was on a bad date. A group of pretty twenty-year-old girls cheered as one of their friends drank a whole mug of beer, spilling half on her top. At another table, a couple had the nerve to be *holding hands*, as if to spite her. The waitresses were walking around smiling, wearing green wigs to celebrate the Irish holiday, serving beer to their happy customers. Saint Patrick's Day was probably a fantastic day for tips. And here she was, stuck with Mr. "Let me tell you about the *real* issue with imported vegetables," seriously considering getting up and leaving.

The problem was, Hannah was bored and lonely, and wanted to find someone to banish a face she'd been seeing a lot in her dreams lately. Mitchell Lonnie, one of the detectives in her squad, had begun seeping into her mind at random moments, and her face would heat up when she thought about him. This would not do. She had to start dating.

Bob Mills, when he shut up, looked like someone she could have some fun with. Perhaps it would be best if she suggested they go to her place before he lost the few shreds of sexual attraction he still had going for him.

But then he started to talk about the Glenmore Park Police Department, and the date was officially doomed. Its score was now eight-point-five David Ferguson.

The police force in Glenmore Park, Bob explained as Hannah nodded in interest, was useless. Glenmore Park had one of the highest crime rates in Massachusetts, and Bob knew firsthand that this was due to police corruption and ineptitude.

"That's terrible," Hannah said.

"They have all this budget … did you know that the Glenmore Park cops are the highest-paid cops in the entire state?"

"Outrageous," Hannah said. "You'd think they'd try to keep us safe, at least."

"Right? I was fined last month for speeding. I swear, I was driving just under the speed limit. I could have fought it in court, but you know how it is. Choose your battles, right?"

"Absolutely. You don't want to go up against a corrupt police force in court." Hannah shook her head in sadness at the deplorable state of the law. "I mean … they probably have all the judges in their pockets."

"Probably? I'd say definitely."

Hannah wondered why she didn't have an extraction plan. Every woman had a friend who called an hour into the date, a phone call that could potentially be turned into an emergency if the occasion mandated. But not Hannah Shor. No … Hannah Shor went into every date as if it was the real thing, the guy she was about to marry.

Well, she and Bob would not get married, would not even have sex, wide shoulders and cute ass notwithstanding. She'd just have to claim she had a headache. He'd probably have a speech about headaches. He probably knew how to take care of headaches.

"Listen," she said, massaging her temple as if the hurricane of migraines simmered there. "I don't—"

Her phone rang. A Saint Patrick's Day miracle. She took it out of her purse. It was an unrecognized number, but that was fine. By this point, she was willing to talk to anyone, just to get out of this date.

"Hello?" she said.

"Hannah?" A familiar voice she couldn't quite place.

"That's right. Who's this?"

"Hannah, it's Naamit."

Right, she realized. Naamit, her mother's friend. She wasn't certain where her mother had befriended the woman. Was it at the synagogue? Or at some sort of Pilates class? The details were hazy, but Naamit and Hannah's mother had been good friends for several years now.

"Hey, Naamit, how are you doing?" she said.

"Not good," The woman said, and Hannah realized she was sobbing. "Hannah, can you come over? We could really use your help."

"Sure," Hannah said, frowning. "What's the problem?"

"It's Abigail," Naamit said. "She's gone."

"What's the address?" Hannah asked.

"23 Lavetta Way."

"I'm on my way," Hannah said, and hung up. "I have to go."

"What is it?" Bob asked.

"A friend needs my help. It's a police matter."

The cogs turned for a few seconds. "You're a cop?" Bob asked.

"Yeah. A detective." Hannah dropped two bills on the table.

"Oh," Bob said.

Hannah stood up. "This was delightful," she said, in a tone that broadcasted that it was as delightful as taxes.

"We should do this again sometime," Bob said.

"Definitely," Hannah said.

Never. Not even if he and David Ferguson were the last men on earth.

———

Hannah was caught off guard when Naamit opened the door. She was dressed in a crimson skirt and black leggings. Her shirt, dotted with little sequins, glittered in the yellow light of the front door lamp. Her lips were dark red, and there were traces of pale makeup on her face, but her eyes and nose were puffy and pink. She had clearly been crying for some time.

"Hannah," she said, sniffling. "Thanks for coming."

"Of course," Hannah said. "What happened?"

"We came back home an hour ago, and Abigail wasn't here! At first we thought she went to a friend's house. But her phone is turned off, and most of her friends don't know where she is."

"Most of her friends?" Hannah asked as Naamit led her inside, into the living room. It was a small space, the furniture simple and worn. Two sofas stood on a faded white carpet, with a round wooden coffee table between them.

"Yes … her best friend, Gracie, isn't answering her phone, and neither are her parents. Ron drove by their house, but it's dark and no one is answering the door."

"I see. Maybe they took Abigail with her friend to see a movie, or something like that?"

"Without telling us?" Naamit said. "I don't believe it."

Hannah had the feeling that was exactly what had happened. Nevertheless, she didn't intend to blow it off. This was a missing child.

"How old is Abigail?" she asked.

"She's twelve," Naamit said, voice wavering.

"Okay, and where were you when she left home?"

"We were at a party," Naamit said. "I shouldn't have left her alone! I wanted to call my mother, ask her to come over, but Abigail kept insisting she wasn't a little girl, that she didn't need a babysitter."

"Uh-huh. A party? A Saint Patrick's Day party?" Hannah raised her eyebrow.

"Well, not really," Naamit said. "It was an office party. And they know we're Jewish, so they made it a Saint Patrick's Purim party."

"Oh, right." Purim was right around the corner. Well, that explained Naamit's costume. "When did the party start?"

"It started at six, but we were a bit late. We only left here at about seven."

"Right. And did you tell Abigail when you were coming back?"

"We said we'd be out until about midnight, but the party ended a bit early. We're a small company. All my coworkers were there, but even with their spouses, there were no more than a dozen people. And we decided to cut it short."

Hannah sighed. So the daughter thought her parents would be out until late at night, she insisted no one should stay with her, and her parents returned home much earlier than they had said they would. Her best friend was missing as well, along with the rest of her family. Hannah was willing to bet that Abigail would walk in any minute, and it would turn out she had gone to a concert her mom hadn't allowed her to go to, or something similar.

"Where's Ron?" Hannah asked.

"He's driving around the neighborhood, looking for her," Naamit said.

"Listen," Hannah said and then paused. "Did you say her phone was turned off?"

"That's right."

If there was one detail that struck Hannah as worrisome, that was it. "Does she turn off her phone sometimes?" she asked.

"No. She's always texting, or talking on it, or something. That thing never stops vibrating."

"And you said Gracie and her parents' phones were on, they simply weren't answering, right?"

"Yes. But I don't think she's with them. She wouldn't have gone somewhere at night without telling me about it first."

Yes, she would, but Hannah saw no reason to argue. "Okay, can you give me an updated picture of Abigail?"

"Of course." Naamit hurried off. Hannah sat down at the edge of one of the sofas and thought back to her years as a teenager. She hadn't exactly been a rebel, but even she'd had her share of misdeeds. Stealing her mom's cigarettes and smoking them with her friend Tina. Getting drunk for the first time at age fifteen, returning home wasted enough to crash into a chair as soon as she walked through the front door. Sneaking out in the middle of the night to meet Gary Jones, the first boy she had ever kissed. She smiled at the memory of that kiss: clumsy and confused, his mouth open, her lips clenched tight, neither of them sure what they were doing.

Where was Abigail right now?

Naamit returned and handed Hannah a small framed photograph. "It's from her last birthday," she said.

Hannah looked at the shy, smiling girl. Abigail was at that awkward age when different parts of the body grew without discussing it with each other. Her feet were big and her arms were long, but her face still had a childlike appearance, with traces of baby fat clinging to her cheeks.

Her auburn hair reached her lower back. Naamit and Ron stood by her side, grinning proudly at the camera.

Hannah dialed Dispatch on her phone. The call was answered almost immediately.

"Glenmore Police Department, this is Candace."

"Candace? Hi, this is Hannah."

"Hi, Hannah!" Candace said cheerfully. She was everybody's favorite dispatcher. Sharp, fast and sweet.

"Listen, I have a missing child case. Twelve-year-old Abigail Lisman left her home sometime between seven and nine in the evening, and hasn't returned yet."

"Okay, description and address?"

"23 Lavetta Way. She's about five feet tall, Caucasian, long auburn hair. She might be with another girl, about the same age, named Gracie…" she glanced at Naamit.

"Durham," Naamit said.

"Durham."

"Okay, no problem Hannah, I'll inform patrol."

"Thanks." Hannah ended the call. Hopefully patrol would locate Abigail and get her home, scaring the living shit out of her. She wouldn't be sneaking out again anytime soon.

Kids did this stuff. Hannah was concerned, but not particularly worried.

"I'll drive around," she told Naamit. "See if I can find her."

"Okay, thank you so much—" A ringtone interrupted Naamit. She went to her handbag, rummaged inside and took out her phone.

"Hello? Yes?" Naamit listened to the caller for a moment, her eyes growing wider. "No. She isn't here either. We called the police; the policewoman is here now. We couldn't get you on the phone, and Ron went by and—" she paused, nodding, her eyes catching Hannah's. "No, of course. I'll let her know. Yes, please."

Naamit put her phone down.

"That was Karen—Gracie's mom," she said, her voice shaking. "They were out for Saint Patrick's Day. Gracie is missing as well, and she still isn't answering her phone. Her parents are on their way over here."

Hannah nodded. "I'll call my partner," she said.

Now she was worried.

TWO

Bernard Gladwin loved his kids dearly. There was nothing he cared for more in the entire world. Nevertheless, they did not make his life easy. And there were a lot of them.

When it was two kids, he'd handled it quite well. He could do a lot with two kids. For example, he could tell one a story while his wife Carmen played with the second. One parent versus one child, which was fair.

In fact, it had seemed so doable that he and Carmen had thought a third child was a good idea.

The thing was, he couldn't have known that three was one too many until they had the third—and by that point, he couldn't really return the baby to the store, could he? Now, with three, he could tell one a story, while Carmen played with the second, and the third tore down the house, stuck forks into electrical outlets, tried to set herself on fire, and threw her brother's toys into the toilet. It was a juggling act he hadn't gotten the hang of yet. He suspected he never would.

He and Carmen were handling another tricky situation: sex. It would be nice to have a bit. His kids thought differently, especially Rory, the baby. Rory was supposedly teething, though no evidence had been provided to support this. He didn't know how to say "I'm teething, please help"—or anything else for that matter. He simply woke up every hour or two, crying hysterically, refusing to calm down. Carmen said he was probably teething. But occasionally Bernard wondered if the baby wasn't just plain evil. At times he spotted a malignant glint in Rory's eyes, one he'd only ever seen in the eyes of psychopaths.

Sex was difficult to approach, knowing it could be interrupted at any moment by a screaming baby. Perhaps it was an evolutionary reflex—reducing the competition. *No sex* meant no tiny brothers and sisters. Bernard considered telling Rory that he didn't have to worry. There would *never* be another brother or sister. Not if Bernard could help it.

This evening, however, was promising. Rory had been sleeping for *three hours straight*, and Gina and Tom did not seem as if they intended to act up. Bernard felt hopeful.

He and Carmen were sitting on the sofa, watching TV. He wasn't even sure what they were watching. His wife was lying by his side, casually, her long legs stretched over him. She had tight black yoga pants on, and the curves of her thighs and ass were between him and the screen, rendering whatever went on there meaningless. He glanced at her face; she stared at the television in fascination, her brown eyes wide open, her lips slightly parted. She wore one of his T-shirts, the wide collar exposing her golden brown skin, the curve of one of her breasts beckoning at him. Yes, it was definitely time. But first, he had to get her in the mood.

"Hey," he whispered. "Wanna have sex?"

She glanced at him. "Good idea," she said, grinning.

Truly he was the master of seduction.

Well, he wasn't the only one who hadn't had sex for almost two weeks.

He leaned over, one hand sneaking under her shirt, the other caressing her cheek. He kissed her gently, his fingers finding something to tickle and squeeze…

His phone rang. He glanced at it.

"Don't you dare," Carmen hissed.

He paused for a second, then grinned. "Of course not," he said, one finger running down the nook between her shoulder and neck. "Do you think I'm crazy?" Whoever it was, they could wait. This was important.

They let the phone ring. Bernard licked Carmen's throat, she breathed excitedly, her back arched, their bodies rubbed against each other…

And then came the sound Bernard dreaded: Rory, crying. The phone had woken him up, and he'd remembered that he was obligated to ruin his father's life.

"Damn it," Carmen muttered.

"Yeah."

"To be continued?" she said, sliding from beneath him.

"Sure," he said, his voice deflated.

She padded off to Rory's room.

Bernard glanced at his phone with hatred. The thing was still ringing. He glanced at the screen. *Hannah*. He picked it up, answering. "Hey."

"Hey, Bernard, am I interrupting anything?"

"And if you are? Will you hang up the phone and leave me in peace?"

There was a pause. "No," she finally said. "Sorry."

"Didn't think so. What is it, Hannah?"

"I have two missing girls. Twelve-year-olds."

He glanced at his watch. It was a bit past eleven. "What time did they go missing?"

"Sometime between seven and nine. There are reasons for concern, Bernard. I don't think they just went to a party."

"Yeah," he said, already walking to the bedroom to get dressed. "It's late anyway. They would have probably come home by now."

"Right … And I know the mother."

Shit. "Where are you?"

"At her house. The mother's."

"Okay," he said, sending an apologetic look toward his wife as she glanced at him, holding Rory in her arms. "I'm on my way."

Hannah sat in the living room, Ron and Naamit in front of her. Ron hugged his wife with his right arm; his left hand picked nervously at the hem of his shirt. He was dressed in white pants and a white shirt, with black spots taped to his clothing—his Purim costume. He must have been dressed as a spotted dog or cow; it was hard to tell. Hannah doubted he even remembered he was dressed in a costume.

Naamit had stopped crying, which was a relief, but her eyes were wide and empty, and Hannah could see the fear in them. She couldn't imagine the terror the woman was feeling. She herself was very concerned. She was aware of some possible anticlimactic outcomes—an older boyfriend, or the two girls going for a walk on the festive streets and getting lost—and she prayed they'd find out this was the case, but she was familiar with other cases.

Pedophiles and perverts, snatching kids and dragging them into dark alleys. Drunk drivers that ran over random passersby and fled the scene, letting their victims bleed to death. Kids that disappeared, never to be seen again, remembered only as a face on an Amber Alert.

And it was Saint Patrick's Day. Beer and stronger drinks flowed freely, and alcohol increased the danger for violence and recklessness.

"Perhaps you should both get dressed," Hannah said delicately. She wished Bernard would get there. He was good with people, could radiate an aura of calm reassurance.

Naamit and her husband looked at each other, seeming to realize that they were still partly in costume.

"I … of course," Ron said. He was a thin tall man with light brown hair and round eyeglasses. His face was a bit elongated, like a character on a screen that did not match the movie's aspect ratio. He got up and then hesitated, turned to his wife. "Do you want to go … or should I…?"

Naamit probably needed her husband to take control, but it was obvious that he didn't want to. He was clumsily trying to find out what she preferred, instead of being the strong spouse who knew what should happen next. Hannah could tell that his intentions were good, but he was trying to let his wife be the strong and commanding one, when clearly all she wanted was to fall apart, and lose control completely.

"You can go," she said, her voice flat. "I'll go next."

He walked into their bedroom, closing the door behind him.

"Maybe I should be searching…" Naamit said, staring at the wall. "I mean … if she's lost somewhere, and she sees my car…"

"It's best you wait here," Hannah said. "She might just come home. Or call your home phone."

"She never does that," Naamit said. "She always calls the mobile."

"Can you show me—" Hannah began, but a knock on the door interrupted her.

They got up together. Naamit walked to the door quickly and flung it open as if she expected to see Abigail standing on the doorstep. But, of course, Abigail wouldn't have knocked.

A couple with a small boy waited outside. Naamit smiled weakly as she saw them.

"Tony. Karen. Come in, please." She stepped back, motioning for them to come inside. The three of them entered hesitantly. Tony was a large man. He was bald, and had a tattoo of a fish on his neck. His face was soft and worried, breaking the tough-guy facade. Karen was slim blonde with full lips. Her eyes were puffy and wet, and she kept sniffling and wiping them with the back of her hand.

"This is Detective Hannah Shor," Naamit introduced her. "She's here to help."

"Do you know anything?" Tony asked. His voice was low and hard, and he had an accent Hannah couldn't quite place. "Did you hear from either of them?"

"Not yet," Hannah said. "But we have police patrols canvasing the streets."

"Why?" he asked.

"In case they're lost," Hannah said. "Or—"

"If they're lost, why didn't they call? Why isn't Gracie answering her phone?"

"They might have misplaced their phones," Hannah said, and then added, "or someone stole them. Mr. and Mrs. Durham, do you have any idea where Gracie went?"

"No," Karen said, her voice brittle. "She said nothing. She was supposed to look after Donny."

The little boy lifted his face when his mother spoke, and Hannah looked at him carefully. He was pale and quiet. His eyes were narrow—almost Asian, similar to his father's—and they looked only at Hannah.

She knelt in front of him. "Donny," she said. "Did Gracie tell you where she was going?"

Hesitantly, he nodded.

"What? Why didn't you say anything?" Tony's voice was steely. "Where did she go? Tell us now!"

Donny shrank backward against his mother. "Tony!" Karen snapped. "You're scaring him!"

Hannah took one of Donny's palms in her hand. His skin was cold as ice. "Where did she say she was going, Donny?"

"She said she was going to meet a friend of Abby's," he said, his voice tiny. "She promised she wouldn't be long. And she told me to call if there was anything wrong." He teared up. "And I called her. Again and again. I was scared! I wanted her to come back home! But she didn't answer the phone! She promised she would answer the phone!"

Hannah stood up, feeling sick. If Gracie had said she would answer the phone, the fact that she hadn't was all the more worrying. She thought for a moment, then said, "Excuse me, I need to make a call."

She walked out the front door. It was freezing outside, and she hugged herself to stay warm. She dialed Captain Bailey, really hoping this would be short.

It only took a few seconds for him to answer. "Hello, Hannah."

"Captain, I have a missing child case here. Two twelve-year-old girls disappeared—"

"No one notified me about a missing child. How did you get the call?"

"I'm notifying you now, sir. One of the girls' mothers is a friend of my mom. Their names are Abigail Lisman and Gracie Durham. One of them isn't answering her phone, the other is going straight to voicemail. There are some indications this is serious."

"What indications?"

"Abigail Lisman turned off her phone, and her mother says she never does that. And Gracie won't answer her phone, although Gracie's brother says she told him to call if anything was wrong."

"Those aren't very strong reasons," Bailey said. "Anything else?"

Hannah hesitated. No, not really, but she had a nasty feeling. "Mostly my instincts," she finally admitted.

"Okay," the captain said, sounding serious. "I'll call Mancuso; she should be notified. The FBI might be able to track the phones much faster than us."

"Do you want me to call her, Captain? It'll save some back and forth."

There was a short pause. "Yes, that would be better. Hang on, I'll give you her number."

"I have it," Hannah said.

"Okay. Keep me in the loop, Detective." He sounded tense. A missing child made everyone high-strung.

Hannah searched for Mancuso's number. It took her several moments, her cold fingers clumsy and sluggish as she tapped on her phone screen. She was shivering a bit by the time Mancuso answered.

"Hello?" The agent's voice was husky, as if she had just woken up.

"Agent Mancuso? This is Detective Hannah Shor from the Glenmore Park PD. We met when we were investigating—"

"I remember you. What's up, Detective Shor?"

Hannah repeated the details she had just given the captain.

"I see," Agent Mancuso said. To Hannah's relief, she didn't sound skeptical.

"I think we need the FBI's help," Hannah said. "This isn't just a case of two girls who snuck out for a party."

"Okay," Agent Mancuso said. "First thing's first. You say one of them isn't answering her phone. The phone is definitely on?"

"As far as I know."

"I'll get the phone company to give us an approximate location."

Hannah blinked. "Just like that?"

"Yes. Let's hope the girl still has it on her, and that the location will be reasonably accurate. Sometimes the error range can be miles. What's the number for the girl whose phone is on?"

"Hang on." Hannah went inside. "What's Gracie's number?" she asked Karen. Karen gave her the number and Hannah dictated it to Agent Mancuso.

"Okay," Mancuso said. "I'll call you back in a few minutes."

The call ended. Hannah turned toward the parents. They were sitting on the living room sofas. There were six steaming mugs on the table. Naamit had changed out of her costume, Hannah realized, and was now wearing black pants and a light blue blouse.

"Who were you talking to?" Tony asked.

"My captain and the FBI," Hannah said after a moment. She wasn't sure if the knowledge that the FBI was involved would reassure the parents or worry them.

Apparently the answer was *both*. Tony and Ron relaxed, while Naamit and Karen clearly tensed up.

"They're helping us locate Gracie's phone," she said, trying to be reassuring.

Tony nodded. "Good."

"I made us all some tea," Ron said, gesturing at the mugs.

Hannah nodded distractedly. She wasn't a tea person. She needed coffee. Tea just made her need to go to the bathroom.

There was another knock on the door. This time, Hannah got to the door before Naamit. Bernard came in, taking in the two couples and the little boy, who all stared at his tall frame.

"This is Detective Bernard Gladwin," Hannah said. "My partner."

Before they could all introduce themselves, Hannah's phone rang again.

It was Agent Mancuso. "Okay, I have a location."

"Where is she?"

"Well, the phone is at the corner of Babel Lane and Kimball Way—or within six hundred feet, give or take."

―――

It was quarter past midnight, just mere minutes after Officer Tanessa Lonnie and Officer Sergio Bertini had begun their shift. They were expecting a rowdy one; Saint Patrick's Day was infamous for overflowing with the worst drunken behavior one could expect. Sure, it was a happy evening, but eventually someone had to deal with the drunks that got into fights or decided they were sober enough to drive home. Tanessa wasn't looking forward to it.

"Look, all I'm saying is, you just have to try it once. If you don't like it, I won't bug you about it again," Sergio told her as she drove slowly down Clayton Road.

"Sergio, I'm not going surfing in March!" Tanessa said, incredulous. This was the third shift he'd spent trying to convince her to share his hobby of playing with hypothermia. "Look around you! It snowed last week! You want to die of pneumonia, be my guest, but why are you trying to take me with you?"

"You wear a wet suit. It's no big deal."

"It's a *wet* suit! I'm freezing my ass off every time I get out of the car, and I'm wearing a coat, two shirts, and a scarf—all of them completely dry. You want me to put on wet clothing and jump into icy water? You're deranged."

"You don't feel the cold!"

"Maybe *you* don't. Your brain is dead; you don't feel anything. Listen, forget it, I'm not going to—"

The crackle of the radio interrupted the conversation. "Four fifty-one, Dispatch."

"Go ahead," Tanessa said into her shoulder mic.

"Four fifty-one, you're needed at the corner of Babel Lane and Kimball Way, to locate a missing child in the area."

"Dispatch, copy." Tanessa said. "Is this about the girls we were told to keep an eye for?"

"Four fifty-one, affirmative."

"Dispatch, we're on our way."

"Who lets their kids wander around at this time of night?" Sergio muttered as Tanessa turned the steering wheel.

"I don't think they let the girls wander around," Tanessa said. "I mean … I used to sneak out when I was a teen. My parents never knew."

"It's neglectful, that's what I'm saying. People should take good care of their kids."

"You can hardly manage taking care of a parrot!" Tanessa said, glancing at a group of young men as they walked down the street, laughing, probably on their way to the next bar.

"Gabriella is a very complicated animal, okay? She has moods!"

"Yeah, well, kids have moods too."

They reached the location, parking the patrol car near a black Dodge Charger and two white Chevrolets. A group of people stood nearby, Bernard's tall figure among them. The big man was hard to miss. He towered over most of the people around him by several inches. Tanessa started as she realized that Captain Bailey stood by Bernard's side. He was focused on a woman in front of the group: Agent Mancuso, whom Tanessa had met once before, shortly after Jovan Stokes had nearly killed her.

Mancuso was an impressive woman, with a commanding presence and a sharp look. She had tawny skin, hardly touched by age, black hair shot through with silvery white, and a beauty mark by her lips that made her face unforgettable. She was talking to the rest of the men and women, her hands in her coat pockets, when Tanessa and Sergio joined them. She paused for a second, nodded at Tanessa, then resumed talking.

"Gracie Durham and Abigail Lisman have been missing for over three hours, so there's a reason for concern. Gracie's phone traces to this area, and we have about a six-hundred-foot margin of error. However, her phone is still on, and we are constantly calling it. When we get closer, we might hear the ringtone."

She glanced around. "We have several apartment buildings and offices here, so we need to check them door to door. Captain Bailey, Detective Shor, and Detective Gladwin will do this, with Agents Fuller and Manning. Start with the gas station, see if anyone there saw anything. The rest of us, including Officer Lonnie and her partner, who have just joined us, will check the alleys, the streets and the playground." She gestured at the dark playground two hundred feet away. "We have no idea if Gracie's phone is still on her, or if the girls are together, and we assume nothing. Okay, let's get going. It's late, and I want to get the girls back to their parents in no more than an hour."

The group broke up. Bailey, Hannah, and Bernard looked toward Tanessa and nodded, their faces grave. They seemed worried. If those experienced detectives were uneasy, they had good reason. Tanessa fervently hoped this shift wouldn't end with her finding the body of a twelve-year-old girl.

"It's nice to see you Officer Lonnie," Agent Mancuso said, her shoulders hunched against the cold. "You seem … well."

Last time they'd met was two days after Tanessa had been kidnapped and nearly killed. She'd had trouble sleeping and eaten almost nothing in the week that followed, so it wasn't surprising that Agent Mancuso thought she seemed much better now. "Thank you," she said. "You, too."

"Right," Agent Mancuso said. "Let's find these girls. I want you two to check the playground. We'll cover the street."

Tanessa nodded, and walked with Sergio toward the playground.

"You know that woman?" Sergio asked her.

"I met her once," Tanessa said.

"She looks badass," he said.

"I think she really is."

The night chill became uncomfortable. It sneaked through Tanessa's collars, the soles of her shoes, and even her multiple layers of clothing. Each breath she took invited the freezing air into her lungs and body. Her nose and ears throbbed.

She hated being cold. It was the thing she hated most about Glenmore Park, the cold winter. She wondered if the girls really were out on the street. If they were, they might freeze to death.

They reached the playground, which was surrounded by a low metal fence. They followed the fence for a few dozen feet until they came to the small opening that served as the entrance. The path inside was muddy, with dozens of shoe prints all over it. Small mounds of snow that hadn't yet melted stood on either side of the path, dimly lit by the pale streetlight. The playground was quite big. There was an area with a merry-go-round, a slide, several swings, then deeper inside there was a basketball court and a long line of trees.

"It's dark in here," Sergio muttered, pulling his flashlight from his belt and switching it on. Tanessa did the same. The beams did little to penetrate the darkness as they stepped through the entrance. Tanessa kept her ears open for the ring or vibration of a mobile phone, but the only thing she could hear were her and Sergio's footsteps crunching on the gravel of the path.

She had once been lost herself as a small child. When she was eight, her mother had taken Tanessa and her brothers for an evening walk. Tanessa skipped ahead, watching her shadow as it grew bigger and smaller in the lights of the street. She didn't notice her mother stopping to talk to someone, probably a fan. Her mother had been an actress back then, and she was stopped by fans for an autograph or a photo almost daily. The street was very busy when Tanessa realized her mother and brothers were no longer behind her. She froze in place, looking for them, fear filling her heart. She'd been on the verge of crying when a man approached her and asked if everything was all right. She still remembered his smell: sweaty, sour, and unpleasant. One of his teeth was blackened. She'd screamed, stepping back, and burst into tears.

Mitchell and Richard were by her side in seconds. They hadn't been far away. They'd all shouted at the embarrassed man, who had probably only wanted to help. Tanessa cried for what felt like hours afterward. It had been the scariest thing that had ever happened to her as a child.

Were Gracie and Abigail alone on the street somewhere, crying? If so, why didn't they answer the phone?

"They're probably in one of the apartments in the area," Sergio said. "Maybe they went to a party."

"Yeah," Tanessa said, but she had a very bad feeling this wasn't the case. It was too late, the girls too young, the fact that they didn't answer their—

"Do you hear that?" she said, stopping in her spot.

"Hear what?"

"Shut up."

"You asked me—"

"Shut the hell up for a second."

They both stood in silence, and she heard it again. A faint tune, far to their right. "Over there," Tanessa said, crossing the frozen ground, her heart beating faster. The beam of her flashlight jumped erratically, searching, then it landed on a small inert body. She ran, nearly slipping on an icy patch, finally reaching the body on the ground. Crouching, she gently moved it to expose the face.

It was a young girl with dried blood on her forehead. She was limp and her skin was pale, almost blue.

"Get an ambulance over here!" Tanessa shouted at Sergio. She put a hand on the girl's chest, lowered her ear to the girl's mouth. The girl's phone chirped somewhere nearby, making it harder for Tanessa to concentrate on the girl's breathing, but finally she could hear and feel it: a faint shallow breath.

The girl was still alive.

Tanessa removed a glove and touched the girl's cheek. It was icy cold. She took off her coat, ignoring the freezing temperature, and wrapped the girl in it, speaking to her softly the whole time. "It's okay honey. We found you. Hang on. Open your eyes. Open your eyes for me. Hang on, help is coming."

THREE

"I'm sorry," the doctor said. "I really can't let you in. This child is exhausted, and we don't want to tax her."

He was bald on top, with tufts of gray hair on either side of his head, and Hannah wanted to grab them and shake him until he changed his tune. "I won't say this again, Doctor," she said through gritted teeth. "There's another girl out there, and we haven't found her yet. This girl might know where she is. I need to question her right now."

"Well … I understand she was found in a park," the doctor said. "Did you search the park?"

Hannah was about to explode. "I know how to do my job, thank you! Now move!" she marched forward, forcing him to move aside, and pulled the double door. It was locked. Beyond it, through the door's tiny window, she could see a corridor lined with rooms, bathed in harsh neon light. A nurse walked slowly, pushing a hospital cart. Hannah thumped the window, emitting a dull thud.

"Open this damn door."

"As I said—"

Agent Mancuso got out of the elevator and marched toward them, already flashing a badge. "Agent Mancuso, FBI," she said. "We need to talk to Gracie Durham right now."

The doctor blinked. "As I told the officer, Gracie Durham is—"

"This is a federal investigation, Doctor. A girl's life is in danger."

He hesitated. "Very well," he said eventually. "But only five minutes. Room 309." He walked to a panel nearby and input a four-digit code. The door clicked open.

"As long as it takes, Doctor," Agent Mancuso said, pulling the door open and walking through it. Hannah hurried after her.

"It's handy, having that badge around," she said, half-running to keep up with the tall woman.

"It has its uses."

They reached Gracie Durham's room and opened the door. The room was beige and cheerless. Gracie, white as paper, lay on a hospital bed with an IV running to her arm. She wore a green hospital gown and was half-covered by a thin blanket. A single fake potted plant stood on a small night table by her bed; it was the only decoration. Her mother sat by her side on a light brown chair, jaw clenched, holding Gracie's hand.

"Mrs. Durham, we need to ask your daughter some questions," Agent Mancuso said.

The woman nodded, sniffling. "Of course," she said. Hannah could see in her eyes that Gracie had already told her something. Something that had a deep impact.

"Gracie, my name is Christine, and this is Hannah," the agent said. "Would you mind if we ask you some questions?"

The girl shook her head.

"Do you know where Abigail is?"

The girl shook her head again. "Some people took her," she said, whispering. "People in black masks."

Hannah felt as if a bee had crawled down the back of her neck. Abigail had been kidnapped.

"Please tell us what happened," Agent Mancuso said.

"We were in the playground," the girl whispered, her voice tiny, barely audible. "And we were just going home when a man showed up. A man in a … a black mask. We ran, and he chased us. Then another man joined him. He also wore a mask. They got Abby. I ran away." She stopped.

"What happened then?" The agent leaned forward, her stance indicating that a series of questions was about to follow. Hannah let her take the lead.

"I don't remember."

"Are you sure there were two men?"

"Yes."

"Can you describe them?"

Gracie shook her head.

"What were they wearing besides the mask?"

"Dark outfits, I think. I don't really remember."

"Did you see where they took Abigail?"

"I think there was a van … but I didn't see them taking her, I was running away … I don't know."

"What kind of masks?"

"Ski masks."

"Can you describe the van?"

Gracie shook her head again.

"Was it white? Blue? Red?"

"I don't know. I don't know!" she said, her voice louder. Tears trickled down her cheeks. "I don't know!"

"Please, she doesn't know any more," Karen Durham said, agitated. "She's just a little girl."

So was Abigail. And she had been kidnapped. Hannah turned toward Karen. "I'm sorry, Mrs. Durham, but even the smallest detail could help us find Abigail. We need to ask these questions, and we need to do it now."

"But—"

"What were you doing there, Gracie?" Hannah asked, ignoring the distraught mother. "What were you doing in the park?"

Eyes wide, bottom lip quivering, Gracie looked at her mother.

"You're not in any kind of trouble, Gracie," Hannah said. "But we need you to answer truthfully. It would help us find your friend."

"We were going to meet Noel." Gracie stared at her blanket, her voice timid. "Abby's boyfriend."

"What is Noel's full name?" Agent Mancuso asked.

"I don't know."

"Where can we find him?"

"I don't know. I have no idea where he lives."

"How long have he and Abigail been together?"

"Two, three weeks, I guess," she said. She seemed to be getting drowsy. "It's hard to tell. I mean … it's not like they went on a date or anything."

"How did they meet?" Hannah asked.

"They started chatting online," Gracie said, her head sinking into her white pillow. "It was a while ago."

"Do you know what he looks like?"

"Yes. Abby showed me a picture he sent her."

"A picture? Did she ever meet him before?"

The girl didn't answer. Her eyes were closed, and she breathed deeply.

"Gracie," Hannah said, shaking the girl by her arm. "Gracie."

Gracie let out a whimper.

"Leave her alone!" Karen snarled, her timidness melting away.

"Gracie!" Hannah said loudly. "This is important! Had she ever met Noel face-to-face before?"

"No," Gracie muttered, her eyes still shut. "Tonight was the first time they were supposed to meet."

"And did he show up?"

The girl didn't respond, but Hannah knew what the answer was. She could see Agent Mancuso knew as well.

He didn't. He probably never existed.

―――

Abigail was shivering. She had wet herself when the rough arms pulled her into the van, the urine drenching her leggings. Now the fabric was soggy and freezing. Her legs throbbed from the cold and itched where the leggings clung to her. She tried rubbing her legs against each other, but that only made it worse, and she whimpered in despair. She wished she could take the damn things off for just a moment, but she couldn't. Her arms were tied behind her back.

She could see nothing; she was surrounded by blackness. When they'd put her there, she had seen that it was a gray room with a chair and a small mattress, on which they dumped her. Then they closed the door, and she was plunged into darkness. Sometimes she thought she could see the outline of the chair, but she wasn't sure if she was imagining it or not. At one point, she felt as if dozens of figures crowded around her, getting closer and closer. She screamed herself hoarse into the rag that had been shoved in her mouth, and then realized it was only her imagination. There was no one there with her. She was alone.

She wanted her mom. She wanted Gracie. She wanted someone to be with her, to tell her it would be all right. At home, she always slept with a small night light on. She wasn't a little girl—she wasn't afraid of monsters—but the light was reassuring when she woke up in the middle of the night. She was desperate for a small light, a tiny light.

She had cried and begged into the rag, not knowing if anyone heard her. She felt as if she were choking, the mucus and tears clogging up her nose, the rag in her mouth blocking her only other airway. Then she blew hard and one nostril opened. She could feel the slimy touch of her mucus on her face, and she rubbed it against the mattress, wiping some of it off, smearing the rest.

Her parents would find her, or the police would. In all the books she had read, all the TV shows she had seen, the cops found the bad guys or the kids managed to escape.

Except…

A few months before, when her parents were out, she'd seen a movie on TV. It was late at night, and she wasn't supposed to watch it. It was rated *TV-MA*, and she had just turned twelve. But it had seemed so exciting, and she figured she was old enough to decide for herself. Kids in class always boasted about watching horror movies, or even adult-only clips online, and she wanted to boast as well.

In the movie, a police officer was investigating the kidnapping of a seven-year-old, and halfway through the movie, he found the boy's body. She switched it off at that point; she couldn't finish. And she couldn't sleep for three nights afterward without waking up screaming. She didn't know how it had ended, but even if they caught the bad guys … the boy was dead.

And now she had been kidnapped. What would they do to her? Would they kill her? Shivers crawled up her spine as she imagined the men in masks coming in with knives, or guns, or ... or ...

She was crying again, her face against the mattress, trying to say "mommy" into the rag, the word muffled beyond comprehension, and she kept saying it over and over and over, as if her mother might hear her and come, like she did back home when Abigail cried for her, and she would hug her and run her hand through Abigail's hair, and tell her it would be all right—

There was light. The door was open, and someone stood in the doorway.

He wore the same black ski mask he'd worn before. Abigail whimpered, shuffling to the corner of the bed as he came closer. Would he kill her now, like they killed that boy in the movie? He had something in his hands—a black lump. She tried to say "Please," but the rag kept swallowing her words, and she coughed and shook her head.

"I'm going to remove the gag from your mouth," the man said. "And if you make a sound, I'll put it back in. Got that?"

Abigail nodded, her eyes wide.

With soft, calm movements, he slid a pair of scissors from his pocket. As the blades of the scissors came closer, Abigail breathed fast through her nose, her eyes following the metal.

He cut the rag with a single snip, and her mouth was free again. She opened and closed it several times, whimpering with relief.

"You're shivering," the man said. "I brought you a blanket." He lifted the lump in his hand. That was what it was: a rolled-up blanket.

"Can you please let me go?" Abigail asked in a meek voice. "Please? I just want to go home."

"If you behave yourself," the man said, "you'll be home in no time. Okay?"

"Okay."

"Good. Do you need to go to the bathroom, or—" He looked at the wet stain on her leggings. "Oh."

Abigail closed her eyes. Would he be angry? Would he think she wasn't behaving herself? She had been scared! It was an accident! But she didn't know what he would think.

"I'll get you a clean pair of pants later," he said. "Here … Stand up."

He helped her stand on her feet. There was a wet spot on the mattress where her urine-soaked pants had touched it. The man flipped the mattress, so that the wet part now faced the cot. Then he turned her around and she heard the scissors snip again, felt her hands loosen.

"There," he said. "You'll behave, right?"

She nodded.

"Okay." He took out his phone and looked at her. "Stay right where you are," he said.

He backed up a few steps, and for one crazy moment she thought about bolting. The door wasn't locked behind him, he was too far to catch her, and … and…

She forced herself to stay still. He'd grab her in no time. He was tall, his legs long, his body muscular. She was just a girl. If she tried running, he'd tie her up again. He would put the gag back in. He'd leave her in the dark.

The phone's tiny light flashed as the man took a photo, then another. Spots danced around Abigail's eyes, and she blinked several times, the room seeming darker. He turned around and began walking out of the room.

"Can you leave the light on, please?" she said.

He hesitated for a moment.

"Please?" she whispered, a tear trickling down her cheek. If the room plunged into darkness again, she would die.

He nodded curtly and left, closing the door behind him. She heard the lock click.

Abigail took off her wet leggings and lay down on the mattress, wrapping the blanket around her. She was still alive. She had light. And she was untied.

She cried again and couldn't stop until, exhausted, she slept.

There was a jackhammer in Naamit's chest. As the hospital elevator climbed upward slowly, stopping at every floor, Naamit wanted to scream, to push everyone out, to dash outside and find the stairway.

No one would tell her anything.

Hannah wasn't answering her phone. The cop who'd showed up at Naamit's home had said Gracie had been found (but *not* Abigail, just Gracie), and was on her way to the hospital. She claimed she didn't know what had happened yet.

Someone knew where Abigail was, and what had happened to her. But no one was talking to Ron or Naamit. Ron had stayed home, waiting for Abigail to return, while Naamit drove to the hospital.

Finally the elevator doors opened on the third floor and Naamit barged out, her eyes frantically looking for anyone who knew what room Gracie was in. Gracie would tell her what had happened. Gracie would—

Her eyes fell upon Hannah, leaving the emergency ward. She was accompanied by the FBI agent. Naamit hurried toward her.

"Hannah," she said, her voice pleading, half-choking. "What happened? Where is Abigail? Is she all right?"

The detective looked at her, jaw clenched, face pale. She didn't smile, didn't put a hand on Naamit's shoulder, did none of the things people do when they try to calm someone down, to tell her there's nothing to worry about.

"Please." Naamit's voice caught in her throat. "Where is Abigail?"

Hannah took Naamit's hand, led her to a bench that sat against the wall. They both sat down.

"Abigail has been kidnapped," Hannah said softly.

Four words. That was all it took to shatter Naamit's world to pieces, to send a new, terrible torrent of fear through her body. *Kidnapped*. Her little girl. In the hands of … of …

"Who … what …?" she stuttered, trying to frame a question that would give her some reassurance, trying to hang on to something.

"It seems like it was a professional kidnapping, planned in advance," Hannah said, her voice low, her eyes looking straight into Naamit's. "That means it wasn't some"—she seemed to hesitate, then plunged on—"some random pedophile, prowling the streets, grabbing a child he happened to see."

Naamit's mind shut out the images this last sentence conjured, knowing well they'd return with a vengeance once she was left alone. "Who, then?"

"We don't know yet," Hannah said. "We're doing everything we can. The FBI are organizing a team to help us investigate. We're preparing to issue an Amber Alert."

Hannah's words stopped making sense as Naamit's hazy mind tried to comprehend what was happening. Amber Alert. How many times had she seen a child's face on TV or online, and thought how terrified his parents were? Losing their own child to a hostile stranger, whose intentions were unknown. Not knowing if they'd ever see the child's smile again. She was that parent.

Much worse, Abigail was that child.

Abigail, who sometimes showed up in her bedroom in the middle of the night because she'd had a bad dream, asking if she could sleep in their bed. Who once, when Naamit had been ten minutes late to pick her up from kindergarten, cried so hard she threw up, because she had been terrified that mommy was gone. She'd been taken by someone who was holding her prisoner, trapped, not knowing what was happening. She was probably crying right now, desperate to return home. Naamit could almost hear her daughter sobbing, her heart torn into a million pieces.

"...the FBI are very good at resolving these cases," Hannah was saying. "You're in superb hands. I know Agent Mancuso personally and—"

"No!" Naamit grabbed Hannah's arm, her fingers tightening. "Please. Hannah. You have to stay and help. They don't know Abigail. They don't know me. Please stay on this..." *case*. Abigail was now a case. "On this case. You're an incredible detective; your mother always says so. You can get my girl back."

Hannah stared at Naamit. She nodded dumbly. "Of course," she said. "We'll all be looking. We'll do everything possible to get Abigail back, okay?"

Get Abigail back. That was what Naamit wanted to hear. Needed to hear. That someone was determined to get her daughter back to her. "Thanks," she whispered.

She stood up, wobbling, and stared at the door to the Emergency Ward. Gracie was there, with Karen. Karen had her daughter back. Naamit loved Gracie—she was the sweetest child—but a wave of anger and bitterness hit her. Why couldn't it have been Gracie that was taken? Why couldn't Karen be the one who was out here, begging for help?

Naamit always took better care of Abigail, always made sure she knew where Abigail was, told her over and over not to trust strangers. Karen and Tony had once told Naamit that kids needed to learn how to take care of themselves. They let Gracie ride on public transportation alone, let her walk home by herself sometimes. Why couldn't it have been Gracie?

She couldn't hold back the tears anymore. She wanted her child back.

FOUR

Naamit opened her eyes to sunlight shining through her bedroom window. Ron was by her side, still sleeping. They had fallen asleep hugging each other, with Naamit sobbing and Ron caressing her hair. Ron never really talked much, and he'd known there was nothing to say that would lessen the fear and pain they both felt.

She looked at her husband's face, so pale and worn, his jaw clenched as he slept. She untangled herself from his embrace and got up, heart sinking when she checked her phone and found no message, no missed call. She had hoped to see a message from Hannah, telling her there was a lead, that the FBI had cracked the case, they had found the kidnapper. Even a message informing her they were working around the clock would have reassured her.

It was just before seven a.m. She had slept no more than an hour and a half, but further sleep was impossible. She plodded to the kitchen and made herself a cup of coffee. She considered making something to eat, but knew it would stick in her throat.

Had they given Abigail something to eat? Her daughter was always so particular about what she deemed edible that she often drove Naamit to fits of anger. As far as Abigail was concerned, only hamburger and tater tots were "good" food. Would the kidnappers bother to bring her what she asked? Would they feed her at all? She felt the tears coming back, but couldn't face crying anymore. She banished the thoughts, forcing herself to think of nothing but the technical details of making coffee. Pouring the dark brew. A flat spoon of sugar. Just a bit of half and half, not too much.

She was sitting in the living room, sipping from her mug, when her phone rang. She pounced on it, looking at the display, already feeling the crushing disappointment. It was just Valerie, a mother of one of Abigail's friends. Naamit had called her last night to ask if Abigail was at their place. She was probably just following up.

"Hello?" she answered. Her voice was weak, trembling.

"Naamit, I'm so sorry! I can't imagine what you're going through! When I saw Abigail's picture I couldn't believe it! The poor girl…"

Naamit tried to understand what Valerie was talking about. How did she know? What picture? And then she realized what had happened.

The Amber Alert. Of course. Abigail's picture was everywhere by now.

She dumbly listened as Valerie kept on talking, telling her how sorry she was, saying how she couldn't believe this had happened, asking if Naamit and Ron needed any help at all.

"Thank you for your call," Naamit finally said. "I appreciate it."

"Please let us know if there are any developments."

"Sure," Naamit said, and hung up. She wondered if Valerie really thought she'd call her to update her about any developments. She shook her head. Valerie was just searching for the right thing to say.

Naamit wondered what she would have said to a parent whose girl was kidnapped? There was no protocol for it. It wasn't supposed to happen to people you knew.

She stared at the phone display. The digits read 7:13. After a few seconds they read 7:14. She kept staring. After an infinity they changed to 7:15. This was what she'd do—just stare at the time moving until her daughter got back.

The phone rang in her hand. She didn't know the number, and she answered immediately, her heart beating.

"H ... hello?"

"Mrs. Lisman? This is Agent Mancuso. Did I wake you up?"

"N ... no. I was awake."

"Good. I wanted to update you that the Amber Alert is being released."

"Yes, I know. A friend called me."

There was a moment of silence. "A friend?" Mancuso said.

"Yes, the parent of ... Anyway, she said she saw the alert."

"Really? That surprises me. I assumed they were only starting now. I guess they got it going faster than I thought."

"Yes." Naamit hesitated. "Is there any other news?"

"Not yet."

"Okay. Thank you for your update."

"Don't mention it ... Are you sure she said she saw the alert?"

"Yes, I'm sure."

"Okay. Thank you, Mrs. Lisman. We'll be in touch."

Naamit put down the phone. She considered calling Valerie to ask where she had seen the alert, but couldn't face the woman's hysterical monologue.

Her phone rang again. Debra. Another mother. She let it ring until it stopped.

Then it rang again. Lyla, this time; her daughter Tammi was in Abigail's class. Naamit wanted to bash the phone, but this was what happened. They just wanted to help.

"Hello?"

"Naamit, I'm so sorry! Tammi was devastated when she saw Abigail's picture. I can't believe they'd do that!"

"Yes," Naamit said emptily. "It's terrible."

"Did you call the cops?"

"I … of course. That's why the Amber Alert was released."

"Oh, an Amber Alert was released? That's great. I've heard those things work really well, they'd find Abigail in no—"

"Wait," Naamit interrupted Lyla, her hand gripping the phone hard. "Didn't you just say Tammi saw the Amber Alert?"

"No," Lyla said. "She saw the photo."

"The photo…" Naamit tried to make sense of it all. "The photo in the alert?"

"No! The photo on Abigail's Instagram page."

Naamit hung up. Hands shaking, she opened the Instagram app on her phone. She didn't follow many people; in fact, she opened the app only once or twice a week.

She didn't need to scroll at all, it was the top post on her feed.

It was an image of Abigail's face, in a dark room. Her daughter's eyes were puffy, her lips twisted as if she was about to cry, her face blotched pink and white. It had been posted using Abigail's account.

The caption beneath said *If you ever want to see Abigail alive, better start preparing the ransom. 3 Million dollars. We'll be in touch. #WeGotAbigail*

Naamit's scream woke Ron up.

Hannah had worked more than eight years in the Glenmore Park Police Department. She could easily sense a change in the department's atmosphere. The brisk speed with which people moved from place to place, the tense faces, the unsmiling countenance of Officer McLure behind the front desk.

"Detective," he said when she walked into the department's lobby. "There's an active situation room in meeting room two. Captain Bailey asked that you join them there once you arrive."

Hannah nodded and quickly headed for the second floor. Meeting room two, which was opposite the squad room, hummed with activity. Agent Mancuso and Captain

Bailey were there, talking over the large-scale map of Glenmore Park spread in front of them. Several people she didn't recognize sat by the table, a laptop in front of each of them. A tech guy was laying wires, trying to connect a complex digital contraption consisting of black boxes, keypads, and a huge screen. Hannah guessed it was the FBI equivalent of a whiteboard and a phone.

"Detective Shor." Captain Bailey motioned to Hannah and she walked over. Mancuso handed her a phone. Confused, Hannah glanced at the screen, and felt a chill as she realized she was looking at an image of Abigail Lisman.

"This was posted on Abigail Lisman's Instagram account last night," Mancuso said. "It wasn't posted from her phone, so we assume the kidnappers got the password from her and posted it using a burner phone. We can't currently locate this phone, meaning it's already offline, but we're working on finding out approximately where the kidnappers were when they posted this."

"Three million dollars?" Hannah asked. "I don't think the Lismans have that sort of money."

"They don't," Mancuso said shortly. "We don't know yet if this is a mistake, or something aimed to throw us off the scent. The image was posted at three-fifteen a.m. We're working under the assumption that Abigail is still alive, and that the picture was taken not long before."

Hannah nodded.

"We've begun to acquire all CCTV footage in the area of the park, and we have men analyzing it, trying to figure out in which direction the van drove away, and what's the license plate. We've done door-to-door questioning within a five-hundred-foot radius of the kidnapping site, and so far we have no witnesses. We're also getting a warrant for a phone dump for the area."

"The Amber Alert?" Hannah asked.

"Dispatched. All airports and border checkpoints have been notified as well," Mancuso said.

"Will you be able to trace any future posts on the Instagram page?"

"Yes," Mancuso nodded.

Hannah looked at the large map on the table. "You're focusing on Glenmore Park?" she asked. "The kidnappers could be in Boston by now."

"They could be in Texas by now," Mancuso said. "We're working all possible angles. Our best bet is to collect as much as we can in Glenmore Park. It looks like the kidnappers were familiar with the girl. We're assuming they live here or work here. If we manage to find evidence that points somewhere else, we'll go where it leads us. Glenmore Park has two main roads through which people are likely to leave. Both have traffic cameras. We're analyzing the feed, collecting license plate numbers, trying to figure out if they left town after the kidnapping."

"Okay," Hannah said.

"We're trying to trace this so-called *Noel* that Abigail and Gracie went to meet," Mancuso added. "We assume there's no such individual, but we want to make sure. We might be able to find the computer or phone that was used by the person using that name."

"The FBI and the police department are working together," Bailey said. "We're currently pairing FBI agents with local patrols and detectives in our effort to resolve this as fast as possible."

"Pairing them to do what?" Hannah asked.

"Collect statements, CCTV feeds, check out leads," Mancuso said. "We've paired you with Agent Ward."

Hannah looked around. "Who's—"

"He's still on his way from Boston," Mancuso said. "Meanwhile, there's something else we need you to do. Naamit Lisman approached me and asked that you update her regarding our progress."

"There is no progress," Hannah pointed out.

"There's always progress," Bailey said, frowning in annoyance. "We need Naamit to be cooperative. The kidnapper will contact her again. When he does, it would be best if she involves us. Please drive over there and reassure her we're doing everything we can."

"Okay," Hannah said. "And then what?"

"If this is a professional kidnapping for ransom, we have some time," Mancuso said. "Abigail will probably be kept safely. But if the ransom letter is just a ruse, we need to act much faster. We need to check all registered sex offenders in Glenmore Park, see if any of them might have done this. You and Ward will do that today."

"Do you think it could be a sex offender?" Hannah asked. "Gracie said there were two men. I don't know of any sex offenders in the area that have been known to work in pairs."

"I agree," Bailey said. "But we can't take any chances. If Abigail has been taken by a pedophile, we don't know how long he'll keep her alive."

FIVE

Hannah met with Naamit and Ron at their home to detail all the effort invested by the FBI and the police. Her descriptions of everything they were doing seemed to fall flat unheard and useless, as though they'd been sucked up into a deep void in the center of the living room. Naamit stared vacantly at her, lost in her own dark thoughts. Ron kept glancing at Naamit worriedly, then at Hannah, his eyes imploring her to say something that would make things better, that would give them a real sliver of hope. Hannah had none to give.

"We don't have three million dollars," Naamit suddenly said.

"I know," Hannah answered.

"If we sell the house, open Abigail's college fund, take a very large loan, we might get to … half a million dollars."

Hannah nodded, not knowing what to say.

"Do you think they'll agree?" Naamit asked. "When they realize we don't have the money? Maybe we can prove it somehow, send them a printout of our bank account? Hannah, there is no way we can get three million dollars."

"I know that, Naamit. We'll figure it out."

"Why did they ask for such a huge amount? You said they were professional. Don't they see that—"

"We don't know yet," Hannah said.

The room lapsed into silence. Then Hannah's phone rang. She answered quickly.

"Hello?"

"Detective Shor? I'm Agent Ward. I'm outside on the street. Next to"—there was a moment of silence—"23 Lavetta Way. Is that the right address?"

"Yes," Hannah said. "Wait there. I'll be out in a minute." She hung up.

"Any developments?" Naamit asked when Hannah put the phone in her bag.

Hannah shook her head. "Just following leads," she said.

"What leads?"

"We need to question some of the … criminal element in the area. One of them could be connected to the kidnapping."

"Oh," Naamit said. She didn't sound reassured.

"I'll let you know as soon as there are any developments."

The couple barely seemed to register her words. She left, relieved to get outside. Her eyes, tired from the lack of sleep, squinted as the bright sunlight hit them. Half-blind, she rummaged in her small handbag, locating her sunglasses. She put them on and the world swam into a relaxed shade of brown. A green Chevy was parked nearby, the engine running. She walked over and knocked on the passenger window. The window rolled down and the driver smiled at her—a shining, perfect smile.

"Detective Shor?"

"Right. Are you Agent Ward?"

"That's me. Come in."

She pulled open the passenger door and sat in the car. It was clean, and smelled of a pine air freshener. Hannah thought of her own car: the empty plastic water bottles on the floor, the small garbage can overflowing with used tissues and snack wrappers. She was happy they were driving in Ward's car.

"You can call me Hannah," she said.

He smiled at her again. He was clean shaven, his skin warm brown, his hair black and cropped short. His shoulders were wide, and he seemed to be tall, though it was hard to be sure, since he was sitting down.

"Okay," he said. "Hi, Hannah."

She waited for a moment, then said, "And I'll just call you Agent, I guess."

"Well, my friends call me Agey," he said, then burst out laughing. "My name's Clint."

"Nice to meet you, Clint," Hannah grinned. His good cheer was welcome after the difficult hour she'd had with Naamit and Ron. "So … We're gonna talk to some perverts? Where do we start?"

He reached a long arm into the backseat and pulled a black briefcase up front and into his lap. Opening it, he rummaged around inside and drew out a beige folder. "Well," he said, inspecting the contents of the folder, "I thought we could start with a guy named … Lionel Cole?"

"Wouldn't it make more sense to start with the heavy offenders?" Hannah asked. "We could start with—"

"Lionel Cole was convicted of three open and gross lewdness acts with children ages nine to fourteen," Clint said, frowning. "That sounds serious to me. And our victim is twelve years old, which fits the pattern of—"

"Lionel Cole was convicted of open and gross lewdness with children because the district attorney wanted to make an example of him," Hannah said impatiently. "The children weren't *victims*, exactly; they were simply there. He doesn't target children. He doesn't target anyone, actually. He just—"

"We can discuss it on the way," Clint said, shutting the folder and shoving it into the briefcase. "I prioritized the list of offenders, but I'd be happy to hear your opinions. Let's start with Mr. Cole."

Hannah looked at him, feeling her face flush pink. "By all means," she said, her voice steely. "Let's talk to this dangerous sexual predator."

―――

Hannah was icily quiet the entire drive to Lionel's house. Agent Ward didn't seem to mind. He was a chatty fellow, and as they drove, he told her about the time he'd tracked down a violent rapist in Worcester. Hannah listened distractedly. The story sounded like a well-practiced tale. She suspected Agent Ward had told it dozens of times, to impress his friends and the women he dated.

She was not impressed.

Finally, they parked in front of Lionel's home. It was in a poor neighborhood, and most of the homes had simple, rotting picket fences or sagging barbed wire around their yard. Lionel's house was surrounded by a six-foot-tall stone wall, which made it stand out. The wall almost completely blocked the view of the house from the street.

Hannah had heard that the entire street had pitched in to pay for the wall.

Clint stepped out of the car and stared at the wall. "Is this his house?" he asked.

"Yes."

"That's a big wall."

"I guess he likes his privacy," Hannah said, knowing very well that it was the exact opposite. The *neighbors* wanted Lionel to have his privacy. Lionel didn't give a damn, and in fact was probably upset about the wall being there.

"Okay, let's go talk to him."

"Sure, but listen—this is important. Don't spook him."

"I'm sorry?" Clint stared at her, looking confused.

"He gets skittish when he's spooked. He might bolt."

"Okay." Clint raised an eyebrow. "I'm not sure what you're telling me here. There's a sex offender in that house. He might know something about the missing girl. And you want me to … what? Talk nicely? So I don't hurt his feelings?"

"Yeah, but we don't want him to run away, because—"

"Detective, we need to get answers! I'm not going to sugarcoat everything I say just to avoid a possible physical incident!"

Hannah grinned. "You're totally right," she said. "I'll follow your lead."

Clint went to the front gate, which was as tall as the wall. He tried the handle, and the wooden gate opened.

"What's the point of this huge wall if the gate is unlocked?" he asked.

Hannah shrugged.

The yard was barren, just hard dirt and some flagstones acting as a path to the front door. The house had uncommonly large windows, and Hannah could see movement through one of them. Lionel was home.

Ward knocked on the door. After a moment it opened.

Hannah knew what to expect, and watched Clint's face as his eyes widened, his mouth going slack. A thin, middle-aged man stood in the doorway, his gray hair long and frazzled, his beard unkempt. He was completely nude, his penis dangling flaccidly as he looked at the agent and Hannah. He didn't attempt to cover himself.

"Yeah?" he said.

Hannah waited for a second. When it seemed the agent was still struggling, she said, "Lionel, I'm Detective Shor. This is Agent Ward from the FBI."

"What's this about?"

"Can you tell us where you were yesterday between eight and ten in the evening?" she asked

"Why?"

"Because we want to know."

"So?"

Clint seemed to wake up from a deep slumber. "We're investigating the disappearance of a young girl," he said, his voice already sharp and angry.

Hannah sighed, and let him go for it.

"So?" Lionel said.

"So, where were you last night?"

"Here."

"Can anyone testify to that?"

"No."

"Can we come in?"

"No."

The agent got louder. "Mr. Cole, a young girl disappeared from a nearby park last night. Do you know anything about that? Did you perhaps see her and think she wanted to have some fun? Maybe grabbed her and—"

"I didn't see any young guhl—"

"You like young girls, don't you, Lionel? You like thinking about them, touching them, fondling—"

Lionel turned around and bolted. Hannah was already running toward the back door, knowing she wouldn't get there in time. She was fast, but not that fast.

He burst through the back door, his penis bouncing up and down as his legs took him dashing straight at the wall. Did he intend to jump over it? It was a difficult jump, even for—

He leaped over it, his hands grabbing the top and pushing him upward like a naked, demented Peter Pan. Hannah grabbed at his legs but they were incredibly powerful. He kicked her away, and then he was gone.

"Where?" she heard Clint shout. He stood in the back door, looking surprised and confused.

"Over the wall," Hannah spat at him. She took a few steps backward, ran and leapt into the air, crashing into the wall, the momentum carrying her to the top. She rolled over it, and landed on the other side, bending her knees, to soften the shock. She looked around, saw Lionel's pale ass getting away as he sprinted with extraordinary speed down Falcon Drive.

Clint landed next to her, his head turning frantically. "There!" he shouted and dashed after Lionel.

Hannah shook her head. Idiot. An enthusiastic idiot, but an idiot nevertheless. He'd never catch up to Lionel—though she had to hand it to Clint, he was a fast runner.

She started running toward Cardinal Drive instead. The two streets intersected, and the way to the intersection was slightly shorter via Cardinal Drive. Hopefully, she would be fast enough to cut Lionel off. Though, frankly, she was skeptical.

Lionel Cole held the very dubious distinction of being the fastest streaker in the United States. His main hobby was running nude, and this was the reason he had so many indecent exposure and open and gross lewdness convictions in his record. The kids he had exposed himself to had simply been there when he went on one of his dashes. But there was a public outcry, because kids should not be exposed to a penis bouncing at twenty miles per hour. He had been charged with multiple cases of open and gross lewdness, and sat in prison for nine months.

And now he was streaking again, with an FBI agent and a detective on his tail.

———

Martha Fitzwilliam drove her car slowly, lost in thought, peering at the road through her thick eyeglasses. Her arthritic hands were acting up again, and she tried to ignore the pain in her fingers as she clutched the steering wheel.

She was on her way to her book club, and she was still trying to think of something to say. Her friend Edith had chosen the book *One Hundred Years of Solitude* for this month's reading, and Martha was cranky about this choice. The rest of the club preferred nice romance novels, or cozy mysteries, and Martha knew Edith had chosen the book just to make herself seem clever.

Martha hadn't even managed to finish it. It was a bizarre novel, full of strange, unexplainable events. When one of the characters, Remedios, inexplicably ascended into the sky, Martha shut the novel in frustration, and didn't bother reading to the end.

The worst of it was that, the month before, Edith had had the nerve to subvert the discussion about Martha's choice, *The Rosie Project*. It was really a delightful book, funny and charming and sweet. Martha had been waiting for the club meeting all week, dying to talk about her favorite parts of the book. But five minutes into the discussion, Edith mentioned something that had happened to her while shopping for a tablecloth, and the book was forgotten.

And now Martha had to think of something to say about *One Hundred Years of Boredom*. She didn't dare talk about just the first thirty or forty pages, because then Edith would know she hadn't read it. But the book had only gotten stranger as she progressed, until she had nothing to say except, "Well, that was a peculiar book."

A movement in the street ahead caught her eye. It was a man, running down the street, wearing a strange beige running suit. He was moving very fast, and Martha hit the brakes, afraid he might suddenly jump in front of her car. He appeared to be in a race with another man, dressed much more formally. She looked at them, transfixed, as they got closer to her car. There was something strange about the leading man's suit.

It wasn't a suit. He was naked.

"Oh my," she said to no one in particular. She squinted, just to be sure, but there was no way around it: he was definitely completely naked.

Martha had seen three grown men naked in her entire life. Her husband George, her son (she'd accidentally barged into the bathroom when he was getting out of the shower), and once, in a very modern ballet, one of the dancers took off his clothes in the middle of the dance. Now, just like that time at the ballet, the blood rushed to her head and she felt slightly dizzy. She thought she should avert her eyes, but it was as if her body refused to respond to her will.

The naked man reached her car and stopped. He laughed—a happy, carefree laugh—and jumped three times in his spot, his penis moving with him, rising as he fell, dropping as he rose. Then he leaped, his feet landing on the hood of her car. She could now only see his legs and the tip of his penis, which was outrageously close to her face. He jumped once more, feet hitting the road on the other side of the car, and dashed onward.

"FBI! Stop!" the man who was chasing him shouted as he ran after him. He was clearly out of breath, his face bewildered. He ran in front of her car and kept chasing the naked man.

Martha glanced in the rearview mirror. She could still see the pale bottom of the naked man as he sprinted away, getting further and further from the FBI agent.

"Oh my," she said again.

She sat motionless in her car for a minute or two, and then started driving again, feeling as if she was moving in a dream. Her mouth quirked into a small smile.

She had a very good story to tell once they started talking about *One Hundred Years of Solitude*.

Hannah ran as fast as she could, cursing herself for not taking her own car instead of riding with Clint. Chasing Lionel on foot was a doomed endeavor. Clint should have gotten his car, but then again, he couldn't have known that Lionel was such a fast runner. Of course, if he had only *listened*…

She reached the intersection with Falcon Drive, and was surprised to see Lionel was still about fifty feet away. Something must have delayed him; he was slower than usual. She had a chance now. She just needed to time things right. She tensed, adrenaline pumping in her blood, her eyes watching him as he got closer and closer. He constantly glanced behind him, a wide, slightly insane grin on his face. Just a bit more … a bit more…

She pounced, hoping she'd judged the distance correctly. Lionel turned his head, noticed her—but he was running too fast, and she was in his way. He tried to swerve around her, but it was too late. She crashed into him, and they both tumbled to the ground together.

Lionel screamed curses at her as she pulled out her handcuffs and pulled his arms roughly behind his back. Clint caught up just as she snapped on the handcuffs. His eyes were wide, and he was breathing like a heavy smoker.

"What … the … hell …" he said.

"Lionel, you'll freeze your ass off, running naked in this weather," Hannah said, pulling him up.

"Let me go!"

"How … How…" Clint still struggled with words.

"Lionel is the fastest streaker in the United States," Hannah said. "He once ran a nude six-hundred-yard dash in one minute and sixteen seconds."

"One minute and fifteen point two seconds," Lionel said, looking hurt.

"Right, sorry. Anyway, as I said, you really shouldn't spook him, he's very skittish."

"Let me go!" Lionel said again.

"Come on," Hannah dragged Lionel back toward his house. "You'll freeze to death if you stay out here naked, and you can't have my coat."

She dragged Lionel behind her as he hurled curses at her and Clint. The agent followed, looking a bit sheepish, which made the whole thing worthwhile.

Finally, they got Lionel back home. Hannah dragged him inside, and the agent came in as well and closed the door.

"Get dressed," Clint said.

Lionel pointedly ignored him.

"I don't think he has clothes," Hannah said.

The house was depressingly sparse and dirty. There was one sofa in the living room in front of an old TV set. Hannah dragged Lionel there and sat him down. Then she took one of the sofa pillows and put it in Lionel's lap, hiding his penis.

"There," she said. "So you don't embarrass Agent Ward. He's very sensitive."

"Yeah, sensitive my ass," Lionel muttered, but he left the pillow on.

"Lionel, yesterday evening a little girl went missing in a park nearby," Hannah said. "Your name came up in the investigation, because of your record."

"I don' take little guhls," Lionel said, looking at the floor.

"It would be helpful if anyone saw you yesterday evening," Hannah said.

"Yeah?"

"Did anyone see you?"

"Yeah."

"Did you run past Tony's Cafe again?" Hannah asked. She glanced at Clint, who looked at her, his eyebrows raised.

"Yeah."

"At what time?"

"About half past eight, I think," Lionel mumbled.

"Okay, we'll check that, Lionel. Stay out of trouble, okay?"

Lionel raised his eyes. "You're not arresting me?" he asked.

Hannah grinned. "No harm done," she said. She helped him up and removed the handcuffs, then left the house.

Clint followed her quietly, and they got in his car.

"So this guy is a regular streaker?" Clint asked.

"Yup."

"So we can check if anyone complained about a naked man running by … Tony's Cafe," Clint said. "And then—"

"There will be no complaint," Hannah said. "Lionel and Tony's cafe are symbiotic."

"I'm sorry?"

"The food at Tony's is crap; the coffee is even worse. People go there because they know there's a good chance they'll see Lionel running past."

Clint stared at her. "Seriously?"

Hannah nodded. "Hang on," she said. She pulled out her phone and located Tony's Cafe's number, then dialed.

"Hello?"

"Hi, this is Detective Shor from the Glenmore Park Police Department. Is this Tony's?"

"Yeah. What do you need, Detective?"

"Just a short question. Did Lionel Cole run past the cafe last night?"

There was a moment of silence.

Hannah rolled her eyes. "I'm not arresting him," she said. "I just want to establish his alibi for a different case."

"Oh, okay. Sure, he was here. Dashed past our front window, faster than the damn Road Runner, his dick bouncing all over the place. I seriously don't know why it doesn't fall off from the cold. It was practically purple. I mean … It's freezing outside. Guy's insane."

"Good. At what time did you see him?"

"Well … can't be sure … Oh, hang on. I was just using the cash register. It was a really funny order, four different people all ordering the spaghetti carbonara."

"Oh, good, can you check?"

"Sure, I'll check. It's weird, you know? Four people, all ordering the carbonara? I mean … sometimes the entire table orders chocolate cake for dessert. That I can understand. But four people, all ordering carbonara? Don't you think that's weird?"

Hannah drummed on the dashboard with her fingers. "It's very weird," she said. "So when was—"

"Yeah, here, found it. They paid the tab at eight thirty-seven, and just then Cole came running past. Man, were they happy. Cheering and clapping like he was some kind of movie star."

"I'm sure they were. Thank you."

"No problem. Tell Cole I said hi."

She hung up. "Okay," she said to Clint. "Lionel Cole's alibi holds up. Who do you think we should check out next?"

Clint grinned, exposing his perfect teeth again. "Tell you what," he said. "I think we should buy some early lunch, and while we eat, you can go over the list and tell me who we should check out next."

"I think that's a good idea," Hannah said.

SIX

Hannah and Clint drove to Red's Pizza, not far from the police department. The waitress led them to a small, square table by the window. Hannah sat down, taking the menu from the waitress and setting it aside. She knew most of it by heart.

"What's good to eat here?" Clint asked, scanning the menu.

"They make good pizza," Hannah said, shrugging. "I've never tried the pasta. They have nice muffins, too, but I don't know if that's lunch material."

"Hmmm. I'll just have a pepperoni pizza."

"Let's order a large one," she suggested. "It's big enough for both of us."

"Sounds great," he said, putting down the menu.

"Wonderful. Can I have your pervert list, please?"

Clint rummaged in his briefcase. "If I had a dollar for every time a woman said that to me … there we go." He handed Hannah the folder.

"Let's see." Hannah opened the folder. She scanned the list of names, printed on a page whose header read: *FBI - Confidential*. "Okay. Your number two is a real piece of work, definitely a pedophile, targets girls between the ages of ten and sixteen … but he's seventy-four years old. I can't see him chasing and grabbing a twelve-year-old girl in the dark."

"Can I take your order?"

Hannah lifted her eyes to the waitress, a young girl wearing heavy makeup and sporting a blatant hickey on her neck.

"A large pepperoni pizza," Clint said. "And soda water for me."

"A Coke for me, please," Hannah said, tearing her eyes off the girl's neck.

The waitress nodded and walked away. Hannah cleared her throat and looked at the list again.

"You're missing two names here," she said.

"These are all the registered sex offenders in Glenmore Park who target children," Clint said.

"Right, except we have two additional sexual offenders who have only been convicted on adult-related crimes, but are known to target young girls as well. Give me a pen."

He handed her his pen. As she grabbed it, their fingers accidentally brushed. He was warm to the touch, his fingers surprisingly soft. She plucked the pen out of his hand and wrote two more names. Then she numbered the list carefully.

The waitress served them their drinks, and Hannah took a long sip from her cold Coke, relishing the taste of the sugary drink, then focused her attention on the page again. Finally, she put the folder and pen on the table and slid them back toward Clint. He took the folder and opened it, glancing at the contents, frowning.

"What?" Hannah asked.

"Just ... trying to read your handwriting."

"Do you have a problem with my handwriting?"

"Not at all! It's very ... artistic. Here, is this a C or a G?"

"It's a P."

"Of course it is. So you think our next stop should be ... Mr. Arthur Patton."

"Yeah. He just got out of jail after two years, he stalked girls online, convicted twice for sexual assault—and he's in his thirties, so he'd have no problem catching up to a twelve-year-old girl."

"But would he kidnap her?"

"Not likely," Hannah said. "But there isn't anyone here that I think would. We don't even know that a sex offender kidnapped Abigail Lisman, especially since Gracie told us there were two men. The predators on this list have never given any indication that they like company."

"Okay," Clint said, nodding. "But we have to check."

The waitress served the pizza to their table, and Hannah took a slice and bit into it, nearly burning her tongue. She puckered her mouth into an O-shape to let out the heat. She finally managed to swallow the bite and quickly took another one.

"Slow down, Detective," Clint said, grinning. "We have a minute or two."

"I'm starved," she said, swallowing. "Chasing nude runners always makes me hungry."

"You were fantastic over there, by the way," Clint said. "I wouldn't have thought you could jump over the wall like that."

"Why not?" Hannah asked, lifting one eyebrow.

"Because uh …" he hesitated, clearly aware of the minefield he'd walked into. He took a bite from his slice, chewing slowly, as Hannah folded her arms and sat back. Finally, he swallowed. "Because of your hair," he said. "I didn't know people with brown hair could jump so high."

Hannah burst out laughing. "Brown hair, huh?" she said. "So it wasn't because I'm short?"

"Detective Shor, I'm appalled," Clint said, holding a hand to his chest. "That's heightism! To me, people of all heights can jump the same. I make no assumptions."

"Okay, okay." She shook her head. "You weren't too bad yourself. You gave Lionel a run for his money, and he's the United States streaker champion."

"How does that work, exactly?" Clint asked, leaning forward. "Was there an actual race?"

"That's what I was told," Hannah said. "I wasn't there, but it must've been quite a sight."

"Did he get a medal?"

"I definitely hope so."

"Is there a world championship?"

"You seem very intrigued with the subject," Hannah said. "Why? Do you want to participate in the next race? It's a very demanding sport."

Clint grinned again. He smiled a lot, more than most people she knew. He had a happy, infectious smile, and it made her relax a bit. She had been tense ever since the day before, when Naamit had called her.

Thinking about Naamit made her feel guilty. Here she was, eating pizza, smiling, *laughing*, while Naamit went through hell, not knowing what was happening to her daughter. Hannah felt as if she should be doing something, but she could only follow the leads she had, and work as closely as she could with the FBI.

"What's wrong?" Clint asked. "Your face went all puppy dog sad all of a sudden."

She shrugged and shook her head. "Just thinking about the case," she said. "I know the mother, and it's getting to me."

"It's the kidnapping of a twelve-year-old girl," Clint said softly. "Of course it gets to you."

"Do you work on a lot of missing children cases?" Hannah asked.

Clint nodded. "Three in the past year. It feels like a lot."

"I'm sure it does."

"What about you?" Clint asked. "What do you usually do as a Glenmore Park detective?"

"Well … the Glenmore Park Detective Squad doesn't have specialized detectives. So … drug dealers, prostitution, murder, theft … pretty much everything."

"Do you like it? I mean your job, not the … prostitution and murder."

"I mostly do," Hannah said after a moment. "It sometimes gets a bit heavy to bear. I thought I'd grow thicker skin, and some days it feels like I did—but then something penetrates, and it stays with me."

Clint nodded, his face solemn.

"This conversation is getting heavy," Hannah muttered. "I liked it better when we were talking about the various pedophiles in the neighborhood."

"Let's change the subject then," Clint said brightly. "How did you celebrate Saint Patrick's Day?"

Hannah blinked in surprise at the topic change. "I don't celebrate Saint Patrick's Day."

"Really? Why not?"

"Because I'm Jewish."

"Oh," Clint paused for a moment. "So you did nothing that day?"

Hannah hesitated. "Not really. What did you do?"

"Nothing," he shrugged. "I wanted to go to the parade; there's a big one in Boston. But work got in the way. So you're Jewish?"

"Yes," she said.

"So you celebrate Jewish holidays like Rosh Hashana, and uh…" he looked lost for a second. "Yom Kippur?"

"Well, technically, you don't really celebrate in Yom Kippur," Hannah said. "You fast and pray."

"Right. So do you?"

"No. I'm not very good with tradition. My dad is, though. He goes to the synagogue, and prays, and everything." Her father's beliefs had intensified shortly after divorcing Hannah's mother, but she didn't feel like sharing that particular point.

"That's interesting."

"Is it?" Hannah asked, her lip quirking upward.

"I think it is." Clint shrugged.

"Are you religious?"

"No, not really."

"Is your family religious?"

"Yes. Catholic. But I'm not."

"Why not?"

"Because my brother died when he was six years old," Clint said. "I was told God took him. And I called bullshit."

"Oh," Hannah said, embarrassed. "I'm so sorry."

"Thanks."

"How did he die?"

"An accident. He was riding his bike, and swerved into the road. No one knows why. The driver wasn't at fault; he was driving within the speed limit. It was just one of those things." Clint laced his fingers together, almost as if praying, and put his hands on the table. He stared at them. When he spoke again, his voice was quiet. "I was eight, and I was riding with him." He raised his eyes and blinked. "I don't talk about it often. Anyway, it happened long ago."

Hannah had a sudden urge to grab his hands, squeeze them, tell him again how sorry she was.

"Let's get going," she said instead. "We have a pervert to interrogate."

Bernard stepped into the empty squad room, his head throbbing. He had hardly slept the night before, and had spent the entire morning with an FBI agent who was more talkative than his Aunt Lorena. And it was hard to beat Aunt Lorena when it came to talking. Bernard finally told the agent he had some urgent paperwork to attend to, just to escape the torrent of words gushing against his weary brain. He shut his eyes, breathing in, enjoying the blissful silence of the squad room.

"Detective Gladwin."

He sighed and turned around to see Agent Mancuso standing in the doorway to the squad room. "Hey, Agent," he said. "Just came in to grab a"—he looked around at the desks, chairs and computers—"thing."

"Can we talk for a moment?" she asked.

"Sure."

She sat down in Mitchell Lonnie's chair. Bernard sat in his own chair, rolling it closer to her.

"We've been questioning the personnel at Abigail Lisman's school," Mancuso said, "and we located a suspect."

"Oh," Bernard said. "That's good. One of the teachers?"

"No," Mancuso said. "I believe you're acquainted with him. Jurgen Adler."

Bernard stared at Mancuso in shock. "There must be some mistake."

Agent Mancuso raised one of her eyebrows. "Why? Don't you know Jurgen Adler?"

"Of course I know Jurgen. What I meant was that he can't be your main suspect."

"Why not?"

"Because he would never kidnap a little girl."

"Really?" Agent Mancuso took a beige folder out of her briefcase, opened it, and scanned the first page. "Wasn't he suspected of bribery and tampering with evidence when you two were partners?"

"He was, but he wasn't convicted, or even charged."

"It also says here that there were some complaints against him—"

"They were dropped," Bernard said. "Look, I know what you're getting at. Jurgen Adler is far from perfect, but he's no kidnapper."

Agent Mancuso sighed and took three printed images out of the folder. She placed them in a row on Mitchell's desk. Bernard looked at the images, feeling sick. A familiar blue Ford Fiesta appeared in all three of them. In one, Bernard could identify Abigail Lisman walking out of a building in a throng of teenagers. In another image he could see Jurgen Adler holding a camera out the driver's side window.

"These are all images taken from the CCTV around the school," Agent Mancuso said. "The pictures were taken on three different dates, all in the past six weeks."

"Jurgen Adler is a private investigator," Bernard said. "He mostly works on getting footage of couples cheating on each other. He's probably following one of the teachers, trying to figure out if he or she is unfaithful."

"Sounds like a stretch," Agent Mancuso said.

Bernard shrugged. "I don't know, stranger things have happened. And Jurgen's no kidnapper. Look, take him in for questioning, and he'll resolve it all in five minutes."

"We are currently following him and tapping his phone," Mancuso said. "We want to see if he leads us to the girl. If we take him in for questioning, his accomplices may disappear."

"He doesn't have any accomplices! You're barking up the wrong tree, Agent."

Mancuso pursed her lips and looked at him, saying nothing.

"What do you want from me, anyway?"

"You were his partner," she said. "You know him better than anyone. We need to know—if we arrest him, will he give up his accomplices? How loyal is he? What makes him tick? We can't afford to blow this lead. We need to know as much as we can about him."

How loyal was Jurgen? That was a good question. Bernard had never fully worked out the answer. When they'd been partners, Bernard had been sure he could trust the man with his life. Then, when the evidence accumulated, Bernard had stood by his partner's side. He did so until the day Jurgen left the force, admitting privately to Bernard that most of the evidence against him was at least partially true.

"Look," Bernard said. "Jurgen's not an easy man to crack. And it's very hard to figure him out. He knows all the interrogation tricks there are. He's one of the cleverest people I've ever known. The investigation against him took months, and they still couldn't make anything stick. He admitted to nothing, even though he was probably guilty."

"If we do arrest him," Mancuso said, "we'll need your help in the interrogation."

"My help? Why?"

"We think your presence might unsettle him."

Bernard hesitated. "I'll do whatever the captain tells me to," he finally said. "But I doubt you'd want me there, Jurgen would be able to read me like a book. He'll know I don't believe that he did it. Sure, I know him, but it goes both ways. Quite frankly, I'm pretty sure he knows me much better than I know him."

"Well," Mancuso said, collecting the images, sliding them into her folder, "I hoped you'd be more helpful. After all, the man put you in a very awkward position. I understand you were investigated yourself?"

Bernard clenched his jaw, containing his temper. "I'll do whatever I can to get that girl back," he said, "and I'll be happy to sit with you and detail my entire history with my ex-partner. But I'm telling you, he's no kidnapper."

"We'll see about that," Mancuso said, standing up.

SEVEN

Hannah's mouth tasted bitter, and she felt as if her entire body was covered in a layer of slime. Some days, no matter how much she showered, she couldn't feel clean. She sat in Clint's Chevy as he drove her back to her car. The lighthearted atmosphere that had surrounded them as they left Red's Pizza was gone. It was evening, and they had visited and interrogated two rapists, a child molester, and a pedophile who was once caught with over seven hundred underage porn clips on his laptop. Hannah hadn't managed to stay calm and distant for long. These twisted examples of humanity at its worst got under her skin, into her bloodstream, piercing her heart.

Clint was quiet as well, his face somber. He moved his lips once or twice, as if muttering to himself, though he said nothing aloud. She wondered if he did this kind of job often, if he'd found that afternoon to be as unpalatable as she did. She was aware that these people existed, but talking to them, seeing the way they reacted when they heard about a young girl gone missing, made it much worse.

And, of course, it was all pointless. Two of them had supplied iron-clad alibis on the spot. The other two hadn't, but they didn't seem likely suspects, and they denied any knowledge. When a kid went missing, it was protocol to pay a visit to the local perverts, and it made sense. But in this case it just felt like slogging through shit for no good reason.

Clint parked the car on the dark street, across from the Lisman's house. They sat in silence for a few seconds, the faint hum of distant traffic the only sound aside from their breathing.

"How are you feeling?" Clint asked.

She shrugged. "Fine. You?"

He turned to face her. "I've been better," he said, his voice low.

She looked at him, found his big brown eyes pointed at her. She quickly glanced away. "Yeah," she said.

"It can get under your skin after a while," Clint said. "I know how that feels."

"Feels shitty," Hannah said, looking out the window. She could see his faint reflection in the pane, still watching her.

"Yeah, it does," Clint said. "Do you want to talk about it?"

She bit her lip. She didn't, but found herself talking anyway. "When I was young, I thought people were inherently good. It's something my mom always told me. That everyone started out with good intentions. And I believed her."

"It's a nice thing to believe."

"It's not. Because when you find out it isn't true, that there are people who can take a ten-year-old child, and push his head against a pillow, and … and … use him, like he's a bit of meat. When you find out this is a thing that actually happens—not far away, but nearby, maybe next door—then you can't believe anything anymore, you have to start building everything from scratch because your entire world view was twisted and wrong, and—"

He touched her arm, and the touch tingled on her skin. She shivered and took a deep breath. "I'm sorry," she said. "I'm rambling. It's been a long day."

"It has," Clint agreed. "It's all right. I don't think you're rambling."

She turned toward him and smiled slightly. "Thanks," she said. "I don't usually have emotional outbursts like that. You got me at my worst."

"I doubt it."

She looked at him, not knowing what to say.

"For what it's worth, your mother was at least partly right. Some people are inherently good. You are."

"You don't know me," she whispered.

"I know you enough."

She stared at her palms, embarrassed.

"Well," he said, clearing his throat. "Thanks for everything, Hannah. Your help was … invaluable."

She nodded. "I wish it wasn't such a waste of time," she said.

"There's no way we could have known for sure," he said.

"Yeah."

The silence between them stretched.

"Do you usually get the kidnapped kids back?" Hannah asked.

"Yes, but…" he hesitated.

"But what?"

"Most kidnappings are resolved fast. Within hours."

"Hours," Hannah repeated heavily. Abigail had been kidnapped more than twenty-four hours ago.

"So … what now?" Hannah asked.

Clint looked at his watch. "It's after midnight," he said. "And I've been awake since six in the morning. I need to get a few hours of sleep. And then we'll see what Mancuso says."

"Right," Hannah said.

"You've been looking for the girl since last night, right? You must be exhausted."

"Yeah."

"Will you be okay to drive home?" he asked.

"Yeah, sure," Hannah said. "It isn't far."

He smiled at her. His smile was sad, tired, and somehow beautiful.

Hannah was struck by a sudden urge to lean over and kiss him. Instead she nodded and offered him her hand. "I hope I'll see you tomorrow, then."

"Probably," he said, shaking it. "Good night."

"Good night," she said, and opened the car door. She hesitated for a moment, then got out of the car, closing the door behind her.

The green Chevy drove away, leaving her alone on the dark street. She wondered if Naamit Lisman was awake. She felt like a terrible person for not going over to check up on them. Instead, she got into her car, and started it. She briefly considered doing as she'd said she would and go home.

But she already knew she wouldn't. So she drove back to the police station.

———

There was no way Abigail could tell the time. There were no windows, her phone had been taken away from her, she had no watch. It could be the middle of the night, or noon, or perhaps early morning.

But her kidnappers made sure to give her food and drink every couple of hours. A sandwich, wrapped in plastic, with the unmistakable taste of shelf time. Bottled water.

The sandwiches and water bottles had been purchased somewhere.

The man brought them. He'd walk in, hand her the sandwich, and walk out—not saying a word, ignoring her requests, her tears, her angry screams. The second time he came, he brought her a pair of dark leggings, to replace the pair she had wet.

She hatched endless plans for escape. At first, she hid all the plastic wrappings of the sandwiches under her mattress, thinking she could somehow make a plastic rope out of them, and strangle her kidnappers. But she wasn't sure how she'd be able to do that, and after tying a few together she found out the plastic tore when stretched. She thought about using her dirty pants for the same purpose, but couldn't think of any reasonable way to do it.

There was a bucket she had used twice to pee in. She considered throwing it in one of the kidnappers' faces before bolting out of the room.

She could crawl under the bed. She would hide under it, and when they came looking for her, she'd … she'd…

But that was the thing. These were fantasies. They made her feel better, in control. She was not stuck in the basement; she was *biding her time.* But when she actually crawled under the bed once, waiting for one of them to show up, her heart pounded. The fear hunched in her throat, like a big fat spider. They'd know she was under the bed; it was the only place in the room she could hide. And then what? Would the woman drag her out, kicking and screaming? Would the man toss the bed aside, lifting her to her feet?

Again she recalled the scene from that movie, where the detective found the boy's body. Had the boy tried to escape? Was that why they killed him? The man said that if she behaved, they'd take her back home.

Hiding under the bed was not behaving. Emptying a bucket of urine on her kidnappers was not behaving. She was smaller than them, and trapped, and afraid. Even if she managed to get out of the room, she didn't know where she was. Was she in Glenmore Park? Could she run to one of the houses nearby, screaming for help? Maybe they'd taken her out of town, somewhere remote, like that summer house that Gracie sometimes went to. Would it really do any good to try to escape if there was nowhere to go?

She wavered constantly, planning her escape one moment, crying for her mom the next. She couldn't calm down, couldn't relax.

The door opened. High-heeled shoes clacked on the stairs. It was the woman this time. She descended the staircase, the dark ski mask hiding her face. She held a plastic-wrapped sandwich, just like the ones the man had brought Abigail before.

"Please," Abigail said, her voice breaking. "Please let me go. I want to go home. I won't tell anyone, I swear. Just let me go."

The woman walked across the room until she stood above Abigail. She held out the sandwich.

"Please," Abigail said again, sobbing. "I'm afraid. I miss my mom and dad. I just—"

The woman's hand moved abruptly, slapping Abigail, knocking her to the mattress. For a moment Abigail lay on the cot in shock, her cheek tingling, numb. Then the pain spread; her cheek felt like it was on fire. She burst into tears, curling on the cot, hugging herself, shutting her eyes, hoping the woman wouldn't hit her again. After a few seconds she heard the woman walk away, climb the stairs, leave the basement.

She touched her cheek, then sobbed as the pain bloomed again. She'd never guessed a slap could hurt so much. Her mom had slapped her once, when she was four years old, and she still remembered that day. But it wasn't even close to what she felt right now.

After a while she calmed down. Her stomach growled. She was hungry. She opened her eyes, and looked around for the sandwich.

It wasn't there. The woman had taken it with her when she left.

Time moved. Or it didn't. Abigail had no way of knowing. The burn in her cheek subsided. Then she heard the key in the lock. For a moment she tensed. Once the door opened, she'd run past whoever stood there. She could run really fast—she was one of the best runners in her class. She had the element of surprise.

The high-heeled shoes descended the steps again.

Her entire body stiffened. She couldn't move. Even as her brain screamed at her that the woman was wearing high-heeled shoes, that Abigail could easily get past her, her limbs felt paralyzed, her heart drumming in her chest, her lungs refusing to take in air, her cheek tingling with the memory of pain.

The woman walked over, wearing the mask. Abigail tried to tell herself that was a good sign. They wore the masks because they didn't want her to see their faces. Because they intended to let her go.

If she behaved.

"Look at me," the woman said, her voice cold and emotionless. Abigail raised her eyes. The woman held her phone, aiming it at Abigail.

Her eyes were brown. Abigail had always thought brown was a warm color, but the woman's eyes were frosty and detached.

The flash blinded her for a second, and then the room was cast back into its dim light. Spots danced in Abigail's vision. The woman put the phone in her pocket, then tossed the sandwich at Abigail's feet.

Long after the woman left, Abigail couldn't move. The sandwich lay on the floor.

———

Agent Mancuso was in the situation room, talking on her phone, when Hannah walked in. Her eyes flickered briefly toward Hannah, and then resumed scanning the large screen that now hung on the wall. It had a map of Glenmore Park on it, and a picture of Abigail in the corner. Three agents sat at the table, staring at screens of their own. One was speaking on the phone as well. They were different agents than the ones who'd been there that morning. The FBI crew worked in shifts.

Mancuso put down her phone and turned to face Hannah.

"Agent Ward reported that you finished interrogating the sex offenders," she said.

"Yeah. Nothing there," Hannah said.

"Good," Mancuso said.

"Any luck here?"

"There is no Noel. It was a fake identity," Mancuso said. "All his comments were posted using the same phone, sent from various spots around Glenmore Park. This phone disappeared completely from the network yesterday morning, and it's safe to assume the kidnappers got rid of it after setting the date with Abigail."

"When did Abigail start talking with Noel?"

"The first connection was three weeks ago," Mancuso said. "He commented on one of her images on Instagram. They began chatting daily two days later, with varying frequency. I've sent all the chat logs to a forensic psychologist—you remember Zoe, right?"

Hannah nodded. Zoe had helped with the Deadly Messenger case.

"Anyway, she's going over the chat logs. Hopefully she'll be able to glean something from them. Noel's phone was first used the same day the first comment was posted."

"So it was bought for that purpose alone," Hannah said.

"Yes. This was planned for a long time."

"Can we find out where the phone was purchased?"

"Not likely, but we're trying," Mancuso said. "We didn't manage to find any CCTV footage of the van. The kidnappers chose their route carefully, avoiding streets with cameras. Thirteen vans were spotted leaving Glenmore Park the night of the kidnapping, and we're now tracking their owners, trying to establish if any of them was used."

"They might have switched cars," Hannah said.

"Yes. If they did, the van is parked somewhere in the city. Your patrol cops are looking for it. Also, a man was seen dragging a young girl forcibly today, on Clayton Road. The girl was screaming and crying."

"What?" Hannah sputtered. "What man? Where—"

"He was arrested and interrogated. The girl was his daughter, and was five years old. Apparently he refused to buy her a new princess doll, and she reacted accordingly."

"Oh," Hannah's shoulders sagged.

"Still," Mancuso said. "I think both the father and the daughter learned a valuable lesson."

Hannah wasn't sure what the lesson was. "What about the Amber Alert?"

"We're getting some calls, and investigating them. Nothing so far." Mancuso shrugged. "I think you and Agent Ward should talk to Gracie tomorrow morning. She was released from the hospital this afternoon, and might be a bit more informative after a night's rest."

"Sure," Hannah said.

"You should get a night's rest, too, Detective," Mancuso said.

"I could say the same about you," Hannah answered.

Mancuso raised her eyebrows, her mouth quirking slightly. "Okay," she said. "If you insist on working till you drop, we have plenty of things to do."

"Can I have a look at the chat logs?" Hannah asked.

Mancuso motioned to a stack of papers on the desk, next to one of the other agents. "Knock yourself out," she said.

EIGHT

Abigail's Instagram profile had one hundred sixty-nine followers—mostly kids from school, some family members, a few kids she'd met online. These followers were all aghast at the ransom letter that appeared on her account. The image of Abigail in captivity was a brutal contrast to the images that were usually found on Instagram. There were no filters. There were no pouting lips, no smiling face, no funny-looking pet.

There was just a twelve-year-old girl held in an unknown location, her face haggard, her eyes red. And the ransom caption: threatening, sharp, with that terrible hashtag. *#WeGotAbigail*. As if the whole thing was some sort of social media joke.

Several of her younger followers cried for hours, scared to leave home. Two had panic attacks. Some parents barred their kids from Instagram, or forced them to unfollow Abigail.

One hundred sixty-nine pairs of eyes, sharing the same horror. On the 18th of March, Wednesday afternoon, another pair of eyes joined them.

When sixteen-year-old Petra Solis came home from school, she found her sister, Joy, sobbing hysterically. Her mother tried to calm Joy down, using the time-tested and proven method of shouting at her to *stop crying already*.

Petra hugged Joy until her sobs slowly petered out, then asked what was wrong. Joy told her she was following Abigail Lisman's Instagram account, and she'd just seen ... something. She couldn't explain what. Instead, she gave Petra her phone.

Petra stared unbelievingly at the image of Abigail, then logged into her own account to share the image.

Petra had three hundred and forty followers. Three of them shared the shocking image of the captive young girl. Between them, those three had a total of one thousand four hundred and twelve followers.

One of *those* followers was a video blogger, or like they called themselves, vlogger. He was very successful, mostly due to his playthroughs of *Minecraft*. When he decided to share the image and mention it on his channel, it was viewed by over a million people.

All of this took a bit less than four hours.

By Wednesday evening, over twenty million people in the United States alone were aware of the images, as well as tens of thousands of people all over the world.

Naamit lay in bed, staring at the ceiling. Ron snored gently by her side. She wondered if he was plagued by dreams as well. If he was, he didn't talk about it. Despite his anxiety and distress, he was sleeping.

For Naamit, the few hours she slept the night before had been the worst so far.

During the past day, she'd talked to friends and family who tried to help. She'd drowned herself in mindless tasks: cleaning, doing the laundry, cooking. Hannah came and gave her an update, trying to reassure her that her daughter was probably still alive. Things weren't so bad during the day.

But night came. She spent hours trying to fall asleep, her mind conjuring images of Abigail crying, or hurt, or dead. And as the minutes slowly ticked by, her imagination became a sadistic entity, tormenting her with horrific thoughts about perverts and psychopaths, and the terrible things that could be happening at that very moment, while she was in her bed doing nothing. When she finally fell asleep, the dreams came. She dreamed she was frantically searching for Abigail at school, hearing her calling for help, but the cries faltered and dwindled away. She dreamed she could hear Abigail beyond a massive door, but couldn't open it. She thumped her fists against it, crying in frustration. She dreamed the FBI came to tell her that her daughter was dead.

Even worse was the last dream. She dreamed that Abigail returned home, safe and sound. Naamit held her daughter in her arms, both of them laughing in joy. When she woke up from that dream, she felt the terrible loss and fear all over again, as if she'd just heard about the kidnapping for the first time.

Abigail had been missing for thirty-six hours. It felt like eternity. Naamit wasn't sure how much longer she could take.

At five in the morning, her phone blipped with a single notification: a new image on Abigail's Instagram profile. Naamit opened the page, her heart hammering, and stared at her daughter.

It was a picture of Abigail stand in front of a featureless gray wall. She looked thinner, and paler. Her legs were unnaturally rigid, as if she was forcing herself to stand. Had those beasts given her anything to eat? To drink? Abigail drank a lot, sometimes a dozen glasses of water a day. Ron said she was a human camel, which always secretly annoyed Naamit. The whole point of a camel was that it could go a long time without drinking.

Were they giving her enough water?

The caption on the image said simply: *3 Million. Soon. #WeGotAbigail.*

Soon. What did they mean by soon? Two days? Three? A week? Either way it was too long; Naamit wouldn't be able to bear it much longer. Either way it was not enough; they would never get that kind of money in such a short time.

They would never get that kind of money in twenty years.

She got up quietly, her movements slow and careful, trying not to wake Ron up. She didn't want to explain where she was going, or why. Not now. Later, she might need to, but not right now. She grabbed some random clothes, and crept out of the bedroom. She dressed in the living room, not bothering with her hair or makeup. Unlocking the front door, she left the house, finding herself the only person outside at four in the morning.

The chill penetrated everything, freezing her to the bone, making her teeth chatter almost immediately. She quickly got into the car and started the engine.

She'd never driven anywhere so early in the morning, as far as she could remember. She found the empty streets strangely soothing. At this hour, just before dawn, the entire city was asleep. She could even believe that her daughter was sleeping, wherever she was.

She parked in front of a large office building on Clayton Road. During the day, finding a parking spot on this street was virtually impossible. But right now the parking spaces were mostly vacant. She stopped the car, leaving the engine running. She needed the heat, despite the waste of fuel. She turned off her phone and leaned back in her seat, waiting.

She sat in the car, frozen like a statue for hours, as the city came to life. Cars began driving past her. Shop owners arrived to prepare their establishments for another busy day. Just across from her, a woman came out of The Warm Bagel. She held a small doughnut in her hand, and chewed slowly, a smile of pleasure on her face.

Naamit realized that tears were clouding her sight. How she wanted to be that woman. She wiped the tears from her eyes and stared straight ahead.

He arrived just before nine. He walked through the main entrance of the building, his face serious and businesslike, his manner brisk. Even now, in her crumbling mental state, she could see how attractive his entire demeanor was. He was a man who had the world around him under his complete control. A man who would take nonsense from no one. A man who, when faced with a crisis, would never flinch.

He was also cold and calculated, prone to anger. He was someone she had been happy to stay away from.

She sat in the car for another forty-five minutes, gathering her courage. She regretted not accosting him on the street, outside his comfort zone. In his office, he would be harder to face.

Finally, she got out of the car and entered the building. She took the elevator to the top floor, and walked into the offices of Koche Industries. The door to his office was closed. His secretary sat behind the front desk, just across from the office door. She turned toward Naamit and looked at her with distant eyes.

"Can I help you?"

"I'm here to see Lance Koche," Naamit said.

"I'm sorry, but Mr. Koche is—"

Naamit strode forward, swinging the door to Lance's office open. The secretary said nothing.

Lance Koche raised his head. He was middle-aged, his hair still mostly black, flecked with gray strands that only made him more imposing. His eyebrows were thick, and pointed in a constant frown above large dark eyes that watched her, betraying no surprise.

"Naamit," he said evenly. "I've asked before, please call before you come here. It's a simple request."

"Abigail has been kidnapped," Naamit blurted, not bothering with any preface.

Lance's eyes widened. There was an emotion she had never seen before on his face. Surprise? Concern? For a moment he seemed almost soft.

"Kidnapped?" he repeated, his voice unusually high. "By whom? When?"

"The FBI don't know who did it," she said. "It happened two days ago, on Tuesday evening." She took her phone out of her pocket, and strode to his desk, turning on the screen. The Instagram app was already open. She showed him the image. "They posted this on her account."

He took the phone gently from her hand and stared at it. "Three million?" he asked, frowning.

"There's another one," Naamit said. "Scroll down."

He did, his frown deepening.

"I can't raise three million dollars," Naamit said.

"Obviously," Lance said shortly.

"I hoped that you could—"

"No."

Naamit caught the sob that threatened to emerge. Lance Koche did not react well to crying. "She's your daughter."

"My biological daughter, whom I didn't know about until two months ago." Lance's voice was cold and steely.

"They'll kill her!"

"I doubt it."

"Are you willing to bet your daughter's life on it?" Naamit asked, the grief and fear morphing into rage. "What sort of monster—"

"Let's make one thing clear," Lance said, raising his voice. "That girl is just a girl to me, nothing more. I don't even know her."

"Don't you want to know her?" Naamit asked. "You will. If she gets back safely, I swear you will."

There was a moment of silence. "I don't have three million dollars," he said, his voice low.

"But you can raise—"

"I can't. It wasn't a good year. Even if I wanted to, I can't pay this ransom."

"Then you can pay some of it! They might negotiate if they know you can pay half or—"

"Your best bet is to let the FBI handle this. They're professionals," Lance said. "I'm sorry, but—"

"I'll tell the FBI that you're her real father," Naamit said, her voice seething with hatred. "I'll tell the press. You'll be the father who let his daughter die because of his greed.

You think this was a bad business year? It's going to get much worse."

Lance's face froze, and she knew she'd blown it.

"By all means," he said. "Tell them. Now, do you want me to call security to escort you out, or will you do it yourself? I don't really care either way."

Naamit turned and ran out of the room, her heart drowning in tears.

―――

Gracie's family lived only five minutes away from the Lismans, but their neighborhood was clearly populated by wealthier families. Their house, like most on the street, had a small, well-groomed yard, and the sidewalk had recently been swept. The path to the front door was lined with pink and white roses. Clint and Hannah surveyed the surroundings before approaching the door and knocking. It was Thursday, late morning, a time for most parents to be at work, for kids to be in school. But the Durham family wasn't like most families this Thursday. They were recuperating from a terrible ordeal. For them, that Thursday morning was a time for healing.

Unfortunately for Gracie, it would also be a time to relive one of the worst nights of her life. Hannah wished she didn't have to question the kid again, but they needed a clear picture of that night. Of the four people who were there, she was the only one available to answer questions.

"Who is it?" a voice asked from behind the door. Karen.

Clint flipped his badge in front of the peephole. "FBI," he said.

There was a moment of silence, and then they heard a lock click, and a latch being removed. The door opened. Karen stood in the doorway, wearing a baggy shirt and worn leggings, her hair a mess. She looked almost worse than she had in the hospital the day before.

"Good morning Mrs. Durham," Clint said. "I'm Agent Ward, and I believe you've met Detective Hannah Shor from the Glenmore Park PD. May we come in?"

She hesitated. "Why?" she finally asked.

"We need to ask Gracie some questions," Clint said.

"Gracie is asleep," she said.

"Mrs. Durham—"

"She woke up three times during the night, screaming," Karen said, her eyes tearing up. "I let her sleep in my lap, like a baby. She needs rest. Please come tomorrow."

"Karen," Hannah said, her tone as soft as she could make it. "Abigail has been kidnapped. The faster we figure out who took her, the better the chance we can get her back."

"But Gracie already told you everything she knew!"

"Yes, but she was medicated, and traumatized," Hannah said. "Please. Think of Naamit. Think of what she's going through."

Guilt was a potent weapon. Hannah had learned how to use it from her mother.

Karen nodded, saying nothing and moved aside to let them in.

Gracie sat on a brown sofa in the living room, clearly awake, gazing at the television. It was muted, and she didn't seem to be paying attention to what was happening on the screen.

"Gracie," her mother said. "These people want to ask you more questions about Abigail."

Gracie looked at them, her eyes watery. "Are you from the police?" she asked.

"And the FBI," Clint said.

"Did you see the image on Instagram?" she asked.

Hannah nodded. "We did."

"Do you think they'll let her go?"

"I hope Abigail will be home soon," Hannah said carefully. Karen went away, then returned carrying a chair. Hannah sat on the chair, and Clint sat down next to Gracie on the sofa.

"What do you want to know?" Gracie asked.

"We want to go over the events of that night again," Hannah said.

"Okay."

"You were at the playground," Clint said. "Do you remember what time you got there?"

"I don't know. A bit before eight. She was supposed to meet Noel at eight."

"And when did the man with the ski mask show up?"

"A few minutes later, I think."

"Can you describe anything about the man?" Hannah asked. "Anything that comes to mind. Did he seem tall? Did he speak? Was he holding something? Did he—"

"He was holding something," Gracie said. "Something white."

"Where did he come from?" Clint asked.

"From the park."

"And where were you?"

"We were sitting on the swing," Gracie said. "Waiting for Noel. I … I convinced Abigail he wasn't going to show up. We were just about to leave. That means he showed up after eight. A few minutes after eight." She looked at them with wide eyes. "That's helpful, right?"

"It really is," Hannah said. "So he was holding something white?"

"Yes."

"You don't know what?"

"No."

"And then what happened?"

"We ran away." Tears began to flow, leaving faint translucent lines on Gracie's pale cheeks. "We were scared!"

"You're doing very well, Gracie," Clint said. "This is a huge help. When you ran, what did the man do?"

"He chased us."

"Did he say anything?"

"I … I'm not sure."

"And then what?"

"A second man showed up. He charged at us, blocking the way."

"Blocking the way to where?" Hannah asked "Where were you running to?" She created a small diagram of the events in her mind.

"Blocking the way back to the street."

"So the second man came from the street?"

"Yes."

"Did you see where he came from?"

"I … I think he came from a van, but I'm not sure."

"Okay," Hannah said, trying to disguise the tension in her voice. "Can you recall the van? Tell us anything about it?"

"N … No."

"Think about the street. Was it well lit?"

"No."

"Okay, but you saw the van. How?"

"I think the van's lights were on."

"Did you see it coming, or was it parked?"

"I don't ... Oh..." Gracie's eyes went distant for a moment. "I think it was both. I mean ... It was parked, and then it got out of the parking and drove to the park's entrance."

"And when looking at it, even for just a tiny moment, did it seem dark, or—"

"It was dark. Like ... black or dark green, I think."

Hannah let out a small breath. The seemingly small detail could be useful in numerous ways.

"And then what happened?"

"We changed directions. We tried to run down a different path. But it was dark, and we couldn't see, and ... and..."

"Yes?"

"I think we split. And they chased Abigail."

"Both of them?" Hannah asked, exchanging looks with Clint.

"Yeah. Both of them. One of them looked at me, but he was definitely chasing Abigail. And ... I don't remember what happened after that."

NINE

Hannah got out of Clint's car. The sleep deprivation was catching up to her. Slumbering for three hours on her desk at the station was not enough.

She shivered slightly. Although it was nearly noon, it was one of those days in which the wind got into every nook and cranny, whistling into ear and nose cavities, snaking down the collar of a loose shirt, breezing through gloveless palms, and generally making everyone miserable. The weather and her exhaustion made her feel tense and short-tempered. She needed a hot shower.

They were back at the scene of the crime, hoping to glean a firm idea of the sequence of events that had led to the kidnapping. She looked at the post office and the gas station down the road. The post office had been closed that night, but the gas station had been open for business. No one there had seen or heard anything.

"We're back at the playground," Clint said. Hannah glanced at him. He held his phone to his ear, frowning. The serious face made him seem authoritative, strong. She suddenly wondered how it would feel to be held by him. He was much taller than her; she could nestle in the hollow of his throat. She flushed, the heat in her face contrasting sharply with the biting wind on her skin.

"I'll give you a full update about the interview with Gracie Durham later," he said, then listened again.

He was talking to Mancuso, Hannah guessed. She banished the thoughts about Clint from her head. She had to be focused right now.

"They're definitely careful," he said after a few moments. "Okay. I'll talk to you later." He hung up. To Hannah, he said, "Mancuso said they traced the phones used to post the Instagram images. Different phones. One image was posted from Boston, the other from twenty miles north of here, somewhere along route 128."

"Both phones turned off once the image was posted?" Hannah asked.

"You guessed it."

They walked briskly into the playground. A single nanny stood above a toddler sitting on the merry-go-round. She pushed it around half-heartedly. They both seemed as if they would rather be someplace else. The toddler looked as if he thought merry-go-rounds were no longer trending in his kindergarten. It was all about slides and sandboxes these days. That was where the cool toddlers were. The nanny simply seemed cold.

"This is where they waited for the imaginary boyfriend," Clint said.

Hannah nodded, looking around with her hands in her pockets. The main path went into the park, snaking between a clump of trees. It wasn't a thick clump; she could even see the street beyond it.

How had it looked that night?

Dark, she decided. Cold. There were small mounds of snow on the ground the night they found Gracie. Now they had mostly melted, and the few that remained were far and between.

"The van parked on the street," Clint said. "Probably over there." He pointed south of the park.

"Why not there?" Hannah asked, pointing north toward the intersection with Clayton Road. "More parking space over there, in front of the gas station."

Clint shook his head. "Checked CCTV feeds from the gas station. They have a security camera aimed directly at those parking spots. There was nothing there."

"Okay," Hannah said, looking at the spot Clint indicated, fixing it in her mind. Then she looked aside and pointed at a tree. "We found Gracie under that tree," she said.

"So … the girls are waiting here, and one of the kidnappers, wearing a ski mask, comes up the main path from the park," Clint said.

"Right."

"The girls run away toward the street, but the second kidnapper rushes them—"

"After parking the van in front of the gate," Hannah said.

"Yeah. He rushes them and they change their direction, running down that way instead," Clint pointed in the direction of the spot where she'd found Gracie. "There's no path. The girls split, and both kidnappers chase Abigail."

"This wasn't chance," Hannah said. "Abigail was the one contacted by the handsome boy. *She* was the one he was supposed to meet. And they both chased *her*."

"Right."

"What if Gracie had escaped? Called for help?"

"I don't know if they planned for it," Hannah said. "But they were pretty fast anyway; it probably wouldn't have helped. So let's see—"

"She told us he was holding something," Clint said. "Something white. What was it?"

Hannah looked at where they'd recovered Gracie, easily sixty feet from the gate. And Abigail was an athlete, she might have gotten even further before they caught up with her. But no signs of a struggle had been found at the scene. Abigail must have been knocked out, or at least incapacitated.

"A rag," she said. "Some sort of anaesthetic."

Clint thought for a moment, then said, "Sounds likely."

"So … one kidnapper hiding in the park, intending to knock Abigail out," Hannah said. "The other one parked nearby in a van, waiting. Abigail gets here with Gracie, he comes over, they run, and both kidnappers chase them, catching Abigail, knocking her out. They carry her back to the van and drive away." She frowned.

"What is it?" Clint asked.

"They planned the rest so professionally: the untraceable lure, the getaway, the ransom note. They completely disappeared. They posted the Instagram pictures from remote locations, using different phones."

"Yeah."

"They're organized, right?"

"Looks like it."

"Why the crappy job here? Rushing both girls with nothing but a rag with some anaesthetic? Chasing them in the darkness through the park? What the hell were they thinking?"

Clint thought about it for a moment. "They expected only Abigail," he finally said. "It should have been a romantic date. If she'd come alone, he could have crept over without her noticing him. It was dark. He might have planned to lure her somewhere with a text, then grab her."

"Makes sense," Hannah said. "But with two girls—"

"Sitting across from each other on the double swing," Clint said.

"He couldn't catch them both unaware."

"They got away with it, though," Clint said. "They messed up, but they still have the girl. And we're still in the dark."

His phone rang, and he fumbled with it for a few seconds before answering.

"Yeah?"

There was a short pause.

"We'll be right there." He hung up. "That was Mancuso. The forensic psychologist is here. She wants to hear what Gracie told us about the kidnapping."

―――

Mancuso and Zoe Bentley were sitting together in the situation room when Hannah and Clint came in.

"Zoe!" Hannah said, grinning. "How are you?"

Zoe stood up, smiling, and shook Hannah's hand. Her dark hair was short, accentuating her long delicate neck. She took a step back, looking at Hannah with her piercing stare.

Hannah found Zoe's eyes to be a bit disconcerting. They reminded her of a predator's eyes, following its prey, anticipating its every move.

"How are you doing, Detective Shor?" Zoe asked.

"Fine! Not bad at all," Hannah said, trying to maintain eye contact with Zoe's piercing, relentless orbs. "Are you assigned to the Lisman kidnapping case?"

Zoe shook her head. "Sorry, I'm afraid not," she said. "I'm working full time on a serial killer case in Texas. Truth be told, kidnapping is far from my expertise, but Agent Mancuso asked me to take a look at your case."

They all sat down. Zoe opened a small folder that was placed in front of her on the table.

"This kidnapping isn't standard," Zoe said. "This ransom letter … I don't think I've ever heard of anything like it."

"Yeah," Hannah said. "So what can you tell us about the assholes who kidnapped her?"

"Well … I've figured out some key notes, but I'd be happy if you could tell me about the kidnapping. Did you talk to the kid who witnessed the entire thing this morning?"

"Yes. Gracie Durham," Hannah said. "And we've gone back to the crime scene to understand her testimony better."

"Good," Zoe nodded. "What did you find?"

Clint brought Zoe and Mancuso up to speed, with Zoe asking a few questions and Hannah interjecting to add some details. When they finished, Zoe drummed with her fingers on the table, thinking.

"So they seemed to have planned this thoroughly," she said after a long pause, "but didn't function well when things didn't align to their plans."

Hannah nodded. "Yeah. We think they didn't expect two girls in the playground, only one."

"Right! And they had no backup plan. It shouldn't have been surprising that Abigail would show up with a friend. And even if they lacked the ability to guess that would happen, they should have had a backup plan if things went haywire."

"So … this indicates they're stupid?" Clint asked.

Zoe shook her head. "No. They're very organized, so I'd say the person who planned this probably has a very orderly mind. It's likely he's in an administrative position. But the lack of planning for unseen occurrences indicates that he's used to being micro-managed. He might have a very demanding supervisor that gives him bite-sized tasks. If the two kidnappers had discussed the plan beforehand, they would have easily thought of the possibility that Abigail would show up with a friend. This shows the planner's partner is probably used to taking orders and doesn't question them."

"So we have a low ranking administrator and a foot soldier," Clint said.

"Do you think they would have stayed in Glenmore Park?" Mancuso asked.

Zoe shrugged. "No idea. Where's the van?"

"We can't be sure. There's no evidence that it left Glenmore Park during the night of the kidnapping, and we have agents stationed at both exists to the highway, monitoring the traffic," Mancuso said. "There are some back roads, but we're working under an assumption that this van never left the city. We think they may have switched cars. So we're looking for it in Glenmore Park."

Zoe bit her lip. "I don't know," she said slowly. "This planner wouldn't have just left this van parked somewhere. That's too disorganized. He would have had a plan for it."

"It could be parked in the garage of a private home," Clint suggested. "They could be Glenmore Park residents."

"Sounds reasonable. As for the note…" Zoe frowned. "There's something sadistic about the delivery. Sadistic and extravagant. The person who sent it thinks he can't get caught, that his plan is infallible."

"Even though they already saw that unexpected things might happen," Hannah said.

"Right. So we're talking about high self-confidence. Also, I've gone through the chat logs with this so-called Noel several times. Whoever wrote this knew how to talk to a twelve-year-old. There are instances where I noticed a small slip-up, the use of a slightly old-fashioned slang word, or missing a basic texting abbreviation, but overall it was pretty natural. I'm guessing the planner is in his twenties. This would also align well with the self-confidence."

"I've known old people to be self-confident," Clint said.

Zoe shrugged. "Usually not to the point of stupidity. Sending a ransom note like this is dumb. It's risky. Again, I'm not sure but I *think* this person is no more than thirty. They're ignoring our attempts at communication, right?"

Mancuso nodded. "We've sent them several private messages and tried to comment on the actual posts. They've ignored it all."

"This is interesting. I initially thought he used Instagram to show off, to get his fifteen minutes of glory. But if that were the case, he'd be inclined to rub it in, to let us know how smart he is. Since he didn't do that, I think this isn't about him at all. This is about Abigail's parents. Whoever sent this wanted to hurt her parents, and he wanted to do so publicly."

"Yeah, he's a real asshole," Hannah said.

"An asshole leaves a nasty comment on your Facebook page, or talks about you behind your back. He doesn't kidnap your child and gloat about it," Zoe said. "This person hates one or both of Abigail's parents. You're looking for someone who knows them."

"Are you sure?" Hannah asked.

"Well, it's hard to be sure in my profession," Zoe said. "But yeah, I'd say I'm pretty sure once you find this person, it'll be someone who knows the parents, and has reason to hate them."

Hannah and Clint exchanged looks. "In that case," Hannah said. "We need to talk to Naamit and Ron again."

Hannah could almost feel the emotional torrents that washed over Naamit and Ron's house as she and Clint parked outside.

"Are you okay?" Clint asked, looking at her with concern.

"Yeah," Hannah said, and sighed. "I just … every time I walk in there without their daughter, I can feel the disappointment and the fear in them. Especially in Naamit."

"Do you know them well?"

"I've met Naamit several times at my mom's house. She and her husband sometimes come to family occasions." She clenched her hands. "I don't really know her well, but she's a very nice woman, and I've heard her talk about her daughter. She's always so proud of her. And protective. I can't imagine what she's going through."

Clint laid a hand on her shoulder. "And you shouldn't try," he said. "Your mom's job is to help her friend cope. It's your job to get Abigail home. You can't do it while trying to empathize with Naamit."

"You're right," Hannah said, drawing strength from his touch. "Come on, let's go inside."

They got out of the car. Hannah, feeling fragile, let Clint lead the way. It was her tiredness, she thought. Tonight she'd have to sleep, even if her mind insisted she shouldn't go to bed before Abigail was found. Clint knocked on the door. After a few seconds, the door opened.

Hannah started in surprise. Her mother stood in the doorway. It was jarring to see her mother's face while she was on the job. Her mom's green eyes, identical to Hannah's, shone in the light of the setting sun, full of sorrow. Her graying hair tumbled to her shoulders, immaculate as always. Hannah took a moment to handle the collision of worlds in her mind.

"Hey, Mom," she said. "We're here to talk to Ron and Naamit."

"Sure, sweetie," her mother said, her voice soft and sad. "Come in."

She led them inside, taking them to the living room. Ron and Naamit sat there, with a woman Hannah didn't recognize.

"Hannah, this is Debra," her mother said. "Debra works with Naamit."

Debra stood up and shook Hannah's hand. She was quite tall, her coal-black hair pulled back in a braid. She would have been beautiful if not for the pockmarks on her skin, perhaps the remnants of a severe case of teenage acne. Her brown eyes were wide, her mouth twisted in worry. "Hello, Hannah."

"Hannah is my daughter," her mother said. "The detective." They exchanged a meaningful glance. Hannah realized they must have been talking about her earlier.

They sat down, and her mother went to the kitchen to prepare coffee.

"Any progress?" Naamit asked, her voice weak. She looked as if she was fading away: paler, thinner, black pouches under her eyes. Ron held her hand, caressing it. Hannah felt for him. He clearly didn't know what to do.

"We have a better description of the vehicle they used," Hannah said "And we're looking for it. We're certain they didn't leave town with it."

"So they're still in Glenmore Park?" Naamit asked.

"That's one of our leading theories," Hannah said, skirting around the truth. "We met with a forensic psychologist today. She thinks that whoever kidnapped Abigail is someone who knows you or Ron."

"Knows us?" Naamit blinked. "What do you mean?"

"She thinks one of the kidnapper's main motivations is hurting you," Hannah said.

"That's terrible!" Debra said, her voice shocked.

"Can you think of anyone who has a reason to hate either of you?" Hannah asked.

"No, of course not," Ron said. "We're not the kind of people who make enemies. We don't get into confrontations. All of our acquaintances are good people. I just can't—"

"We want to make sure no stone is left unturned," Clint said. "I'm sure your friends are good people, but try to think of any argument you might have had, any disagreement."

Ron shook his head slowly.

"What about that man you fired?" Naamit asked abruptly. "What was his name? Hal!"

"That was three years ago," Ron said, frowning. "And he wasn't a bad man, he would never have—"

"What's his full name?" Hannah asked.

"Hal Moore," Ron said. "There were layoffs at the factory. I was in charge of six men, and my boss said I had to fire one, so I fired Hal. But it was a long time ago."

"We have to make sure," Hannah explained again. "Anyone else? Could be someone in your family, perhaps someone from long ago, could even be someone you went to school with, someone you dated…" Hannah felt Naamit tense up, and turned to look at her. "Anyone you've dumped? Anyone who had a crush on you…?"

Naamit shook her head. "I'm sorry," she said.

"You might think it isn't important," Clint said, "but you'd be amazed at the strange things people do over seemingly small matters."

Silence filled the room. Hannah's mother walked in with two mugs in her hands. "Agent Ward, I wasn't sure how you take your coffee—"

"Thank you, but we have to get going," Clint said, standing up.

Though she wanted the coffee, Hannah stood up as well. She'd buy coffee at the nearby Starbucks.

"If you think of anyone else, please let us know," Hannah said. She looked at Naamit as she said it. She wondered if it had only been her imagination. It almost seemed as if the woman was hiding something.

They left the house, walking to Clint's car, when a voice called after them.

Debra followed, her high heels tapping on the paved path. "Please wait." She caught up and cleared her throat. "Naamit is a good person," she said. "Too good. She can't see what's in front of her eyes."

"What can't she see?" Hannah asked.

"We work in a small HR company," Debra said. "Five of us. Naamit started working there after all of us, four years ago."

Hannah nodded, waiting.

"Our manager quit a year ago, and the owner decided to promote Naamit," Debra said. "She earned it. She's a brilliant woman and incredibly dedicated. And she's a great manager."

"But someone doesn't agree," Hannah said.

Debra nodded. "Melanie Pool thinks she should have been promoted. She undermines Naamit every chance she gets. She's hated her ever since the promotion."

"Thank you," Hannah said. "We'll check it out."

"Naamit is my best friend," Debra said, her eyes tearing up. "I … miscarried two years ago, and she was there for me. She was there for me when my bastard husband left me. I can't stand watching her suffer like this."

"We'll do what we can to get her daughter back safely," Hannah said softly.

"Thank you," Debra sniffled. "I … I should probably go inside. Your mother says you're an amazing detective. I know you'll get Abigail back."

She turned around and walked inside.

"Okay," Clint said. "We have two names. Melanie Pool and Hal Moore. Who should we check first?"

"Neither sounds very promising," Hannah muttered. A thought flitted in the back of her mind. A new lead.

"Well, we should still check them out," Clint said. "Zoe said that—"

"Hang on," Hannah said. "Earlier … We talked about the van. And Zoe said she didn't think they'd just abandon the van. That it's too disorganized, right?"

"Yeah, and I said that maybe it's parked in their garage."

"Right. But they've been very thorough in erasing any trace leading to them, dumping their phones, wearing ski masks … these guys are careful."

"What's your point?"

Hannah narrowed her eyes. "What about getting rid of the van in a junkyard?" she said.

TEN

It was Howard Carson's fortieth birthday, and he was excited for the surprise the guys would set up. Well, hardly a surprise by this point; they'd been ordering a stripper for any of them who turned forty, ever since Tony's memorable birthday. Still, there were shades of surprise. She could be dressed as a cheerleader, or a cowboy, jump out of a cake, or a big box, kinky or vanilla … there really was a large variety to choose from. Of course, his wife would not approve of his friends' gift, which was why he mentioned to them several times that he'd be working late on his birthday. In his office. Alone.

He was dealing with some paperwork, although frankly his progress was slow—almost nonexistent, due to the excitement clouding his mind. He hadn't been close to another woman's naked breasts in years, aside from his wife's. He knew there would be a lap dance if he wanted one, and the prospect made him dizzy.

He opened a bottle of beer, his third in the past hour, and took a long swig. When someone knocked on the door, he nearly knocked over the bottle on his desk in his hurry to get up. He walked to the door.

"Who is it?" he asked, his voice slightly high, grinning foolishly as he peeked through the peephole.

At first he was disappointed. There was a large black man in a buttoned-up gray shirt and black pants behind the door—definitely not what he expected. But then he noticed the woman by his side. She was a sweet thing, petite, with dark brown hair and the cutest mouth. She was not every man's taste, but Howard loved small women, and his friends knew that well.

The large man flipped open a badge. "FBI," he said. "Please open the door."

Howard's grin widened. So this was the surprise. An "FBI agent." The black man was probably her sound guy and security, there to make sure the customer didn't touch the goods. Carson could respect that. It was a crazy world. Being a stripper was a hazardous occupation.

He opened the door and motioned them inside. Then he walked over to his desk, and got his chair, dragging it to the middle of the room, where there would be plenty of space for a lap dance. He sat down, smiling at the stripper expectantly.

"Mr. Carson?" she asked.

"That's right," he said in a jocular tone. "But you can call me Howey."

She raised her eyebrows. "Mr. Carson, I'm Detective Shor from the Glenmore Park PD, and this here is Agent Ward, from the FBI."

"Good, good." He slapped his palms against his thighs. Great roleplaying on that woman. He was glad he'd prepared a large cash tip in advance.

"We wanted to ask you a few questions," she said. "Regarding … are you all right?"

"Couldn't be better!"

"You seem a bit flushed." She narrowed her eyes. "And you're shaking. Are you nervous about something, Mr. Carson?"

"Oh, no, I assure you," he grinned. "Howey Carson is quite thrilled about this."

"Uh … Okay," she said. "Mr. Carson, we're looking for a vehicle that was left in your yard. A dark van."

"And what will you do if you find it?" Howey waggled his eyebrows. He hoped the guy would hit the *Play* button soon. The anticipation and role-playing were exciting, but he could already imagine the naked thighs of the woman riding him, her breasts thrusting in his face.

"Sir, this specific van would have been delivered on Tuesday night or Wednesday morning," she said.

For a moment he kept grinning, still imagining her creamy, naked skin. Then some details registered. First, this wasn't a very good disguise. She wasn't wearing anything sexy, not even makeup. Second, there really had been a dark van on Tuesday night, and quite a memorable one at that.

This was not a stripper.

He wasn't aware of his erection until the moment it wilted to nothing in his pants.

"Mr. Carson?"

"Y-yes. Yes, of course." He got up, feeling shaky, and fumbled with the papers on his desk until he found the right form. "There," he said. "I have it here. Chevrolet Express. Registered to a Mr. John Smith."

Agent Ward and Detective Shor exchanged glances as he held out the form. Shor took the single sheet from his hand and read it quickly.

"It says *scrapped*," she said.

"That's right," Howard said. He felt sad.

"What does that mean?"

"It means it was scrapped for metal and sold."

"Do you usually scrap usable cars?"

"No, but that's what the man asked for," Howard said, "and he paid well."

"What did you do with the scrapped metal?" Detective Shor asked.

"I sold it to a warehouse I work with."

"What about the rest of the car?"

"I sold the engine to a different client. The rest was disposed of."

"Can you describe—" Shor was interrupted by a knock on the door.

Howard sighed as he walked to the door and pulled it open. There was another cop in the doorway.

"Come in," he said despondently. "Your friends are already inside."

She walked inside, her high heels tapping on the floor. She was tall, thin, and blonde, wearing a very short skirt and fishnet stockings. In her hand she carried a portable stereo.

It took Howard only a moment to understand what was going on. "Hang on—" he began.

"Mr. Carson?" the girl asked in a soft silky tone. "You have been a very bad boy." She looked at the agent and the detective and winked.

"Please listen, I need to—"

"I'm afraid I have to put you under arrest," she said, "for being sexy."

She hit *Play*, and soft, rhythmic music filled the room. She put the stereo on the floor, pouting at Howard the entire time. He froze, mortified, unable to stop the scene unfolding around him. Both the detective and the agent were staring, bemused expressions on their faces. They didn't look as if they were about to intervene.

The stripper wiggled in a way Howard might have found alluring fifteen minutes before, her fingers crawling to the top button of her shirt. Before this atrocity could go any further, he crouched down and hysterically pressed all the buttons on the portable stereo until it stopped playing.

"Please," he said, breathing hard. "I'm in the middle of something here."

"Oh," the stripper said. "The dude who called told me six-thirty, so…"

"Agent Ward," Shor said to her companion, "being sexy is not illegal in Massachusetts, so this isn't really in my jurisdiction. Is it perhaps a federal offense?"

"Not that I know of," Agent Ward said.

"You're in luck." Shor smiled at Howard sweetly. "I don't think you're under arrest after all. But we do need to ask you some further questions Mr. Carson."

Howard nodded glumly. *Worst birthday ever.*

"Okay," Shor said. "So this man calling himself John Smith comes here on Tuesday evening, wants to scrap his van—insists, in fact, that his van be scrapped and not sold for parts—and pays extra for that. Can you describe the man who identified himself as John Smith?"

"Sure," Howard said. "He was a bit taller than me and wore dark clothes. And a ski mask."

"A ski mask," the agent said, his voice dry.

"Yeah."

"He never took it off?"

Howard shrugged. "It was a cold night."

The stripper cop spoke up. "That sounds very suspicious."

Shor grinned. "Just like Officer … what's your name?"

"Candy," the stripper said.

"Like Officer Candy said, that sounds suspicious. Didn't it strike you as odd?"

Howard sighed. "Look, people have strange requests, okay? I don't pry into their personal business. If the car is registered to them, I do what they ask me to."

"You said it was a cold night," Agent Ward said. "What time did he come here?"

"About nine, possibly a bit later," Howard said.

"That's very late," the detective said.

"He called a few hours in advance," Howard said. "He said he'd come late. I waited for him."

"Sounds like the dude was trying to get rid of a hot car," Candy said. "And John Smith? That's a fake name."

"Officer Candy, you're sharp. You'll get far," Shor said. "Was there anyone else with him? Anyone waiting outside?"

"There was no one with him," Howard said. "I don't know if there was anyone outside."

"There must have been," Candy said. "Otherwise, how'd he get home? Did you see who picked him up?"

"Uh…" Howard hesitated, unsure if he should really answer questions from the stripper. But Shor and the agent were looking at him, unfazed. "I didn't see who picked him up. Maybe he took a cab."

"Did you see—" Candy said.

"Thank you, Officer Candy," Shor said. "I think I can take it from here." She turned back to Howard. "I need the name of the warehouse you sold the scrap metal to, the details of the client you sold the engine to, and the form this guy filled out. And if you have security footage from that night—"

"I don't," Howard said, feeling very sorry for himself. He could never go to a strip club again, without this dismal occasion popping into the front of his mind. They'd ruined strippers forever.

"Well, we need everything you have from that night. I'll have no problem getting a search warrant." Detective Shor grinned widely. "We can have Officer Candy deliver it."

"No need." Howard said.

He got up, and gave them copies of all the paperwork he had on that car while Candy watched with wide eyes.

As the detective and the agent turned to leave, Candy asked, "Do you want your birthday dance now?"

Shor turned back. "It's your birthday?"

"Yeah," he answered, staring at the floor.

"Well, happy birthday!" she said cheerfully and walked out the door with the agent following her.

———

It was dark as they drove back, the night sky cloudy enough to swallow the moon. No one lingered in the streets; everyone had been driven inside by the biting cold. The chilly air managed to slither its way into the car's interior, but Hannah felt warm. The thrill of the chase pulsed in her blood as she reviewed what they'd learned. They had a plausible chain of events, and the details of the van used for the kidnapping. Would that lead them somewhere? Perhaps, if the kidnapper hadn't been careful when he'd bought it.

Tension tightened her body, and her fists clenched as she sorted through the evidence in her head, trying to look for unasked questions, for missing puzzle pieces, for leads and threads.

"Are you okay?" Clint asked.

Her jaw was clenched. "Yeah." She tried to relax. She smiled at him. "I get very intense when I'm on a case. It can drive my partner insane."

"Your partner?"

"Detective Gladwin. Have you met him?"

"No."

"You'd like him. He's a lot more easygoing than I am."

Clint smiled back. "Who said I like people who are easygoing?"

"Well, people generally do," Hannah said.

"I enjoy your intensity," Clint said, his voice low.

Hannah flushed, trying to ignore the tiny shivers on the back of her neck. "Thanks." In the small space of the car, Clint's scent enveloped her. He wore a subtle cologne that reminded Hannah of cedar trees and rainfall. Once again she imagined him holding her, but this time the images were much more vivid. She could almost feel his fingers brushing against her cheek, his lips touching her skin.

"Want to talk about the case, hash out the details? We can do it over dinner. It could help you relax a bit. If you're feeling too … intense."

She glanced at him—his handsome face, his wide shoulders—and could feel her body reacting, changing its rhythm. Her brain quieted as her heart took the lead, thrumming excitedly.

"What did you have in mind?" she asked.

"I don't know." He let his eyes linger over her. All of her, not just her face. "Is there anywhere good around here?"

"Sure," Hannah said. "Turn right here."

He did. "Are you cold?" he asked. "We can turn up the heat."

"No need." She shivered slightly, but not from the cold. "Turn left at the next intersection,"

"So ... where are we going? Not that pizza place again, right?" Clint asked.

Hannah didn't answer, staring at herself in the passenger window. She raised her hand to tuck a loose strand of hair behind her ear, then hesitated and let her hand drop to her lap. Her mind bubbled with images and feelings. Her nerves were sensitive, almost raw.

She was nearly certain Clint wanted her, too. Was she imagining it? Did he casually flirt with everyone? She tried to think of the conversation with Zoe, earlier. Had he acted the same as he did when he spoke with her? Had he half-smiled at Zoe like he did to her? She thought he hadn't, but wasn't completely sure.

The car turned slowly onto Laguna Street, a small residential area close to the police station. There was a small grocery store there, which Hannah occasionally visited to buy some bagels or hot rolls. It was closed now, which was totally fine.

"Park the car in there," Hannah said, pointing at the small alley where trucks parked when delivering their supplies to the grocery. It was bathed in shadows, mostly hidden from the street.

To her relief, Clint didn't argue, or ask why. He simply followed her instructions, pulling into the small alley. He stopped the car. The engine humming silently.

Hannah turned to smile at him. "This is it," she said.

He looked around him, then at her, saying nothing. She leaned closer to him and switched off the car's engine. Their faces were only inches apart. Clint looked at her, his lips slightly parted, his dark eyes intense. Hannah tilted her head just a bit, leaning in to brush his lips with hers. As their lips met, she felt a rush of excitement and heat washing her body. Her tongue dipped forward slightly, finding his. She still wondered, in the back of her brain, if he might suddenly push her away. She backed away just a bit to study his face, and he grabbed the back of her head, pulling her closer, returning her kiss just as intensely. He grabbed her waist, his fingers strong and insistent as he pulled her body toward him.

She hooked a leg over him, straddling him, both hands stroking his body in hunger, her fingers exploring his skin. She let out a low breath as his hand crept under her bra, brushing over her nipple. She quickly took off her shirt, banging her arm against the steering wheel, not caring about the discomfort, or the cramped space, ignoring the cold and giving herself away to pleasure.

―――

Still in his lap, she grinned at him. Both of them were naked, though Clint's pants were bunched at his ankles.

"Check out the windows," he said.

She glanced at them and laughed. All the car windows were completely fogged up; it was impossible to see anything through them. The driver's window had a small imprint in the condensation, in the shape of her palm. She vaguely remembered leaning against it as waves of pleasure shook her body. How very Kate Winslet of her.

"I think you can take me to my car now," she said in a sleepy voice.

"Okay."

They were silent for a few moments.

"I kinda need my legs to do that," Clint finally said. "And it'll be hard to see the road with your body blocking the view."

"Do you have a problem with my body?"

"Only when I'm trying to drive."

"Fine," Hannah sighed. She returned to her own seat and started looking for her discarded clothing. Her underpants were on the dashboard, her shirt and pants on the floor. She couldn't find her bra.

"We'll look for it in the parking lot, where there's light," Clint said. He wore his pants and his shirt, though he still hadn't buttoned it up. She took another glance at his chest. Those FBI agents sure kept themselves in shape.

"Sure," she said. "We'll just try fishing for my bra by the police station. If my boss shows up, we'll tell him we're looking for evidence."

Clint started the car, and turned up the heat, waiting for the windows to clear up. "So you're going home now?" he asked.

"Well, it's getting late," she pointed out.

"Yeah."

"You're welcome to follow me there," she said. "I can make us some spaghetti."

He smiled at her. "That sounds delicious."

Abigail woke up to the sound of the door creaking. She lay on the bed, her eyes still shut, her mind and body numb, submerged in despair and fear. She couldn't face her captors anymore, couldn't face the sight of the basement. As long as her eyes remained closed, she could imagine she was in her own room, lying on the bed, waiting for her mother to call her for dinner. Except her room didn't have the smell of dust, mold and urine the basement had. And her bed wasn't as hard or uncomfortable.

She heard the footsteps. It was the man again. The man was less awful than the woman. She hated them both, but she hated the woman much more. She heard him come closer, then stop.

"You didn't eat," the man said. She opened her eyes, turned toward him. He looked at the floor, where the last two sandwiches lay, untouched. She had no appetite anymore, couldn't bring herself to swallow the dry, tasteless sandwiches. She also barely drank. Drinking led to using the bucket in the corner, which she hated. She could feel her body weakening, her head pounding as it always did when she skipped a meal. But she didn't care.

The man held a third sandwich in his hand. He looked at it, then at her, his masked face unreadable.

"You need to eat," he said.

Abigail made a small motion. It was meant to be a shrug, but lying on the bed was not the ideal position to shrug.

He sighed, then bent and picked up the two uneaten sandwiches. He left the room with all three sandwiches in his hands, locking the door behind him.

Abigail tried to go back to sleep. There was nothing good about staying awake. When she slept, time went by. Perhaps someone would find her. Perhaps her kidnappers would return her home. Time was her friend. She thought about Gracie. It was strange, she hadn't thought about her friend up to that moment. They had tried to escape the kidnappers together. Had Gracie made it? Was she back home, wondering what had happened to Abigail?

She would have done anything to talk to Gracie. Her friend could always make her happy. She had such a positive outlook on life. She'd have pointed out that the kidnappers kept her fed and masked their faces. They clearly intended to set her free in the future. She would probably quote a statistic about how most kidnappings ended well. Gracie always had statistics up her sleeve. Abigail almost smiled, imagining Gracie's face as she said, "You'll be home in no time, and you'll be the most popular girl in school! *Everyone* will want to hang out with Abigail Lisman, the girl who was kidnapped."

Time moved by. The door opened again. She ignored it this time, keeping her eyes closed, her head facing away.

Except the smells made her change her mind. It was the smell of baked dough and cooked cheese, a smell any kid knew by heart. The smell of pizza.

She opened her eyes. The man stepped to her bed, holding a pizza box in his hand. She sat up, and he laid the box on the bed and opened it. The pizza was still hot and steamy. The box was green and red, with a logo she didn't identify, but the implication of all this was clear.

She was being held somewhere near a pizza place. That meant she was in a city, maybe even Glenmore Park. If she managed to escape, she could get somewhere safe, call the police or her parents.

"Eat," the man said.

A sliver of hope crawled into her mind, and with it came her appetite. She realized she was famished. The pizza smelled amazing. She picked up a slice with a shaking hand, and took a large bite. The taste was exquisite. This was the best pizza she had ever eaten in her entire life.

The man fished around in a plastic bag slung on his arm and pulled out a can of Coke, which he handed to her. She wolfed down the pizza slice, then opened the can and drank, enjoying the sudden sugary rush. She picked up a second slice of pizza and bit in, and her face rose to meet the man's eyes.

He looked at her strangely. It was difficult to know what he thought. People always said you could spot an emotion in someone's eyes, but Abigail was realizing that if a person was masked, if she couldn't see the person's mouth, or nose, or forehead, she just couldn't figure out what he felt.

She swallowed the bite she'd taken. "Thank you," she said.

"You're welcome," he said. "Better?"

"Yeah."

"Good. It's important that you eat."

"Are you going to send me home soon?" she blurted out.

He hesitated for a moment. "Soon," he finally said. "Yes. Not today, but soon."

Abigail nodded and took another bite. She wondered if he was telling the truth. Should she try to escape? There was a pizza place nearby.

The man pulled out his phone and aimed it at her. The flash blinded her and he put the phone away.

"Why are you taking all those pictures of me?" she asked.

"To let your parents know you're alive."

Her parents knew she was alive. She hadn't realized how worried she was about them not knowing. If they knew she was alive, they'd never stop looking for her.

He didn't have to tell her that. It was an act of kindness.

"Thanks," she said.

He nodded and got up. "Don't eat too fast," he said. "You might get sick."

She grabbed the third slice of pizza. As he locked the door behind him, she allowed herself, for the first time in a couple of days, to smile.

———

By Thursday, over fifty million people all over the world had been exposed to Abigail Lisman's images.

People began reacting. #SaveAbigail was trending on Twitter. Comments flooded the images on Abigail's Instagram. Redditors, that odd breed of folks who hung out on the site reddit.com, marshaled to find clues in them that could pinpoint her location.

And then someone figured out that she had been kidnapped on Saint Patrick's Day. A lot of pictures had been taken that evening, selfies of drunken people at parties, in bars, and on the street. The citizens of Glenmore Park were asked to share images and videos from that evening, to save Abigail. Because if they didn't share those images, it was tantamount to wanting Abigail to *die*.

Soon there were a lot of images to pore through.

One of those images was a selfie of a hugging couple, suffering from that malaise of the selfie age, where heads always seemed to be too close to each other. In the background, several people could be seen—including two girls walking down the street. They were fuzzy, unfocused, but it was still easy to see that they were small, no more than thirteen. The shapes of their bodies, the length and color of their hair and skin easily matched to other images in their Instagram profiles.

Abigail and Gracie.

ELEVEN

"I spy with my little eye, something beginning with *J*," Agent Perkins said.

Agent Bob Tyler glanced at him, unamused. This joke was getting old, and it wasn't funny the first time. Perkins insisted on using it every time they went on a stakeout together.

They were in their white Chevy with its sparkling clean interior. At Tyler's insistence, they'd had the car washed yesterday. A stakeout in a clean car was infinitely better than a stakeout in a dirty car. Now, sitting back, smelling the pine air freshener, he thought even Perkins could see that this was better.

"Well? It begins with a *J*," Perkins said again.

Jurgen Adler was fifty feet ahead of them, in his own car, an ugly blue Ford Fiesta, doing nothing. He had parked there about ten minutes before, and the agents following him were quick to stop their car. Tyler wondered what he was waiting for. Was he meeting someone? Perhaps the kidnapper? Tyler sure hoped so. The FBI had been trailing Jurgen for the past two days, with no tangible results so far.

"Give up?" Perkins asked.

"Is it a Jeep?" Tyler asked.

"No," Perkins beamed at him. "It's Jurgen Adler."

Tyler ignored him. Perkins was a decent partner, he really was. Sure, he had his quirks, but who didn't? The important thing was, he was a good guy, and Tyler could trust him blindly when things got out of hand.

So he had a stupid sense of humor, and was a bit racist. So what? Tyler's previous partner had had bad breath. That might sound like an insignificant flaw, but spend fourteen hours in a vehicle with the guy, and you'd consider instant retirement.

He looked out at the stores lining the street. In front of them, the man who owned the flower shop, Hummingbird Blossoms, was talking to a woman near a large display of bouquets. The explosion of colors stood out on the gray, drab street. It must be nice to work in a flower shop all day, selling things that made people happy. When he'd been younger, Tyler had brought flowers to his wife every week. She was always so thankful when she got them. Why had he stopped? He resolved to start buying flowers again.

"His name is a bit weird, isn't it?" Perkins said.

"Why?" Tyler asked distractedly. He knew where this was going, but this discussion would open a whole can of racist worms he didn't want opened. Racist worms were the worst. This made him think of a joke.

What's worse than finding a worm in your apple?
Finding a racist worm in your apple.

Perkins's sense of humor was apparently infectious.

"Well, Jurgen isn't a Japanese name, is it?"

"I don't think so."

"But this guy's Japanese."

"He's half-Norwegian, half-Chinese," Tyler said wearily.

"Yeah, well … still. I mean he looks like—"

"It's just a name," Tyler said. "My parents nearly named me Sauron. That doesn't mean I came from Mordor."

"Seriously? They considered calling you Sauron?" Perkins asked.

"It was an option on the short list."

"How long was the short list?"

"It had three names," Tyler said.

"Wow. Lucky break for you, there."

Tyler nodded. "It sure was," he agreed. "I mean … growing up being called Sauron would have been … terrible."

"Bob is a really nice name, though."

"Thanks."

They sat and looked ahead at the blue Ford Fiesta.

"Could have been cool, though," Perkins said. "To say my partner is the dark lord."

Jurgen Adler sat in his 2012 blue Ford Fiesta, waiting for Heather Gibbons to emerge from the bank. He'd been following her for the past hour, wondering if she was on her way to meet her lover. Her husband was almost certain she had a lover, and he wanted Jurgen to give him some evidence he could use when filing for divorce. Up till now, Jurgen hadn't been convinced this lover existed, though his Spidey-sense tingled. Something was definitely off with Heather. She had a secret. And in Jurgen's line of work, a secret nearly always meant a lover.

"Isn't there a movie actress named Heather?" he asked aloud. "Who was it? Do you remember, Sharon?"

Sharon was Jurgen's car. As an ex-cop, Jurgen was used to having a partner to talk to during his stakeouts. But now, as a private investigator, he sometimes spent long hours with no one to talk to. Unlike his somber, silent Norwegian father, Jurgen loved to talk. So he talked to his car.

He tapped his steering wheel, chewing his lip. "Heather Graham," he finally said. "She was awesome in *Austin Powers*. And in *Hangover*."

He sneezed and fumbled for his box of tissues. He was still a bit under the weather. He had spent the past week mostly in bed, trying to get over a bad bout of the flu. He hated having a cold more than almost anything else. He hated it when his nose was runny, like a case of God's plumbing malfunctioning. He hated it when it clogged up, making him choke and snore when going to sleep.

Right now, due to the fact that he'd never bothered with a trash bin for his car, the entire floor was carpeted with used tissues. The tissues he used were white or pink, and he felt as if he was driving in the midst of a field of crumpled, snot-filled petunias. He wiped his nose, squashed the paper, and tossed it over his shoulder to the backseat. Once he was over the cold, he'll clean the car until it sparkled. He just had to get over this horrid, nose-destroying virus.

He looked out at the street. George, the owner of Hummingbird Blossoms, talked to a young woman who nodded, pointing at various bouquets. She was quite beautiful, and Jurgen stared, wondering how it felt to hold her, to kiss her neck, to caress her thighs. It had been a while since he'd broken up with his last girlfriend, and he felt lonely. Sharon, for all her fantastic qualities, was not enough.

He sighed and looked back at the bank.

"There we go," he said, tensing up. "She's leaving. Better get ready, Sharon, we're about to hit the road."

Heather really regretted snorting the last half gram of her cocaine stash.

She usually waited until noon, which was the most difficult time of the day, before her daily hit. That way, she had half the day to look forward to that wonderful moment, and then the middle of the day was quite nice. She'd spend the afternoon watching TV, so the down wasn't so hard.

But that morning her husband had looked at her and asked how her diet was going. And she didn't need a decoding ring to figure out what he meant by that. *You look like a pregnant whale, Heather*—that's what he wanted to say. And that's what she heard. Once he had gone to work she hurried to her dresser, located the last bit of coke she had left, and inhaled it as fast as she could.

Now it was nearly noon, the effect had worn off, and she was out of cocaine. She had to go meet her dealer, get some more.

She quickly headed back to the car, the three hundred dollars she had just withdrawn tucked deep in her purse. As always, after the cocaine buzz faded she was left depressed and anxious. She could feel the eyes of the surrounding people. Could they see the redness of her nose? Did they know what she was doing?

You are horizontally tall, Heather.

She opened the door to her car and got inside, feeling heavy and clumsy. Not for the first time, she wondered if all the money she spent on cocaine would not be better spent on a gastric bypass surgery. She sat still, on the verge of tears, hating herself.

You are queen-sized, Heather.

A woman stood just across the street, buying flowers. Heather looked at her thin, sexy body, her long legs, that tiny waist. She hated that woman. She hated her even more than she hated herself.

She had to get some cocaine. With a shaking hand, she switched on the engine. She was always terrified when meeting her dealer. Would today be the day she was arrested for buying drugs? Had the police tapped her phone, monitored the short text she had sent her dealer? Her anxiety fought with her depression over who would get more real estate in her brain. Currently, her anxiety was winning.

She pulled out of her parking spot. She needed to get this over with.

Jurgen was the first to admit that when it came to tailing cars, his skills were a bit underwhelming. When he'd been a cop he hadn't done it often, and when he had, his partner was usually the one driving. Now, as a private detective, he had to do it *all the time*, and he hated it.

The two bullet-points for tailing a car were: don't get spotted, and don't lose your target. Completely absurd. Either you did something, or you didn't. That was like telling someone to eat a large dinner, but to make sure he stayed hungry. Couldn't be done.

So his style for tailing a car was simple. He stayed far behind his target, but once he felt he was losing it, he panicked and sped up until the car he was following was two feet ahead of him. At which point he would realize he was too close, and hit the brakes. As far as he could tell, the reason he wasn't spotted more often was that people couldn't believe anyone tailing them would draw so much attention to himself.

When Heather's green Audi pulled out, Jurgen waited for a few seconds. When he finally decided to pull out, traffic seemed to thicken, and he couldn't merge into the lane. He finally hit the gas and swerved into traffic just in front of an incoming van, which honked. The driver screaming something Jurgen couldn't make out.

He cursed, worried about the number of cars between him and Heather. Worse yet, there were three green cars in front of him, and though he thought he knew which one was Heather's, he wasn't completely certain. One of them turned right at the next intersection and he nearly followed it, just because of an irrational worry that he got the green cars mixed up. But no, it wasn't even an Audi, and anyway it was more like olive green, and Heather's car was lime green.

Finally, traffic thinned, and he could positively spot Heather's head in the driver's seat in front of him. He slowed down, the car behind him almost ramming into him, honking as well.

"What's his problem, Sharon?" he said, craning his head to make sure Heather was still there. "It's his fault. He shouldn't have been so close."

He followed Heather for another couple of minutes, growing quite proud of his cool driving. Then he sneezed.

It was one of those "everything must go, geyser erupting" sneezes, and he fumbled helplessly for the box of tissues. Finally, he grabbed a handful of used tissues from the floor, and wiped his nose and hand with them. Another low point of the day.

Looking back up, he realized he couldn't see Heather anywhere.

"Damn it!" He hit the gas, zigzagging between cars, spotting her just as she turned right. He was in the left lane, and as he crossed both lanes furious honking erupted around him.

And now he was too close again.

"What the hell … is he drunk?" Fowler asked as their Chevy followed Jurgen's Ford. The man drove like a panicky teenager on the first day behind the steering wheel.

"I don't know," Tyler said, frowning. He had read Jurgen's file carefully, and it hadn't mentioned drunk driving anywhere. But who knew?

They tailed Jurgen's car from afar, watching traffic swerving out of his way, people shaking their fists at him. And then he suddenly swerved and turned right, disappearing down a side street.

"He spotted us," Tyler said speeding up. "He's trying to shake us loose."

"We have to stop him!" Fowler said. "If he gets to the girl—"

"I know," Tyler muttered. Now that Jurgen knew the FBI were on to him, this could spin out of control. They could have a hostage situation before long.

No. This had to end now. They'd bring Jurgen in, interrogate him, find out the location of the girl.

They turned right. Jurgen zigzagged ahead, getting further away. The street was packed with traffic, and Tyler could see no way around it. They were losing him.

"Call in the chopper!" he barked at Fowler. "He's getting away!"

———

Everyone around Heather kept honking. The jarring noise was making her frantic. She could hear brakes squealing behind her, and yelling. Something was definitely off. Was it possible that the police really had intercepted her text? Were they chasing her even now? She glanced in the rearview mirror. There were a lot of cars, but no squad car. Could they be following her to get to her dealer? She didn't want her dealer to think she had ratted him out!

She accelerated, and several cars behind her also seemed to accelerate. Was it just her anxiety acting up? It didn't feel like it.

She got closer to the street corner where she and her dealer met, but she decided to avoid it, drive around a bit, make sure she wasn't being followed. Her dealer would appreciate her caution. She turned left at the next intersection. A few seconds later she heard honking behind her again. By now she was crying. She had to get on the highway. She'd lose them on the highway.

As she drove, she realized she was muttering to herself. She prayed to God, swearing that if she managed to get back home safely she would never do cocaine again. She'd try the Dukan diet; she hadn't tried that one yet. She'd become a better wife and stop wasting their money on drugs.

She reached the highway and got on. It was relatively clear, and she felt as if the traffic behind her calmed down.

Which was when she heard the helicopter.

It flew right above her, *following her car*. Her muttering became hysterical as she pressed the gas, then decided to give herself up, hitting the brakes, then panicking and accelerating again. This was a nightmare! Would her husband see the car chase tonight on the news? See her car on the highway, a tail of squad cars following her?

Sure enough, the sirens began screaming around her. The police closed in.

———

As far as tails went, this one was insane. What was she doing on the highway? Did her lover live in a different city? Why were the police following her? Was that really a helicopter flying low above them?

Jurgen was way out of his depth. All he had wanted were some pictures of Heather with another guy. He didn't need any trouble with the police. God knew they were already looking for a reason to take him down.

He slowed down, pulled aside, waiting for the patrol cars and the helicopter to pass him by—at which point one of the patrol cars stopped behind him, brakes squealing, and another one blocked his way out. A white Chevy stopped just a few feet behind the squad cars, and two men leapt out of it, holding guns aimed at his car.

"FBI!" one of them shouted. "Get out with your hands up!"

Jurgen blinked, then switched off the engine. Carefully and slowly, he opened the door.

"I'm getting out!" he shouted. "I am unarmed!"

The two FBI agents didn't look as if they were about to lower their weapons. He really hoped he wasn't about to get shot. He had no idea what was going on. He got out, hands above his head, and turned around.

"Freeze!" one of them shouted, and he did. Rough hands grabbed his arms and pulled them behind his back.

"Jurgen Adler, you are under arrest," one of them said, and the angry metal bite of handcuffs pressed on his wrists.

He wasn't sure what had just happened, but it was a huge mistake.

Heather stared in the rearview mirror with tear-stained eyes, watching the police surrounding the blue vehicle. She let out heavy shuddering breaths and slowed down, ignoring the irritated honking of the cars in her lane as she drove at a steady speed of forty miles per hour on the highway. Finally, she got off at the next exit and parked the car on the side of the road. She shook uncontrollably as she rummaged in her bag for her phone. At first she couldn't even tap the message, couldn't steady her tapping finger. Finally, she managed to send a message to her dealer.

Can't meet. Almost got caught by the police.

She added a sad face to the message for good measure. Then she set the phone aside. What would her husband say about all this?

Her husband could go to hell, she decided. Next time he asked about her diet, she'd tell him that.

TWELVE

Hannah walked briskly into the police station. Clint was waiting for her by the reception desk, wearing a tailored gray suit and a blue tie. His face was serious, his customary smile gone. When he'd called her earlier, it wasn't to talk about the incident in the car, or the one later, in her bed. There was a development in the case. He'd asked her to come to the station as soon as possible.

"What happened?" she asked as she joined him. "What's so urgent?"

He walked toward the stairs and she followed him.

"We arrested Jurgen Adler," he said in a low voice.

"What?" she asked, her tone rising. "Why? Didn't you want to follow him from a distance?"

"According to the agents tailing him, he spotted them and tried to shake off the tail. They were worried it could devolve into a hostage situation."

Hannah was nearly running up the stairs, trying to keep up with Clint's fast pace. "And where is he now?"

"Here. Agent Mancuso instructed me to interrogate him as soon as possible. She thinks his partners might find out he's been caught, and decide to get rid of Abigail and flee. Your chief agreed to let me interrogate him in your interrogation room."

"Did Agent Mancuso ask for me to question him as well?" Hannah asked.

Clint hesitated. "No," he finally said. "But I thought you'd want to be involved."

Hannah nodded. She did want to be involved. She also suspected Clint had broken some kind of FBI protocol by calling her without updating his superior.

"I want to lead the interrogation," Clint said. "We don't have time to do it right. We need to intimidate him; it's the fastest way to get results. People assume the worst when they're held by the FBI, and it often makes them crack faster."

"Jurgen is not the type of guy who cracks easily," Hannah said. "I agree; we can't do this slowly. I think it's best to ask him why he followed—"

"He doesn't know what we have on him, and I prefer it remains that way."

"But if you want fast results, there's no point in beating around the bush. We should ask him why he followed Abigail."

"I'd rather not," Clint said shortly as they got to the interrogation room. He opened the door, and Hannah walked inside, her shoulder brushing his.

On a scale of one to ten, where one was the balloon-decorated room of a boy who just turned five, and ten was a solitary confinement prison cell, the interrogation room at the Glenmore Park PD was an eight. The walls were black up to waist level, where they turned dirty white. A one-way mirror adorned one wall, reflecting the harsh light of the single light bulb that hung directly above a small metal table.

Jurgen Adler sat behind the table, his hands cuffed. Hannah and Clint sat down on the other side.

"Mr. Adler," Clint said. "I'm Agent Ward, and this is—"

"Detective Hannah Shor," Jurgen said, his voice sounding strangely nasal. "We know each other. Hey, Hannah."

Hannah nodded, her face blank.

"Mr. Adler, we know that—"

"Can I have a tissue?" Jurgen said. "I have a cold, and my nose is kinda dripping all over the place."

"We'll bring some in a few minutes," Clint said. "Mr. Adler, where is Abigail Lisman?"

Jurgen blinked. "Abigail Lisman?" he asked. "The little girl? Isn't she home?"

"She was kidnapped several days ago, as you know very well," Clint said sharply. "Where is she being held?"

"She was kidnapped?"

"Oh, come on, Jurgen," Hannah said, irritated. "Don't play dumb. She's been all over the news, on bulletin boards, in—"

"Hannah, I've been sick in bed for the past week," Jurgen said, his eyes wide. "I didn't know! When was she—"

"Mr. Adler, answer the question. Where is Abigail Lisman?"

"I swear, I don't—" Jurgen suddenly sneezed, covering his face with his hands. "Argh," he said, removing them from his nose. There was phlegm on his fingers and right cheek. "Cad I pdease hab a tissue?"

Hannah walked out of the room, went to the restroom, and got a roll of toilet paper. She returned to the interrogation room, slamming the door behind her, and handed him the roll.

"Thank you," Jurgen said, cleaning his face and fingers.

"If Abigail Lisman is hurt, you'll never leave federal prison," Clint said, his words clipped and sharp. "But if you tell us where she is—"

"I don't know where you got the idea I was involved," Jurgen said, placing the bunched up toilet paper on the table. "I don't know where she is. This is all news to me. If I had heard about her kidnapping, I'd have gone straight to the police."

"Why?" Clint asked. "Do you know who has her?"

Jurgen leaned back. "I forgot how damned uncomfortable this chair is," he muttered. "Why did you arrest me?"

"Who has Abigail Lisman?" Clint barked at him.

"For God's sake, Jurgen, we have photos of you following the girl," Hannah said, irritated. Clint shot her a furious stare which she pointedly ignored.

"Ah," Jurgen said. He blew his nose into another piece of toilet paper. "So that's it. Yes, it's true, her father hired me to follow her."

"Why would Mr. Lisman hire you to follow his daughter?"

Jurgen shook his head. "Not Mr. Lisman. Her biological father. Lance Koche."

There was a moment of silence in the room.

"You didn't know that?" Jurgen asked dryly. "A girl has been kidnapped, and you didn't even check with her parents? What kind of investigation—"

"Mrs. Lisman didn't tell us—" Hannah began.

"For God's sake, Hannah, look at the girl's damn pictures. Does she look anything like the Lismans? Yeah, she has her mother's ears. And probably her chin. But that's where it ends." He raised his eyebrow. "Bernard would have figured it out. Isn't he involved with this case?"

"Why did Lance Koche have Abigail followed?" Clint asked, ignoring the question.

Jurgen shrugged. "He mostly wanted pictures of her. With her friends, at school. I don't know. I got the impression he had never met her before. Lance Koche is a sneaky bastard. Perhaps he was trying to figure out if he really wanted to meet his daughter."

"Mr. Adler, I will only say it one more time. If you know where Abigail Lisman is and—"

"Talk to Lance Koche," Jurgen said, his voice raised. "He'll corroborate my story. I was only hired to take photos of the girl. I didn't know about any kidnapping until just now."

He sneezed again, and Hannah flinched as something wet hit her neck.

"I'be beed bery sick," Jurgen said into another piece of toilet paper. "I habed't beed out of bed the whole week."

―――

They drove Clint's car to Lance Koche's office, Clint seething behind the wheel. Hannah let him be; she wasn't about to apologize for doing her job, and obviously she'd gotten results, and fast. The FBI—Clint included—seemed to be eager to pin the kidnapping on Jurgen. Hannah could understand their point of view. He was the perfect suspect, except that she knew him, and even more importantly, Bernard knew him well. Bernard said Jurgen couldn't be involved, and that was enough for Hannah.

She glanced at Clint. He was frowning, his jaw locked tight. There was something attractive about his fury, but she missed his smile from the night before.

"You didn't even wait ten minutes before doing precisely what I told you not to," Clint finally said.

Told? Hannah raised an eyebrow, but let it slide. "He isn't our guy, Clint. And he had some vital info."

"He still might be our guy," Clint said. "He could be buying time for his partners, and thanks to you he knows what evidence we're holding, so he knows how to play us."

"Lance Koche wasn't surprised when we called him about Jurgen," Hannah pointed out. "He knew who we were talking about."

"He could have hired Jurgen for anything!" Clint spat. "And it doesn't matter! I told you not to say anything about the photos, and you did it anyway."

There was that *told* again. "You're not my superior. We're working together."

"You're my local police contact, and your main purpose is—"

"This is the place," Hannah said. She didn't like where the argument was going, and was relieved at the opportunity to change the subject.

"Fancy building," Clint muttered, parking the car on the sidewalk.

It was. Lance Koche worked in a modern office building, its surface a grid of blue tinted windows. It managed to inspire an equal amount of superiority and bad taste, jutting up along Clayton Road like an alien monolith. Hannah realized that, despite passing by the building thousands of times, she had never stepped inside.

"Eighteenth floor," she said, looking up. "Let's go."

They got out of the car and walked side by side. Hannah once again found herself half-running to keep up with Clint's pace. It was getting annoying. She expected him to adjust his pace to accommodate the fact that his legs were about twice the length of hers, but he was either blind to that fact or simply didn't care. Whatever the case, she was breathing hard when they got to the elevator. Neither of them said anything as they waited.

Finally, the elevator arrived on the ground floor, and got in. As it drifted upward, Hannah wondered why she found it so awkward to be in this small space with Clint, especially considering that just the day before she'd ridden him naked in his car.

Lance Koche's office, like the building it was in, was designed to impress and intimidate. All the furniture had a polished, cold look to it, most in various shades of white or metallic blue. His secretary, a blonde woman with frighteningly long eyelashes, and hair so straight it seemed to be made from metal as well, asked them to wait a few moments while Lance finished an important business call.

Hannah doubted there was a call. She was certain Lance Koche was the type of guy who made almost everyone wait when they met him.

Finally, just as she was about to barge into his office, the door opened. A tall, middle-aged man with silvery hair stood in the doorway.

"Agent Ward? Please come in."

They both entered the office. Lance sat down behind a desk made of heavy-looking, dark wood. It was clean and organized, with a few papers lying in a metallic tray and a small laptop sitting in the middle of the wooden surface.

"How can I help you, Agents?"

"Mr. Koche," Clint said, without bothering to correct Lance about Hannah's title, nor bothering to introduce her. "Did you hire Jurgen Adler a few weeks ago?"

"Yes."

"Can you tell us why?"

"What did he tell you the reason was?" Koche asked.

"I'd prefer it if you tell us yourself," Clint said.

Koche glanced at Hannah for the first time. There was something in his face. Worry? Anxiety? He covered it well, but Hannah could spot the bags under his eyes, the slight tremor in his lips.

"I hired him to follow my biological daughter," Koche said. "Abigail."

"Abigail Lisman," Hannah said.

"That's right."

"Who was kidnapped last week."

"That's right."

"Why didn't you approach us when you first heard about your daughter's kidnapping?" Hannah asked.

"She's not my daughter," he said sharply. "She's my *biological* daughter. I didn't know she existed until two months ago. I didn't come to you because I didn't find it relevant, and I was under the impression that the girl's mother had enough problems on her plate."

Hannah looked at him intently. Was he lying? Could he have been involved in the kidnapping somehow? And if so, why?

"When did you hear about Abigail's kidnapping?" Clint asked.

"Naamit Lisman was here yesterday, to ask me to pay the ransom."

"And what did you say?"

"I said I can't afford it, and that I'm not inclined to pay such an amount for a girl I don't even know."

Asshole, Hannah thought. "How did you find out Abigail was your daughter?" she asked.

"Her mother told me," Koche said, his mouth twisting in apparent annoyance. "She showed up here, to tell me she got pregnant from our one night all those years ago, and that now she wanted me to pay for her daughter's private school tuition."

"And what did you say?"

"I demanded a paternity test. It wasn't the first time a woman had tried to get me with this trick. They say they're on the pill, then suddenly it turns out they're pregnant and I'm supposed to pay the bills."

"Did she do a paternity test?" Hannah asked, curbing the desire to punch him.

"She did one, and e-mailed it to me. The results were positive. Abigail is my biological daughter. I verified the authenticity of the results with the hospital, and then I said I would think about it."

"Why did you have her followed?" Clint asked.

"Because I was interested," Lance said, shrugging. "I never had children, and here was one all grown up. I wanted to know how she turned out."

"So you hired a private detective?"

"That's right."

"You could have just approached her, or asked her mother to arrange a meeting."

"I could have."

"When did you hire Jurgen Adler?" Clint asked.

"One minute." Lance picked up the phone on his desk and pressed a button. "Megan," he said. "Can you come in for a second?"

The secretary entered the room, her feet making a light tapping noise on the hardwood flooring. She wore high heels, Hannah realized, even though she was plenty tall without them—probably five ten. Hannah guessed that Lance Koche expected his secretary to wear high heels. She was young, slim, blonde, big brown eyes. The perfect cliché.

"Yes Mr. Koche?" Megan asked.

"When did I meet with Mr. Jurgen Adler?"

She pulled out a small tablet and tapped on it with a long, pink manicured fingernail. "On the 22nd of January."

"And when did Naamit approach you?" Clint asked Koche.

"A week before that. She didn't have an appointment, so Megan won't be able to—"

"On the 13th of January," Megan said. "It was Monday, the week before."

Lance Koche's lips curved slightly upward. "There you go," he said.

"And Jurgen gave you the photos?" Hannah said. "Did you meet with him again?"

"I met him once, when he came for the first payment," Koche said. "After that he sent me the photos by mail, and I paid him with a bank transfer. Megan will happily supply you with the pictures and the transfer paperwork."

Megan glanced at her boss and nodded. Hannah, following the woman's body language, guessed that Koche occasionally had sex with his secretary.

"You're very cooperative," Clint said.

"I want my daught … Abigail Lisman to come home safely. I'm not a monster. I'll do anything I can do to help."

"Except for paying the ransom," Hannah said dryly.

"Anything within reason," Koche amended. "Like I said, she isn't my daughter. I don't see you going to any other rich people around here, asking them for the ransom money."

Clint nodded and stood up. "Thank you for your time."

"If you have any more questions," Koche said, "please call."

In the outer office, Clint gave Megan his e-mail address, so she could send him the pictures and the wire transfer paperwork. Then he and Hannah got back in the elevator.

"Well, Jurgen is clearly off the hook," Hannah said.

"Not necessarily," Clint said. "He's hired to follow Mr. Koche's daughter, and six weeks later she's kidnapped? Quite a coincidence. What if he figured out he could easily kidnap the girl and ask Koche for ransom? Perhaps he saw something in her that made him think this would be easy money."

"You're reaching," Hannah said.

"And you're blind," Clint snapped. "You're just desperate to get him off the hook, no matter what, because your partner told you he's innocent."

Hannah said nothing, though the words jabbed at her. He was right, of course, and it infuriated her.

Abigail took a large bite from the cheeseburger and chewed it slowly. It was sublime. This time she was smarter—took small bites, ate it slow. After she had eaten the pizza, she'd nearly thrown up the entire thing, feeling sick from eating too fast and too much.

She took one of the French fries and put it on her tongue, letting the salty taste sink in.

"You like McDonald's," the man said. He sounded satisfied, though his mouth was still hidden behind the mask.

"I love hamburgers," she said. "It's my favorite food. And I really like cheeseburgers! I don't eat them at…" she hesitated for a second. "At home."

"Why not?"

"Because they aren't kosher," she said simply.

"Oh!" he said in surprise. "Do you want me to get you a hamburger without cheese?"

"No, it's fine, I don't care," she said hurriedly, tightening her grip on the cheeseburger. "I eat cheeseburgers when I'm at my friends' houses. And bacon. My parents eat kosher, but I don't mind at all."

"Okay. And the fries are good?" he asked.

"Uh-huh." She nodded. She liked to dip them in ketchup, but he hadn't brought any. She considered mentioning it, then changed her mind. "They're really good. You want one?"

He laughed. It was strange, hearing his laughter without seeing his mouth. His laughter was low, and sounded heartfelt. "No need. I'll eat later."

"It's weird, eating alone," Abigail said. "At school I eat with my friends, and at home I eat with my family."

He was silent for a second, then said, "Yeah, sure, why not. I'll take one."

She held the French fries container up and he took one. He rolled up the bottom part of his mask, exposing his mouth, and ate the fry. Abigail tried not to stare. For some reason, she'd imagined he had a beard, or that he was unshaven, but the bottom half of his face was completely smooth. His lips were a bit full, his teeth very white.

After finishing the fry, he smiled, and the small gesture made her feel much better. "That really is good," he said. "I should eat McDonald's more often."

Abigail moved aside a bit, sitting on one side of the cot. "You can have more, if you want to," she said.

He sat next to her. "Just one more," he said, and grinned. She suddenly got the impression that this man smiled a lot.

He took another one and ate it. Abigail finished the cheeseburger and took a long sip from the large plastic cup. Her mom never let her drink Coke, not since she'd read that if you put a tooth in a cup of Coke, it disintegrated after two days.

"Thanks," she said. "For the meal."

"No problem."

"What day is it?" she asked.

"It's Friday," he said. His mask was still rolled up above his mouth. He didn't seem to notice.

Abigail nodded and tried to figure out how long ago she'd been kidnapped. Only four days? It felt like an eternity. She tried to remember what classes she took on Friday. English, for sure. And science. She hated science class, but sitting in class right now—next to the window, the sun shining outside, other kids around her—suddenly sounded like paradise. An involuntary sob emerged from her mouth.

"What? What happened?" The man asked.

"I want to go home!" she cried. "I miss my parents. And my..." a sobbing fit caught hold of her throat, preventing her from talking.

"You'll be home soon," the man said, his voice softening. "Not much longer."

"What if ... what if something happens?" Abigail asked between whimpers.

"Like what?"

"I don't want to die!"

"Hey!" he said. "You're not going to die! Why would you die?"

"You said ... you said if I don't behave..."

"But you're behaving very well," he said. "You have nothing to worry about."

"*She* doesn't think so. She slapped me. I think she hates me. What if she hurts me? I'm scared." She was losing control, talking while crying, her words becoming unintelligible.

"No one hates you. Listen, Abigail, you'll be home soon. Nothing will happen to you, I promise."

It was the first time he had said her name, and it calmed her down. "Okay," she said.

He clumsily put a hand on her shoulder. "Just a few more days, okay?" he said. "And then you'll be home."

She took a deep, shuddering breath. "Okay," she said.

THIRTEEN

Hannah stared dumbfounded at what used to be the situation room. The large screen on the wall was gone, as was the strange FBI switchboard, the map, and the three interchangeable agents that had sat around the table. Only some wires remained behind, snaking across the floor and ending abruptly at nothing.

Had they moved to another room? Why hadn't anyone notified her? She took out her phone, already searching for Clint's number, then hesitated.

She put the phone back in her pocket and walked across the hall to the squad room. It was empty as well—not surprising since it was Saturday, and still early in the morning. She'd woken up just after five a.m. She'd tried to go back to sleep, but her mind had already kicked into high gear, cataloguing the leads she needed to follow, prioritizing them. Finally, she'd gotten up and driven to work.

The door to the captain's office was open, and through it she could see the light switched on and signs of movement. She crossed the squad room and entered his office.

"Captain?" she asked, barely able to see him beyond the mounds of paper on his desk.

"Good morning, Detective," the captain said. He sounded tired. "Please, sit down."

Hannah craned her neck to see the captain's face above the paperwork. There were piles and towers of forms, reports and Post-its in various shades and sizes, all over the desk. They collapsed into each other, creating shapes that resembled mountains more than stacks. Small cups of coffee sat in various strategic spots around the desk, long forgotten, some growing mold.

Carl, the man who cleaned their office, had countless arguments with Captain Bailey about this desk, which he claimed was a fire and biological hazard combined. Hannah sat down in one of the chairs and rolled it to the side, so she could see the captain without the desk and its burdens interrupting her line of sight.

"How are Mr. and Mrs. Lisman?" he asked, folding his hands and leaning backward.

"As well as could be expected," Hannah said. "The Instagram posts are a blessing and a curse. It gives them fresh hope when they see one, but the captions are becoming more and more threatening, and they're getting very scared."

"Those posts are also making this case very famous," Bailey said. "It was on Fox News and CNN yesterday."

"I heard," Hannah said.

"My father used to say that a story that grows wings might become either an eagle or a duck," Bailey said.

Hannah blinked and said nothing. Captain Bailey's father had some confusing idioms.

"Agent Mancuso called. The case is no longer under her direct control. It's too public."

Hannah shrugged. FBI politics didn't concern her.

"The FBI moved the situation room to the FBI main office, in Boston."

"That's ridiculous!" Hannah said sharply. "Do they expect us to drive to Boston and back every day? The case is here. The family is here."

The captain looked at her, his expression unreadable. "I wasn't under the impression that they wanted us to drive over," he said.

"What?"

"We aren't invited to the party anymore, Detective. We'll keep helping as much as we can, of course, but the main task force won't be here. You will no longer work with Agent Ward on the case. Your main responsibility in this case now is to support the family."

"What?" Hannah said, the word spat from her mouth like dirt.

"Orders from above. Agent Mancuso has a lot of respect for you."

"Does she?" Hannah said, and thought about her argument with Clint. "Are you sure this isn't because of something Clint ... Agent Ward told her?"

Captain Bailey raised his eyebrows. "She hasn't mentioned anything like that."

"Captain, I need to be involved in the case. Naamit expects me to—"

"Mrs. Lisman expects you to do what's best for her daughter. Currently, what this means is letting the FBI do their job, and helping whenever they ask."

"But they're screwing up! They're stuck on the notion that Jurgen Adler is somehow connected. They can't get the kidnappers to answer their messages. I can't let them—"

"Detective Shor," Bailey said, his voice hardening. "Get it together."

Hannah took a deep breath and clenched her lips.

"It looks like the kidnappers are preparing to send the ransom drop details," Bailey said. "Our leads have run cold. Abigail Lisman has been missing for almost *four days*."

"There are two people we have to investigate. Melanie Pool and—"

"Hal Moore," Bailey said. "Jacob and Agent Fuller interviewed them yesterday. They both have alibis. Hal Moore was actually in Canada at the time of the kidnapping. I can forward you Jacob's report."

Hannah tightened her fingers on the arms of her chair, gritting her teeth.

"It's mostly a waiting game now, Hannah," Bailey said softly. "There's nothing much we can do anymore."

"Do you think Jurgen Adler might be involved?" she asked.

Bailey sighed. "I was Jurgen's captain for over a year," he said. "And I failed to see what was in front of my eyes. The man can be charming as hell, and he was a good detective. But he's morally bankrupt. Quite frankly, I thought the entire internal investigation was a mistake until I saw the proof mounting. I was blind once with this man, and I don't intend to make the same blunder twice. If the FBI thinks that he has something to do with the kidnapping, it might very well be true."

"I'm scared we won't get her back," Hannah said, half whispering.

Bailey nodded, his eyes softening. "So am I. But there's nothing else you can do about it."

Glen Haney raised the binoculars to his eyes again. He sat in his mom's car, two hundred feet from the kidnapper's house. He had chosen the location beforehand, using Google Maps. It was far enough so they wouldn't spot him, but with a clear view of the house. It was also just past a curve in the road, and behind a large tree, so he was mostly hidden from passersby.

In any case, if anyone asked him what he was doing there with a pair of binoculars, he had an answer prepared: he was bird-watching. He had a bird guide at hand. He would tell anyone who bothered asking that he was looking for white-winged crossbills, which had been spotted around Glenmore Park.

He wasn't really bird-watching. He was kidnapper-watching. The rare breed of "twelve-year-old girl kidnapper" had been spotted in Glenmore Park, and Glen was the first to figure out where he was.

He scanned the front of the house through the binoculars, already well-acquainted with the layout. A driveway, leading to a closed garage door. The entrance to the house just next to the garage—a brown door, simple lock. One window, shuttered and dirty. A front yard with a failed attempt at a lawn, several lonely clumps of grass in the midst of barren ground, weeds sprouting everywhere.

He wondered again if Abigail was in the garage. He was almost certain she was inside the house. He had seen the kidnapper arriving a few hours ago, carrying a small-sized pizza box and a carton of grape juice. Glen doubted the man drank grape juice, and he didn't have kids. Not according to Glen's extensive research.

Just like most of the people online, Glen had found out about Abigail three days ago. He was one of the first Redditors to join the frantic subreddit analyzing the images taken that day in Glenmore Park, and speculating about the chain of events. He'd seen the famous picture of Abigail and Grace walking down the street together. He'd seen the images in the Instagram feed.

And then he'd picked up a strange detail no one else had noticed.

At first he'd rushed to the subreddit, heart thumping, about to share the discovery with his fellow Redditors, preparing for his five minutes of fame and thousands of upvotes … but then he hesitated.

Five minutes of fame was all very nice … but he could have more. Maybe, just maybe, he could find out who the kidnapper really was. He began an intense online search, involving a hacker acquaintance in his research. Six hours later, he stared at the image of the presumed kidnapper. Four hours after that, he had the kidnapper's address.

It was enough. Perhaps that was the moment he should have contacted the cops, or the FBI. But he was concerned with the illegal hacking—and besides, would they even believe him?

Wouldn't it be much better if he simply saved the girl? Delivered her to the police?

And frankly, wasn't this what he had always wanted? A chance to be a hero? To save an innocent child from the clutches of a malicious kidnapper. To be a vigilante?

He made plans, prepared well—Glen was a great believer in preparations—and took off in his mom's car early in the morning. He left her a haphazard note on the kitchen table, apologizing and promising to call by evening.

And now he waited. The kidnapper had arrived home three hours ago. Glen hoped he would leave the house soon, but he was prepared to spend the night in the car if needed. The man would surely leave in the morning.

Except … there he was! Glen lifted the binoculars to his eyes. The garage door opened; the man's car emerged and turned left, away from where Glen waited. The car got further away, and the garage door slowly closed. That meant Abigail probably wasn't in the garage.

Time to act. Glen got out of the car, his backpack slung on one shoulder, and casually walked to the house. This was the crucial moment. Would he be able to get in?

As he reached the front door he opened his backpack, finding the kit. He had been practicing for years. This was one of the things he most loved doing away from his computer: picking locks. He'd amassed his lock-picking kit over three years, had taken an online course, practiced almost every day. He had over a dozen locks and lock cutaways at home, and he knew how to pick them by heart. It was time to use his skills to save a life.

Glen wasn't concerned about the lock; he was more worried about someone noticing him and calling the cops. But now, as he worked the lock, he realized that his anxiety was affecting his fingers. He trembled slightly, the tension wrench shaking in his hand. He wedged it in the lock but couldn't seem to get the pressure right. His palms started sweating, and the tool felt slippery between his fingers. Finally, he straightened, taking a deep breath. A small voice in his mind yelled at him to turn around, go to the police, show them what he had found.

He shut the voice away. He closed his eyes and took a few deep breaths, forcing himself to relax. He tried to think of something else. There was a girl in his Spanish class, Breanna. He'd been fantasizing for more than three months about asking her out. He'd been fantasizing about other things related to her as well. Wouldn't she be impressed when he became the guy who saved Abigail Lisman? He imagined her eyes, full of admiration, her hand as it held his, her lips parting ...

It was best if he stopped there. He still needed his wits.

Smiling, Glen wiped his palms on his shirt. Then he bent to his task again. This time his hands were steady, his mind clear. The lock was simple. The pins were standard. He wedged the tension wrench in and applied slight pressure. Then he inserted the Bogota Rake into the lock and began moving it forward and back patiently. It only took a couple of minutes before he felt the pins set and the tension wrench budge. He twisted the wrench to unlock the door, and he was in.

He entered the house, closing the door behind him silently. If the man came back, he'd hear the garage door opening, and he'd dash outside. If that happened, Glen would call the cops. He wouldn't try a second time.

He looked around, moving from room to room. The apartment was a mess—dusty living room, dirty kitchen, a sink full of dishes, a half-eaten sandwich on the table, no plate.

A single closed door. He tried the handle.

Locked.

She was behind this door; he was certain. Why else lock a door inside your own house? He inspected the lock. An easy job. He got to work on it, his ears alert to the sound of the garage door. At one point a car drove by outside, and his heart froze, but the garage door remained closed and the car passed the house by.

Finally, another click, and when he twisted the door handle, the door opened. A few stairs led down. He began descending.

"Who are you?" a voice asked. A girl's voice.

His eyes acclimated to the dim light, and he could see the figure of Abigail Lisman sitting on a cot in the middle of the basement. He'd found her! His heart rate quickened." My name is Glen," he said. "I'm here to rescue you!"

Such simple words, uttered so many times in various movies or books. He had never believed he would say them himself.

The girl didn't move. "Are you a cop?" she asked.

"I … what? No, I'm not a cop. Come on!" When she still didn't move, he asked, "Did he tie you to the cot?"

"No." She shook her head and stood up. She trembled. "What if they come back?"

"We'll hear the garage door," he said, impatient. "Come on, let's get out of here before that happens!"

She took a few halting steps. Glen smiled at her, then turned back to the stairs. He went up three stairs, frowned, and turned back to Abigail again. "What do you mean, *they*? Only one man lives here."

"There's a woman," Abigail said. "She comes here, too."

"A woman? I only saw—" The words died in his throat as her eyes widened, as her mouth opened in horror. She stared over his shoulder.

He turned around, and a terrible pain blossomed in his chest. He tried to shout but no sound emerged. He was choking. He tried to breathe in—the pain was terrible—and then something sharp plunged into him over and over again, his stomach feeling as if it was being torn apart, his eyes barely registering the woman standing just above him. A pair of cold, empty brown eyes. His feet couldn't hold him anymore, he was falling down the stairs, hearing the girl screaming, the door slamming above him plunging the room into darkness.

He moaned, trying to tell the girl to help him up, that something was wrong with him. He couldn't breathe, he couldn't move, and everything was fading. He couldn't see anymore, he could only hear the girl muttering over and over:

"She killed him, oh God, she killed him, oh God, I saw her face, I saw her face, I saw her face…"

FOURTEEN

Mitchell parked his car at the edge of Cypress Street, near the medical examiner's gray Nissan Altima. He sighed and rubbed his eyes, still half-asleep. The phone call from Dispatch had woken him up at two-fifteen a.m., and it took the dispatcher a few tries before she managed to convince him he really did have to wake up. He regretted not buying a cup of coffee on the way.

He opened the car door, and the freezing air outside immediately chilled him half to death. He fumbled for his coat, which he had tossed in the back seat, and put it on. Then he got out of the car, swearing he'd find a different job soon, and walked toward the crime scene.

Tanessa stood on the sidewalk, looking at him with pity in her eyes as he shambled toward her. Beyond her stood a red Honda with its trunk open, a few people huddled around it.

"Hey," he said hoarsely.

"Mitchy, you look like hell," she said.

"That's Detective Mitchy to you, sis. You'd look the same if someone woke you up in the middle of the night and dragged you across half the city."

"I'm always awake in the middle of the night," she said.

"Yeah, well, no one told you to be a cop. What do we have here?"

Her eyes became serious. "At one-fifty a guy called Dispatch, saying there was a dead body in the trunk of a car on Cypress Street. I arrived at the scene ten minutes later, found the car with the trunk open, a dead body inside. The guy who called in was nearby, completely stoned. It's difficult to make any sense of what he's saying. As far as I can tell, he claims he walked past the car, noticed the trunk open, and called us."

"Uh-huh."

She shrugged. "That's what he said, Mitchell. I was busy securing the scene, didn't have time to interrogate him. Officer Bertini is talking to him."

"Yeah, okay. When did Annie and the rest get here?"

"A few minutes before you did."

"Did Jacob get here yet?"

"Nope." She handed him the crime scene log. "Sign here, please."

He scribbled his signature on the page, then walked over to the Honda. There were three people standing around the trunk. Annie Turner, the medical examiner, was wearing a thick orange coat which almost exactly matched her hair color. She peered over her glasses into the trunk, holding a small flashlight. The crime investigation duo, Matt Lowery and Violet Todd, stood by her side. Violet was taking pictures of the open trunk. Matt was bending inside it, busy with something.

Mitchell approached the car and looked into the trunk. "Aw, shit," he muttered. The dead body belonged to a young man, maybe sixteen or seventeen years old. He was dressed in a sky-blue sweater with a large brown stain all over the front. His eyes were closed, his skin pale, and there was a large bruise on his right cheek. Matt was scraping something on the bottom of the trunk into a small paper bag.

"Gloves, Detective," Violet said, tilting her head toward a box of latex gloves on the floor. Mitchell slid two of them on and stepped forward, looking inside the trunk again.

"Hello, Detective," Annie said, her eyes focused on the body.

"What do we have here, Annie?"

"Young male, stabbed several times," she said, pointing her flashlight at the young man's stomach. "He was alive when stabbed, and died soon after. At least one of his lungs was punctured." She pointed the flashlight at his mouth, where a brown smudge trickled from the side of the victim's lips. Dried blood. "The body is in full rigor mortis. Signs of lividity on his right cheek, but he was lying on his back when he was found. Detective, can you help me roll him to his side?"

"Sure," Mitchell said. "Matt, can you step back for a second?"

Matt moved aside. Mitchell grabbed the body by the arm. It was solidly stiff, and the feeling was unnerving. Overcoming his queasy stomach, Mitchell helped Annie roll the body onto its side. Annie lifted the sweater, exposing the victim's skin. There was a large dark bruise all over the dead kid's back.

"Lividity marks on his back as well," Annie said. She lowered the sweater. "You can put him back."

Mitchell carefully positioned the body back in its original position. "Okay," he said. "So, lividity on the side, and on the back as well. That means the body was moved a few hours after the murder, right?"

Annie took a step back from the car. "Right," she said. "See how the body is bent, but the legs are almost straight?"

"Yeah."

"Rigor mortis had already started to set in before they moved the body. They had trouble bending the legs to fit the body in the trunk. That's why it's mostly bent at the waist. I assume they moved it about…" She chewed on her lip for a moment. "Three to five hours after death."

"Can you estimate time of death?"

"Only very loosely. Rigor mortis and the lividity indicate at least twelve hours and no more than twenty-four. It's freezing out here, and it was cold during the day as well, so the body cooled much faster once the car was on the road. Its current temperature is 70.6, so somewhere between…" Her lips moved silently as she made some calculations in her head. "Twelve and eighteen hours ago," she finally said.

Mitchell glanced at his watch. "So between eight a.m. and two p.m.," he said.

"Right," Annie nodded. "I'll be able to give you a better assessment once I do the autopsy."

"Okay," Mitchell said. "Did any of you find a wallet on the body, or any kind of identification?"

"No wallet, no phone" Matt said from within the trunk. He straightened, though considering his height this didn't mean much. Mitchell was used to see Matt from above; he was one of the shortest people Mitchell knew. Matt had once told him that from his vantage point, he always saw who trimmed his nose hair and who didn't. Ever since that day, Mitchell always hesitated when summoned to a murder scene, wondering if he should stop for just a second to do some trimming.

"I'll try to check the fingerprints, see if we get a match," Matt added.

"I'm sure you will," Annie blurted.

Mitchell glanced at her, raising an eyebrow. She stared at Matt, her lips slightly parted. Matt looked back at her, his eyes piercing and suggestive. He took a small step toward her.

"We will, if he's in CODIS," he said, his voice soft.

"Right," Annie whispered huskily.

Mitchell glanced at Violet, nonplussed, and she rolled her eyes, her mouth quirking in amusement.

"Yeah," Mitchell said loudly, breaking the moment. "Let me know what you find out. Is there anything else I should know?"

Matt cleared his throat. "No," he said. "But I haven't gone over the car yet. I'll update you later."

"Good," Mitchell muttered and stepped away. He looked over at Officer Sergio Bertini, who was talking to a thin man in dirty jeans and a worn hoodie. The man shook his head repeatedly.

Mitchell hesitated for a moment. Jacob was certainly taking his time. Usually he got to a crime scene much faster. Mitchell wondered if he should wait before talking to the guy who'd made the call.

Better not, he decided. There was no point in wasting time. He approached the two men.

"Officer." He nodded at Bertini.

"Detective." Bertini nodded back. "This man is the one who called Dispatch to let them know about the body. His name is Joe."

"Hello, Joe," Mitchell said.

"Yeah, hi," the man said, shaking his head slightly. "I called the police because, y'know, it's a murder. I mean, that's terrible, and such a young boy, but now I really have to go, it's getting very late, and I have to work tomorrow. The officer here said I had to wait for the detective, so I waited, because, y'know, I want you to catch the asshole who did this, but now I really have to go. I'm sorry, I really have to go." He wrung his hands. His eyes shifted constantly. The man was incredibly thin, his skin pale and oily. One of his front teeth was missing, the others various shades of yellow and brown, and there were several dark blisters on his lips.

"Joe, what's your last name?" Mitchell asked.

"Uh … Williams," Joe said. "Joe Williams."

"Uh-huh," Mitchell said skeptically. "Can you tell me what happened?"

"Well, this guy here already asked me that like three times, y'know? I was passing through, on my way home when I noticed the car parked here, and the trunk was open. So I looked inside, and saw the dead guy. I immediately called the police, because, y'know, I was horrified. It's terrible. A terrible thing."

"Can you tell me what you were doing here at two in the morning?" Mitchell asked. "You were going back home? Going back from where?"

"The bar. I was going back from the bar. I drank a beer in the bar."

"Which bar?"

Joe blinked. "I don' remember the name. It's a bar nearby."

"Can you explain how we can get there?" Mitchell asked.

"I'm really tired, y'know. I want to go home. I have work tomorrow, and I really need to sleep a few hours before that. Look, that's what happened. There's nothing more."

"Did you see anyone around the car?" Mitchell asked. "Anyone on the street? Did you see how the car got here?"

"No! Just what I said, y'know?"

"Right," Mitchell sighed. "The thing is, Joe, this is a murder investigation and—"

He overheard Jacob's voice behind him, talking to Matt and Annie.

"Hang on," he said. He turned around. Jacob stood by the trunk, his iconic fedora on his head. He stared into the trunk, his hands in his pockets.

Mitchell headed over to talk to him. The victim's hands were already bagged, and Matt was in the front seat of the car, dusting the steering wheel for prints. An ambulance had parked by the rest of the cars, and two men were unloading a stretcher from it.

"Hey," Mitchell said, his voice low.

"Hey, Mitchell," Jacob said. "Sorry I took so long. Amy's a bit sick." Amy was Jacob's teenage daughter.

"Oh, I'm sorry," Mitchell said. "Is it serious?"

"I don't think so." Jacob shrugged, though his eyes were distant and troubled. "Probably just the flu. But she has a very high fever so…"

"Do you want to go home, take care of her?"

"Marissa is with her, and I'm needed here," Jacob said. "What did Fin have to say?"

"Who's Fin?" Mitchell asked.

"The crackhead you were talking to. His name is Fin."

"Well, for one, he told me his name was Joe," Mitchell said. "He said he just walked by, saw the car parked at the curb with the trunk open, and called us."

"Uh-huh. What a charming story."

"I was just about to pry the truth out of him," Mitchell said.

"Sounds good," Jacob answered. "Let's do that."

Both of them approached Fin, halting only when they were really close, towering above him.

"Hello, Fin," Jacob said softly.

"Hello, Detective," Fin muttered, staring at their shoes.

"Detective Lonnie said you've been telling him a very nice story," Jacob said

"Not very nice. I mean, a man was killed, y'know? Terrible business. That's why I called the cops, y'know? Because—"

"I think it is nice, because in this story you're a model citizen who did the right thing, and expected no reward. I think that's very encouraging. It makes me believe a man can change." Jacob smiled a small smile, his cold blue eyes drilling into the man, who shrank under his gaze. "Who would believe that Fin, a guy I've busted at least six times for burglary and possession of narcotics, would be so upstanding?"

"Yeah, y'know? I'm really straightening up. I'm in this group, and I have this sponsor and everything. I didn't like what I've become, y'know? That's why—"

"Fin, look at me," Jacob said.

Fin raised his eyes.

Jacob looked at him intently. "That's a bad burn you have on your lower lip," he said. "Looks painful."

Fin's eyes began glancing around nervously.

"In fact, your lips are covered with burns, but this one looks really fresh," Jacob said. Mitchell took a look at the blistered lips. One of the sores was pink, glistening.

Crack users often burned their lips when smoking the stuff. They used metal cans as pipes, and the metal got very hot.

"Empty your pockets, Fin," Jacob said.

"No, I don't need to. You have to have probable cause to search me and—"

"This is a murder, Fin. Do you think I care about your drug stash? If you don't empty your pockets, I'll arrest you for murder and you'll spend the next twenty years in jail. Empty your damn pockets, now!"

Fin sniffed. He put his hand in his pocket and drew out a few bills and a couple of what looked like silvery pebbles. Crack rocks were usually wrapped in aluminum foil.

"Two rocks," Jacob said. "And you've just smoked a third. That's sixty dollars' worth of crack, and you even have forty dollars in your other hand. Why, Fin, you've hit the jackpot! Congratulations!"

"Yeah, well, y'know, I have a job now and—"

"Shut up," Jacob said tiredly. "I don't have time for this. Let me tell you a different story. You can correct me if I'm wrong, okay?"

"'kay," Fin mumbled, looking back at the ground.

"You were walking here to meet your dealer with a fresh, crinkly twenty-dollar bill in your hand," Jacob said, his voice sharp. "Who knows, maybe you even got it at your new job! And then you noticed this nice car. A very pricey car, for a street like this. And lo and behold, the car was unlocked. You, being the industrious fellow you are, opened the car—"

"I didn't open the car—"

"Fin, before you say any more, remember that we're dusting the car for prints, and we have yours in the system. Now, what were you about to say?"

"Nothin'."

"Okay. You opened the car, looking for anything easy to pilfer, and then popped the trunk open. Here's where things got bad—you found a body in the trunk, right?"

"Yeah, and then I called the cops, y'know? Because it was terrible. I mean, yeah, I guess I opened the car because I wanted to see if I could find out who the owners were, let them know they left their car unlocked. But then when I opened the trunk, I realized it had a dead body inside, and I called the cops."

"Well ... that's not how you tell a story, Fin," Jacob said softly. "You don't rush to the end like that. There has to be a twist, to make the story interesting. The twist here is, before you called us you searched the body, and you found the guy's wallet. It had eighty dollars inside. You took the money, went to your dealer, bought three rocks, and smoked one. You probably wanted to smoke the other two as well, but your conscience bugged you, so then you called us. Isn't that how the story goes?"

Fin shrugged. "The wallet was in the trunk next to the body," he finally said. "I didn' search the body for money. I'm not that far gone."

"Okay," Jacob said. "Where's the wallet?"

Fin led them to a trash can a few hundred feet away. Inside, they found the wallet. Mitchell picked it up and opened it, found the victim's driver's license inside.

"Glen Haney," he said. "The kid's name is Glen Haney. He's seventeen years old."

FIFTEEN

The Honda in which Glen Haney's body was found was registered to Betty Haney, whose home address was in Portland, Maine. Mitchell considered calling the local police, asking them to inform the woman, then hesitated. It seemed wrong, somehow. Sure, she wasn't even in the same state, and he could easily dump this unpleasant task on the local cops, but it seemed right that he should be the one to bear the news. It also occurred to him that Glen Haney might have been killed in Portland, and his body dumped two states away just to muddy the killer's tracks.

He glanced at Jacob. His partner was watching the medics move the body to the ambulance, his expression unreadable.

"I think we should inform the mother ourselves," Mitchell said.

"Yeah?" Jacob said. He sounded distant.

"Listen," Mitchell said carefully. "It's best if I go, inform the mother. You can go back home, be with your daughter. It's probably better for one of us to stay in Glenmore Park anyway, just in case."

Jacob turned to face him, a mixture of gratitude and worry on his face. "Yeah," he said. "That's probably a good idea."

"I'll call you in a few hours," Mitchell said. "Let me know if Matt or Annie find out anything new."

"I will."

Mitchell got back into his car and drove away from the crime scene. He turned on the radio, setting it to *WERS*. He didn't normally listen to live radio, preferring to handpick from his own collection of indie rock albums that he'd amassed in his phone over the years. But he was going on a long drive up the coast, on his way to deliver the most terrible news a parent could ever receive. This time, he preferred to delegate, and assign the task of song picking to someone else.

The roads were empty, and he got to Route 128 in less than fifteen minutes. The night traffic, lone cars on a wide highway intended to contain so many more, made Mitchell feel glum. He usually loved driving at night, when the world was asleep, but the face of the dead seventeen-year-old kept invading his thoughts. He almost turned the car back at one point, his determination to do the so-called right thing wavering. But he didn't, and kept driving.

He slowed down on the bridge in Portsmouth, glancing at the water deep underneath him, the surface reflecting the city lights. He thought about Jacob, back home tending to his sick daughter, and a pang of loneliness hit him. He turned up the volume, and the car filled with a *Frightened Rabbit* song

He nearly missed his exit to I-295, and had to swerve quite sharply, his sleepy eyes widening in alarm as a truck honked at him. But the truck was actually quite far away, the driver only cranky at Mitchell's abrupt maneuver. At the next gas station, he stopped and bought himself a huge cup of coffee.

When he finally reached Portland, he was utterly exhausted, disgusted by his own idea of driving all this way with hardly any sleep, just to deliver the bad news himself. Would it have been that bad to let the local police do the job, then call a few hours later to ask some questions?

He found the address easily, a red brick three-story house on West Street. The sky began to brighten, the stars slowly blinking out of sight as he knocked on the door.

WEB OF FEAR

Curt Haney looked at his wife Betty, her face twisted in horror and confusion as Detective Mitchell Lonnie from Glenmore Park explained that their son was dead. Betty let out a whimper, her hands flying to her mouth, smothering what was perhaps a scream of pain. Curt's vision misted; his wife swam out of focus as, for the first time in years, his eyes filled with tears.

They hadn't seen the body, but the detective had shown them a picture of the car, and another of Glen's driver's license. He said they would be contacted later by the morgue to identify the body, but didn't elaborate on if he meant the Glenmore Park morgue or the Portland morgue.

What had Glen been doing in Glenmore Park?

Glen often disappeared for a day or two, though it was the first time he'd taken Betty's car without asking first. Curt had been furious when he found out. He'd left Glen two angry voicemails. Now Curt wondered if a cop would listen to those voicemails, thinking that Curt had been a bad father. Curt wondered about that himself quite often. Even now he was thinking about small details, like the voicemails or which morgue the body was in, instead of mourning his son.

Glen had always confused Curt. He was so different from the child Curt had been. He was quiet, and could spend hours in his room online, a pastime that often resulted in heated arguments—or, to be fair, heated monologues, in which Curt would shout at his son, telling him he should do something with himself, while Glen looked at the floor and mumble his agreement.

Had Glen known that, after those tirades, Curt often felt guilty? After the last time, Curt had crept to Glen's room at two in the morning, and kissed his son's forehead as he slept. Had Glen felt it? Curt hoped he had.

"I'm sorry, but it would be really helpful if you could answer some questions," Mitchell said.

The three of them were standing in the entrance hall of their home. They had asked Mitchell to come in, because it was cold outside, but they hadn't offered him a drink or asked him to sit down.

Curt wasn't about to do it now. He wanted the man to leave. "Could this wait?" he asked, his voice hoarse. "We need a bit of time to—"

"It would really help us to find out who did this if I asked the questions now," Mitchell said. "It won't take long."

"Okay."

"Do you know what he was doing in Glenmore Park?"

"No," Curt shook his head. "He just left a note that he'd be gone for a couple of days."

"Did he often do that?"

"Sometimes," Curt said. He was about to say Glen usually asked before taking the car, but stopped himself. What did it matter?

"Did your son seem agitated lately, or worried about something?"

"Not that I noticed," Curt said.

"He kept to himself," Betty said, her words trembling. "He spent most of his time online, or he'd go to his friend's house." She suddenly covered her face with her hands, crying uncontrollably. Curt hesitantly laid a hand on his wife's shoulder.

"Which friend is that?" Mitchell asked.

"A girl," Curt said. "Yelena something. Uh … Petrov. Yelena Petrov."

"Was she his girlfriend?" Mitchell asked.

"I don't think so," Curt said. "They were just friends."

"Do you have her phone number?" Mitchell asked.

"Yeah," Curt said. "I'll go look for it." He was reluctant to leave his wife alone, afraid she'd crumple to the floor. He led her inside and helped her sit down on the couch. Then he went to get his phone, located Yelena's number, and gave it to Detective Mitchell.

The detective rattled off a few more questions, but Curt had nothing to say that could help. He didn't really know anything. He tried to convince himself most parents didn't know much about their children as they grew older, but he was still ashamed.

He wondered, if he had been more insistent, had been a larger part of his son's life, would Glen be alive today?

———

Mitchell sat in his car, sipping coffee from a plastic cup, weariness making him feel heavy and sluggish. He glanced at his own reflection in the rearview mirror. He looked awful.

He knew he was usually considered handsome by his acquaintances. He had thick, wavy black hair, perfect tawny skin, wide shoulders, and a muscular body. He cultivated the look of a man who knew what pain and suffering was, with sorrow and wisdom in his eyes. He did it mostly by trimming his eyebrows to achieve the desired effect.

Right now, though, his hair was a complete jumble and his jade-green eyes were red tinged, with dark pouches underneath. His eyebrows were a mess, and his face didn't look sad and wise. He just looked slightly confused.

The conversation with Mr. and Mrs. Haney had been predictably depressing. The only useful thing he'd gotten was Yelena Petrov's number. On the phone, Yelena had told Mitchell she was home, and he'd said he would drop by in half an hour.

He had wisely used that half hour to eat a small breakfast at a local cafe, and consume as much coffee as humanly possible.

He sighed, brushed a hand through his messy hair, and got out of the car. He threw his empty coffee cup into a trash can and walked over to Yelena's home. She lived in a beige-colored building, with peeling paint and boarded-up windows on the bottom floor. Yelena lived in one of those bottom apartments. Mitchell climbed a few concrete stairs and walked down a short, paved path between two of the buildings, avoiding discarded plastic bags and candy wrappers. He finally arrived at the door and knocked.

The door was opened almost immediately by a pale, chubby girl. Her hair was oily and unkempt, her face heavily pockmarked. She wore a shirt with a faded Star Wars print. There was a brown stain on the collar. Her pupils were the size of pinpricks, and she smelled of cannabis.

"You the detective?" Yelena said.

"That's right," Mitchell said.

"Yeah, okay," Yelena nodded.

"Can I come in?" Mitchell asked.

"Yeah, man, Sure, come in."

Mitchell followed her to a dirty living room that consisted of a tattered blue couch, a gaming console, and a large, flat-screen TV.

"So you said this is about Glen, right?" Yelena asked, plopping on the couch. "Is he like … in trouble?"

"Something like that," Mitchell said carefully, still standing. "When did you last see Glen?"

"I don't know," Yelena said, narrowing her eyes. "Last week, I think."

"You think?"

"Yeah, He was definitely here last Monday. What is it? Glen's all right. Whatever you think he did, you're wrong."

"Do you know where he went this weekend?"

"I didn't know he went anywhere."

"When did you last talk to him?"

"Do you mean like talk-talk?"

Mitchell thought about it for a moment. "Yeah, or chatted, or interacted on snapchat, or whatever."

"Three days ago."

"Did he seem tense, or worried, or—"

"So listen, man," Yelena interrupted him sharply. "You say you're a detective, but you haven't even shown me your badge. I think I should talk to Glen before I answer any of your damn questions. So I'd like you to get out now. I'll call you if Glen says that—"

"I'm sorry," Mitchell said, as gently as he could. "Glen is dead." He pulled out his badge and showed it to her.

Yelena stared at the badge, and then looked away. "Oh," she said.

"You don't look very surprised," Mitchell said.

"Yeah, well, I am," Yelena said, her voice subdued. "I just don't have a very expressive face."

She looked back at Mitchell and cleared her throat. "How did it happen?"

"He was stabbed," Mitchell said. "His body was found in his mother's car."

"Oh, man," Yelena said.

"His parents told me Glen sometimes disappeared for a day or two, every once in a while. Do you know why?"

"Yeah, man, he'd sometimes go see some friends he met online somewhere. He was a very friendly guy."

"Did he ever mention any of those friends threatening him in any way? Were any of them violent?"

"I don't think so. Oh man, can you wait a second?" Yelena got up, ran into the bathroom and slammed the door behind her.

Mitchell waited patiently. After a while he sat on the couch, ignoring the aggressive aroma of pot that stuck to its surface. Fifteen minutes later, just as Mitchell was about to check if she was all right, Yelena emerged from the bathroom. Her face was wet, her eyes red.

"Sorry, man," she said. "It's just … Glen was my best friend."

"What can you tell me about him?"

"He was really smart. Kept learning new things all the time. Like, he would do those online courses to learn how to draw, or how to build stuff, or pick locks, or play music. He played guitar really well. Learned it online. Most of the people I know, they're kind of lazy. But Glen had this … I dunno. Like inner energy. He drew that." She pointed at the wall. There was a small canvas painting of Yelena's street, with Yelena leaning against one of the buildings. "See how detailed it is? Glen had a real eye for details. He noticed *everything*."

Mitchell looked at the image carefully. As far as he could tell, it had been painted with water colors. He had no eye for art, but he could tell there was a lot of skill there.

"Do you know where he went this time?" he asked.

"No, he didn't tell me he was going anywhere."

"Did he usually tell you?"

Yelena shrugged. "Sometimes."

"Did Glen seem worried about anything lately? Did he seem on edge for any reason?"

"Nah, not really. I mean, his parents kept hounding him to get off his computer, but I don't think it was that big of a deal."

"Can you think of anyone who'd want to harm him?"

"Not really."

"Can you think of any reason why someone might dump his body all the way in Glenmore Park?"

Yelena raised her eyes quickly. "Did you say Glenmore Park?"

"Yes."

"That's where Abigail Lisman was kidnapped."

"That's right."

"Aw, shit, man. Sure, come on. I'll show you." Yelena got up, suddenly energized, shaking her head, muttering to herself. She led the way to a small, stuffy bedroom that contained a mattress covered with stained sheets. There was a small laptop on the mattress, and a plastic zipper bag full of weed. Yelena dumped herself on the mattress and opened the laptop.

Mitchell raised an eyebrow and pointed at the weed. "This yours?" he asked.

Yelena glanced at it. "Yeah," she said. "It's tea."

"Uh-huh."

"Smell it, man."

Mitchell sighed, picked up the bag, opened it, and smelled it. Jasmine. It was the best-smelling thing in the apartment.

"I like to drink tea, man. Anyway, you're not here to bust me for tea, or for weed, right? Check it out." She opened a browser and browsed to a Reddit page. It was a subreddit Mitchell identified immediately: the subreddit dedicated to Abigail Lisman's kidnapping.

"There," Yelena pointed at the screen. "RollingPunches, that's him. He got really obsessed with this case. Kept messaging me about it, trying to get me to join the thread."

"Did you?" Mitchell asked.

"Naw, man, I don't dig those crowdsourced policing threads. They always get things wrong, and get all worked up about nothing."

"But Glen was involved."

"Yeah. But he stopped messaging me about it after a while. And see here? He last posted two days ago."

"Okay," Mitchell said, frowning.

"Glen was really in to this," Yelena said. "He might have figured he'd be able to find some more info in Glenmore Park."

"Yeah," Mitchell said, his mind kicking into high gear. "Could be."

SIXTEEN

Hannah sat in the squad room, listening as Mitchell detailed his visit to Portland. He yawned constantly, and occasionally lost his train of thought, staring into the distance like a thoughtful, grazing cow. But his eyes sparkled with determination, and Hannah could tell he felt that incredible buzz that comes with finding a good lead.

Hansel and Gretel got it all wrong. You don't follow the breadcrumb trail back home. You follow it into the forest, until you reach the gingerbread house and arrest the witch.

Captain Bailey was in the room as well, listening with rapt attention to the details of the case. The usual background noise of the station was muted and drowsy, as it always was on a Sunday morning. Only those who had to be on duty were present in the building, and even they tried to do as little as possible.

Hannah should have been at home too, but the quiet and loneliness of her home got to her. She'd nearly called Clint to invite him over. Then she thought *he* should be the one to call *her*. So she did the only thing she could think of, and drove to the station. She was the first to show up in the squad room, followed closely by the captain, who had come to meet with Mitchell.

Eventually Mitchell's outline of events came to an end, or maybe he just fell asleep with his eyes open. In any case, he was suddenly quiet.

"Okay, then," Bailey said. "Our murder victim is connected to the Lisman kidnapping."

"He's more than just connected," Hannah said. "It sounds like he was on the right track, and was murdered because of it."

"Not necessarily," Bailey said. "There are other explanations."

"It's highly unlikely that he was searching for her and just got killed by chance," Hannah said.

"I wouldn't know about highly unlikely," Bailey said. "The kid drove to a city he didn't know and started poking his nose where it didn't belong. My father used to say, never lift a rock without putting your scorpion helmet on first."

The concept of a scorpion helmet gave them all pause.

"So, what, you think he just ran into a drug dealer or something while looking for the kidnapper and got himself killed?" Hannah asked.

Bailey shrugged. "We can't discount the possibility, but I can think of an even more plausible explanation. Maybe the kid really did have sharp instincts. He began suspecting someone with a criminal past. But unlike us, he didn't have a gun and a badge, and when he started throwing accusations he found himself dead in a trunk."

"We can't ignore the possibility that he really was on to something," Mitchell said. "Tracking the murderer here could lead us to one of Abigail's kidnappers."

"That's true," Bailey nodded.

"The FBI should be notified," Hannah said. "They should take over the case."

"Let's not get ahead of ourselves here," Bailey said, raising an eyebrow.

"Captain," Hannah said. "The FBI has resources we don't. If this has a bearing on Abigail's safety, we can't be pigheaded. I mean … sure, we could offer our help. But I really think we should let them know right now. It could have real impact on their investigation."

Bailey leaned back in the chair, his face thoughtful. Finally, he said, "Okay. You're probably right. Here's what we'll do: Detective Lonnie will go home and get some sleep, because he's getting drool all over my squad room floor."

Mitchell blinked and yawned again, then nodded.

Bailey continued. "Hannah, you should talk to either Agent Ward or Agent Mancuso—"

"Agent Mancuso is probably a better choice," Hannah said hurriedly.

"Okay. Update her on our preliminary findings. She isn't directly in charge of this case, so I assume it'll take them some time to reach a decision regarding this. For now, we keep investigating it. The body was found less than twelve hours ago; the trail is still reasonably warm. We don't want to waste time. I'll try to get authorization for overtime for the lab and the morgue as well. If this case is related to the kidnapping case, it's crucial we resolve this case as soon as possible."

"Sounds good," Hannah said.

"I'm so glad you approve of my management skills. Now, Detective Cooper is at the hospital; his daughter's fever was very high and they had to get her to the emergency room."

Hannah tensed. "Is she okay?" she asked, worried.

"Yeah. Apparently it's just a bad case of the flu. She isn't in any danger. But that means one of the detectives in charge is currently not on the case. I want you to temporarily pair with Detective Lonnie on this investigation. You're the closest to the Lisman case, so your knowledge will be valuable. Bernard and I will help as much as we can."

Hannah nodded, relieved that she was back on the kidnapping case, even if temporarily so.

"Where do we stand on leads?" Bailey asked.

There was silence in the room. Everyone looked at Mitchell. His eyes were glazed and unfocused.

"Mitchell!" Hannah snapped.

"Wha?"

"Leads," Bailey repeated. "On this case."

"Oh. Uh … we know the guy who called Dispatch to report the body met his dealer nearby."

"The dealer could have seen who drove the car to that spot," Bailey said.

"Do we know who the dealer is?" Hannah asked. "Mitchell. Mitchell! Do we know who the dealer is?"

"Not yet," Mitchell said sleepily.

"Find the dealer's name," Bailey told Hannah. "Interrogate him. Maybe he saw something. And get those lab reports. I want more info on this case before the FBI steals it from under our feet."

To Hannah's surprise, Agent Christine Mancuso suggested meeting in person instead of talking on the phone. She was just visiting the Lisman family, so she was nearby. They agreed to have breakfast at Red's Pizza.

Despite being five minutes away, Hannah was late; she was breathing heavily, her pulse racing, by the time she got to Red's Pizza. Agent Mancuso was already seated at a table nearby and waved her over. She had a small espresso cup in front of her. Hannah sat down and grabbed a menu.

"I hope you don't mind, but I already ordered," Mancuso said. "I need to be in Boston in a couple of hours, so I don't have much time."

"Sure, no problem. I'm sorry I was late," Hannah said, scanning the menu quickly. "I think I'll just have a muffin and a cup of coffee."

Mancuso frowned. "You should inform the waitress. I'm not sure telling me about it is very helpful."

"I was just sharing," Hannah muttered, her face flushing. "Okay."

Hannah put the menu down. "So … We found out something related to the Lisman case."

"What is it?" Mancuso asked.

"A young man named Glen Haney was found dead—stabbed—in the trunk of his parents' car on Cypress Street. It's one of the worst areas in Glenmore Park."

"Yeah," Mancuso nodded. "I know where that is."

"Glen Haney lives in Portland. He was one of the Redditors who are trying to find Abigail Lisman."

"Uh huh."

"We think he was here following a lead. Or he decided to come here to be closer to the case. And then he got killed."

Mancuso nodded. The waitress approached them, carrying a huge round tray. Hannah stopped talking as the waitress laid a large pepperoni pizza in front of Mancuso.

"One pepperoni pizza," she said cheerfully, and turned to Hannah with a smile. "What can I get you?"

"Uh…" Hannah stared at the huge steaming pizza tray. "A muffin," she said, her voice a bit higher than usual. "And coffee?"

"Sure!" The waitress nodded. "Anything else?" She glanced at the large pizza.

Hannah looked at it as well. Her muffin seemed completely inadequate. "No," she finally said. "That's all."

The waitress left, and Mancuso grabbed a slice and bit into it. "You can have a slice if you want," she said, after swallowing.

Hannah stared at her. "No. Thanks." The idea of eating pizza first thing in the morning made her queasy.

"Okay," Mancuso said. "Dead Redditor."

"Right."

"Why do you think this has anything to do with the kidnapping?"

"Well … I think it's very possible he was on to something, and it got him killed."

"Is it?" Mancuso's eyebrows quirked and she took another huge bite from her slice.

"Yes. Don't you?"

"Did he post anything illuminating about the case before disappearing?"

"I don't think so, but—"

Mancuso interrupted her. "He didn't. You want to know how I know that? Because I read all the posts on that subreddit. And they were far from illuminating. Some of them were downright dangerous."

"Yeah, but maybe he wanted to be sure before—"

"One of the most popular posts there fingers a man named Abdul Baasit as a suspect in the kidnapping. Do you know what their proof is?"

"No," Hannah said.

"He's a Muslim. Truly great minds at work. It has over fifty upvotes."

"It's the internet," Hannah said. "Of course it draws mindless assholes. But that doesn't mean that—"

"Hannah, you know as well as I do that the most likely scenario here is that this Glen fellow drove over here, accused some drug dealer of the kidnapping, and got killed."

"Damn it, Mancuso, you can't just ignore this!"

Mancuso finished her slice and took another. "I'm not ignoring anything. But I think the FBI has resources that random people on the internet don't. We have over fifteen agents working on this case, and dozens more involved. Due to its publicity, it rose to the top of the pile. If those Redditors found something, we would have noticed it as well."

"That's classic FBI superiority," Hannah said sharply. "You just assume you're better."

"We *are* better," Mancuso said, leaning forward, her eyes narrowing. "And better funded as well. A man has been killed. That's terrible. But do you really want resources pulled away from this case because of it?"

Hannah remained silent, seething.

The waitress approached them and put a small cup of coffee and a plate with a single muffin in front of Hannah. The muffin plate was completely dwarfed by the huge pizza tray. It looked like a Sesame Street demonstration of "big and small."

"Okay, listen," Mancuso said after she finished chewing. "I'm not the one making the call. Maybe I am being a patronizing Fed, bloated by her own self-perception." She grinned, and the rage in Hannah's heart subsided slightly. "I'll talk to the person in charge. See what he thinks."

"Okay," Hannah said.

"Who's in charge of the murder case?" Mancuso asked.

"Detective Lonnie and I."

"Then what are you so angry about?" Mancuso asked, her grin widening. "You'll catch the killer in no time." She shoved the rest of the pizza crust into her mouth and chewed contentedly.

Hannah watched Fin's eyes as they constantly shifted right and left, as if searching desperately for something. Perhaps his eyes were looking for the next crack rock. Or maybe they were simply searching for some way to escape the two detectives blocking the view.

The noon sun hit the back alley of the burger joint, exposing the numerous cracks in the walls, the uninspired graffiti, the trash-infested ground.

Fin worked as a dishwasher at the restaurant. Mitchell had joined Hannah, and they'd driven over to interrogate him.

"We're not going to arrest anybody," Hannah said. "We're just interested in the murder. Your dealer might have seen something."

"I have no dealer," Fin said.

"Don't try my patience, Fin. we found two rocks in your pocket," Mitchell said sharply.

"That was an illegal search," Fin mumbled. "You can't arrest me for that."

"Wanna try me?" Mitchell asked.

"We don't want to arrest you, Fin," Hannah said. "Just give us the name of the dealer."

"I don't know his name."

"Oh?" Mitchell said. "Do you call him Mr. Dealer, then? His nickname is good enough, Fin. Give me something, so I don't have to haul your ass into jail. It's hard to get crack inside."

"I just saw this guy, and I knew he sometimes sold crack, so I bought some. I don't know his name, I swear!"

"I believe you," Hannah said softly. "But we need to find him. He might have been a witness to the murder. He won't even know you're the one who told us. We'll tell him we saw it on a security camera."

"There are no security cameras on Cypress Street," Fin said. "People make sure of that."

"What people?" Mitchell asked.

"I don't know. I just heard what people told me."

"Okay, I'm losing my patience," Mitchell said to Hannah. "This guy isn't talking. You know what? I think he killed that boy for his money. Let's arrest him for murder. Boom, case closed, we can go home."

"I didn't kill that boy!" Fin said, panicking.

"I'm sure you didn't," Hannah said, her eyes sad. It wasn't an act. He was pitiful, his fingers trembling, lips blistered beyond repair, teeth rotting, clothing tattered. He couldn't be older than thirty, but he looked as if he was sixty. She sighed heavily. "But we really need to catch the guy who did this. So just give us the—"

"You know what?" Fin said, his voice rising high. "You want to take me to jail? Do it. Because I'd rather spend the next twenty years in prison, than have my throat cut tonight."

There was a moment of silence in the alley. The noise of a truck rumbled in the distance. Fin's eyes stopped shifting for a second as he looked at them both, his jaw clenched tight.

"Let's try this again," Mitchell said. "Last night you bought some crack on Cypress Street. What was your dealer's name?"

———

"Damn it," Hannah muttered as they got back in the car. "I thought he'd give the name up eventually."

Mitchell shrugged. "Nothing we can do about it. Let's go back to the station. We can start checking out the Reddit page, search Glen's social networks, see if there are any leads there."

Hannah glanced at him. This was Mitchell's favorite approach: go online, find leads there. It often led to good results; he was very good at ferreting out connections and interesting details from the internet.

But Hannah preferred physical leads. It was what had attracted her to this line of work in the first place. She definitely hadn't expected to spend so much time behind a desk.

"Hang on," she said. "Let's think about it for a second. The dealer was hanging around Cypress Street. Who controls that area?"

"The Hasidic Panthers dominate the drug business on the entire southern side of town," Mitchell said. "So, I guess we're talking about Rabbi Friedman."

"Why don't we talk to him?"

Mitchell stared at her. "You want us to ask Rabbi Friedman to finger the dealer who worked that night? Do you think he'll just take a look at the roster for that evening, and tell us the name of the employee in question?"

"It's all theoretical. We just want to find Abigail. We aren't looking to arrest anyone for selling drugs."

"Hannah, we're talking about crack," Mitchell said sharply. "This isn't marijuana; we can't just look the other way."

"Well, there's no harm in talking to him," she said.

"I think you're actually the first person to ever say there's no harm in talking to Rabbi Friedman."

"After that we'll go do your thing with the computer."

"My thing?"

"You know what I mean."

"Fine," Mitchell grumbled as he started the engine. "Don't blame me if we'll find ourselves on the bottom of the ocean with lead dreidels chained to our ankles."

Hannah bit her lip as they drove, occasionally glancing at Mitchell. Whenever they were together lately, she was unusually tense and on edge. She realized the car smelled of Mitchell. Probably even more so after his trip to Portland and back.

She liked his smell; it was sweet and fresh, and made her feel warm all over. Had his smell affected her like that a year ago? She doubted it. She wasn't even sure she'd ever even noticed his smell a year ago.

She should call Clint. She liked him, and the fact that they didn't work together anymore only made a relationship more feasible. He hadn't called her since Friday. Was he mad about Jurgen's interrogation? Probably, just a bit. Hannah hoped he'd get over it. Clint didn't strike her as a guy who could hang on to a grudge for long.

"Here we are," Mitchell said, parking the car.

Rabbi Friedman lived in a large, two-story house with a generous front yard, complete with a wide white table, four chairs surrounding it, and a plastic tanning bed. Hannah tried to imagine the rabbi or his wife on the bed, and her mind rebelled against the impossible images. No one ever used the tanning bed, she decided.

It felt strange, approaching the door of the Friedman mansion without any cover, without a warrant or a plan. Though Hannah had been to the house four times before, this was the first time she'd come just to talk. She hesitated before pressing the doorbell.

After a moment, a voice called from behind the door. "Yes?"

"Detectives Shor and Lonnie to see Rabbi Friedman," Hannah said.

There was a moment of silence, and then the voice said. "Do you have an appointment?" This was where Hannah would normally brandish a warrant, or threaten to break down the door.

"No," she said. "But we really need to talk to him. It's important."

"Hang on," the voice said.

They waited.

"This was a bad idea," Mitchell said. Hannah didn't answer.

The door finally opened. A woman in a long dress stood in the entrance, wearing a scarf around her head.

"Please," she said. "Come in."

She led them inside and down a large hallway into a lavishly furnished room. "The rabbi will soon join you," she said, gesturing at a cream colored sofa, then left.

Mitchell and Hannah sat down, exchanging looks. They waited in silence for several minutes until the man of the house came in.

Rabbi Friedman was a wide man, though his body hinted at a deep muscular frame. His blue eyes were large and cold, overshadowed by two incredibly thick eyebrows. His black beard was very rich as well, and even as he sat in front of them he was already stroking it. It was a strange mannerism of his; he would constantly touch his beard, as if trying to verify it was still there, and would occasionally yank it when irritated.

"Detective Shor," he said in a deep, vibrating voice. He glanced at Mitchell. "And the *pisher*. Visiting me on a Sunday. Isn't this the police's day off?"

"Hello, Rabbi," Hannah said. "We were hoping you could help us with a case."

"Really?" His eyes went wide. "Help you? That's a first."

Hannah cleared her throat. "A young man was found dead on Cypress Street. The man who found the body was meeting his drug dealer there."

The rabbi caressed his beard. "Terrible business. How does that relate to me?"

"We were hoping the drug dealer saw the killer," Mitchell said.

"*Nu?* What am I supposed to do about it? You're the detectives, go and ask him!"

"We don't know who the drug dealer is," Hannah said.

"Ah," the rabbi said, the tugging of his beard becoming more pronounced. "And you came here to ask for my guidance? Perhaps hoping I'll throw in a good word with *Hashem* up above?"

"We … What?" Mitchell looked at him confused.

"Because I can't see any other reason for you *nudnikim* to show up at my door! Why would I know anything about a drug—"

The door suddenly opened, and an old frail woman of maybe eighty years poked her head inside. Her entire face was an impossible network of crinkles and liver spots, except for her eyes, which were blue and penetrating, almost identical to the rabbi's.

"Baruch!" she said in a sharp voice. "Yemima made pasta again. Pasta!"

The rabbi's hand left his beard, and his face transformed into a mask of horror. "Momma," he said. "I am busy right now, and—"

"I told you to talk to her. All this pasta is making me constipated! I told her, but the *balabusta* will not listen to me!"

"Yes, Momma, I will talk to her—"

"And it tastes like *drek*. I can't eat this food. If she would let me cook, I could make my chicken soup."

At the mention of the chicken soup, the rabbi's face became deathly pale. He stood up quickly. "No need!" he said. "You should rest. I will talk to Yemima. She will make very good food, no more pasta."

"Something with prunes!" his mother quacked at him. "For my constipation."

"Yes Momma, of course, Momma." He ushered her out of the room and slammed the door behind her. Sweating profusely, he fumbled in his pockets until he located a handkerchief and wiped his forehead.

"This season," he muttered, glancing at Hannah. "Every year, a month before Pesach, my mother comes here to stay with us. It's enough to drive a man mad! Do you celebrate Pesach with your family?"

"Y-yes," Hannah said hesitantly.

"It is very difficult! Makes me think we should have stayed in Egypt. Did we really have it so bad there? *Mein Got*. And my wife just bought twenty packages of pasta. Twenty! She said she had coupons. Of course we eat pasta every day, we have to get rid of the *hametz* before Pesach. Even I am constipated by now!"

He sat down, breathing deeply, while Hannah tried to recuperate from the realm of too much information she had been thrown into.

"Right," he finally said. "So you have a murder investigation. Okay. Go on, *shlep*. Find your murderer, so that we can sleep safe at night, knowing the police are looking after us."

"Rabbi," Hannah said. "The killer. We think he is the man who kidnapped the Lisman child."

The rabbi looked at her sharply. "Abigail Lisman?" he asked.

Hannah nodded.

The rabbi began caressing the beard again. "I see," he said.

"Her bat mitzvah is next year," Hannah said.

"Yes," the rabbi said shrewdly, looking at her. "And you thought you'd come here with your Jewish-cop, Goy-cop *shtick* and the rabbi will help?"

"She's just a little girl," Hannah said.

"Harrumph," the rabbi said. It was the first time Hannah ever heard someone *say* Harrumph. "Okay, give me a moment. I don't know how I can help with drug dealers, of course, but someone from the congregation might know something." He stood up, opened the door, and walked out of the room.

"Did you see his face when she said chicken soup?" Mitchell whispered.

"Shut up," Hannah hissed at him. "Not now."

"I thought Jewish people liked chicken soup!"

"It depends."

"Depends on what?"

"Depends if your parents make you eat the chicken. Now shut up."

They waited for several moments more until the rabbi returned. "Okay," he said. "I made a few calls. I don't know about any drug dealer. But a man I know works nearby, and he didn't see anything. However, he said there was a homeless *nebech* wandering around. Peter something?"

"Peter Bell?" Mitchell asked.

"That's right."

"And does the … man you know think that Peter saw something?" Hannah asked.

"He wasn't sure. But he thought it was possible."

Hannah stood up, and Mitchell followed suit. "Thank you, Rabbi," she said.

"You're welcome, *meydale*," he said, nodding. "I hope you find little Abigail and get her home safely."

"There," Hannah said, pointing at the sidewalk. Twenty feet ahead of their car, Peter Bell paced along with his usual, shambling gait.

Peter Bell was one of Glenmore Park's biggest failures. Due to Massachusetts's freezing winters, the mayor had decided to divert funding to make sure that shelter was supplied to all the homeless in the city between October and April. It worked reasonably well. A flexible timetable for signing in and a blind eye for pets made sure no one slept outside in the winter.

Except for Peter Bell.

He refused to explain why he wouldn't stay in any of the shelters. He didn't drink too heavily, and didn't do any drugs. Occasionally, on particularly cold nights, the cops would be instructed to keep an eye for him, and arrest him for loitering if spotted. Once in jail, he'd be supplied with warm soup and admonished for his incessant loitering. He'd be released the next morning.

Hannah, like the rest of the cops, knew him from her days as a patrol cop on the graveyard shift. She still saw him here and there, though she hadn't had a good reason to talk to him for the past three years, since she became a detective.

Mitchell parked the car, and they both hurried after Peter. He was walking hunched over, hugging himself like he always did, his long legs jerking sharply as he paced, as if his control over them was not absolute. When they caught up to him he halted, looking at them with his soft eyes.

"Hello, Peter," Mitchell said.

He stared at the flagstones. "'ello," he muttered.

He was dressed in a thick black coat, a gift from one of Glenmore Park's merciful citizens. His head was a tangled mess of long, gray-brown hair that grew all the way to his chin, where it intermingled with his beard. His lips were cracked, his teeth yellow.

Right now, he looked even more tired than usual. Hannah's heart panged, and she wondered yet again if there had been a moment in time at which Peter could have been saved. Maybe there was. Maybe he could still be saved even now.

"Peter," Mitchell said. "Can we ask you something?"

"Yeah, I guess."

"Were you on Cypress Street last night?"

He raised his eyes and looked first at Mitchell, then at Hannah. "Yeah," he finally said.

"Did you perhaps … see a man park a Honda in the middle of the night?" Hannah asked, lowering her expectations. Even if he had, he probably wouldn't remember.

"Yeah," he said.

"You did?" she asked in surprise.

"Yeah. I was cold, because someone stole my blanket, so I was walking, instead of sleeping. I saw the man park the Honda."

"Do you remember what he looked like?"

"Yeah."

Hannah stared at him in amazement. She could hardly believe their luck. "Really? How?"

"He wore a black mask. That's why I remember him. People usually don't wear masks."

"Oh," Hannah said, deflating. Damn. "Can you tell us what he did?"

"Yeah," Peter said. "He parked the car. Then he got out and closed the door. And then he walked away from the car."

"That's it?" Mitchell asked.

"After walking a few steps away from the car, he took off his mask," Peter said.

"And you saw his face?" Mitchell asked.

"Yeah."

"And he didn't see you?"

"People mostly don't see me," Peter said. "Even if they do, they don't really notice."

"Can you describe his face?"

"Yeah."

"Can you describe it to a sketch artist?"

"Yeah, I guess. Do we need to go to the police station for that?"

"It would be better, but if you don't want to—" Hannah began.

"I don't mind."

"Okay." She nodded and gently put a hand on his shoulder. "Come on, we'll take you there."

———

The sketch artist agreed to come in, despite the fact that it was the weekend. He showed up at the station half an hour later with his laptop, and chatted with Peter as he turned it on. Peter answered his questions hesitantly at first, then his confidence slowly grew; his tone became more certain. The artist began making a series of sketches on screen, matching faces to Peter's detailed descriptions. Hannah watched the process, hoping Peter's memory was as good as he claimed.

She remembered that he'd said someone stole his blanket, that he was walking around because he was cold, so she left the station and drove over to the local Walmart, about ten minutes away. She hesitated in the bedding section, torn between several blankets.

When she bought bedsheets for herself, she was mostly concerned about the patterns and colors. Trying to buy a blanket for a man sleeping on the street was quite different. She needed something that wouldn't draw attention, that wouldn't make him a target. But she also wanted a blanket that wouldn't tear easily, and that wouldn't look terrible when grime inevitably began to cling to it.

She finally found a grayish-brown blanket that she decided would do the trick. She bought it and returned as fast as she could to the station.

Mitchell was there alone; the sketch artist and Peter were gone. Mitchell held a sketch in his hand: the face of a middle-aged man with thinning hair, thick lips, and a strong chin. Mitchell tried to match it to their collection of mugshot pictures. He told Hannah that Peter had left only five minutes before she got back.

She ran back outside and got in her car, circled the nearby streets several times. The sun set, plunging the streets into another cold night. Peter Bell was nowhere to be found.

SEVENTEEN

On Monday morning, Hannah began working on the case whiteboard in the squad room. To avoid contaminating the case with preconceptions, she decided to address it as the Glen Haney murder case. She avoided any mention of Abigail, aside from the Reddit thread Glen had been involved with. First she drew the timeline, starting three days before the murder so she could add the time of his first post on the Reddit thread.

She also included the last post on the Reddit thread; him leaving his parents' home on Saturday the 21st; the murder, between eight a.m. and two p.m. that day; and the discovery of the body on Cypress Street the following night.

She opened Violet's e-mail containing the crime scene pictures and sent a few to the printer. Then she located the sketch of the man Peter Bell had described. They hadn't succeeded in getting an exact match in the mugshot book. The sketch had been distributed to all patrol cops, with no result so far. She taped it carefully to the board. Then she made herself a cup of coffee as a reward for a good start.

She was standing over the printer, coffee cup in hand, when Mitchell entered the room.

"Good morning!" he said. There was a slight uptake in her heartbeat as he spoke. She hated herself for it, and resolved to call Clint and set a date for that very night.

"Hey," she said, focusing intently on the printer. The thing was ridiculously slow.

"Filling the whiteboard?"

She nodded. "Yeah." She needed to feel the sense of progression that came with populating the board. She was *getting* somewhere. Specifically, to a point where there would be no space left on the board.

"Talk to Matt and Annie yet?" he asked.

She glanced at the clock. "Not yet. I'll do it now."

"I can call them if you want."

She smiled at him briefly. She wasn't used to working with him, and they didn't have assigned roles in the partnership yet. But when she worked with Bernard, calling the morgue and the crime investigation unit was her thing. "It's fine," she said. "I'll do it. You should start with the…" she hesitated. Would he feel like she was dominating the case if she told him what to do? Who was lead detective here? "Uh…"

"Then I'll look into the subreddit where Haney was active," Mitchell said, already sitting by his computer. "See if there's any clue to what he was doing in Glenmore Park."

"Good," she said, relieved.

He was acting so casual and cool. Was she the only one bothered by their roles in this investigation? Usually, the experienced detective took lead in the investigation. That meant Bernard was lead detective in their partnership, and similarly, Jacob was lead with Mitchell. But she and Mitchell had gone to the police academy together. She'd been promoted to detective only six weeks before him.

Perhaps the choice of lead detective should be dictated by the case? She was probably the one in charge of the kidnapping case … but Mitchell caught the call for the murder case. And anyway, the kidnapping case was now primarily being investigated by the FBI. So it should probably be Mitchell.

Would it have bothered her if it was someone else, someone who didn't make her feel weird whenever he stepped into the room?

She ground her teeth in frustration. This neurotic mind loop was getting her nowhere. Mitchell was already deeply focused on his monitors, and she was doing nothing. She snatched the crime scene printouts and began tacking them to the whiteboard with vengeance.

Once she was done, she sat down at her desk and picked up the phone. She dialed Annie's number and waited. It rang for a long time, and she was about to hang up when Annie finally answered.

"Hello?" Annie said, sounding out of breath.

"Annie? It's Hannah. Is this a bad time? I thought you were working."

"Yeah, no … I mean it's a good time. Uh … I can talk."

"Right," Hannah said hesitantly. "I was calling about Glen Haney's autopsy report."

"Yeah?"

"You never sent it to me. And usually we meet at the morgue, to go over the findings, and—"

"Right! I'm sorry, I'm a bit out of focus this week. Sorry. There's no real reason to come to the morgue. The cause of death was loss of blood. The victim was stabbed four times. The first two stabs were in his chest. The first tore through his right lung. The second wasn't deep; the blade hit the ribs, making a superficial cut. The third and fourth were in his abdomen—one hit his kidney, the other his liver."

"Okay," Hannah said, thinking. "How tall was the victim?"

"Just under six feet," Annie said.

"So the killer was tall, if he stabbed him in the chest, right?"

"That's what I thought at first," Annie said. "But actually, the angle of the first two stabs indicated he would have to be seven feet tall."

"That's very tall."

"Yeah. I think it's more likely the killer was standing above him. The third and fourth stabs weren't as deep as the first stab. That seems to indicate that the killer found it a bit difficult to plunge the knife into his stomach from where he stood, which also indicates higher ground. Also, he had several abrasions all over his body, indicating a very rough tumble."

There was a short pause in the conversation.

"Stairs," Hannah finally said.

"That would be my bet," Annie said. Her breathing became strangely husky. Hannah suddenly suspected Annie wasn't in the morgue at all.

"Do you have a more accurate time of death?" Hannah asked.

"Um…" Annie's tone became a bit high. "Hang on, I need to … uh … I'll just … give me a second…"

Hannah waited for a bit. She heard some fumbling, and a male voice saying something. Then there was the sound of a door shutting. "Okay," Annie finally said. "Right. Time of death."

"Are you checking the chart?" Hannah asked, smiling to herself.

"No. I remember. The time of death was between eleven a.m. and two p.m."

Hannah noted it. "Right," she said. "Anything else?"

"Stomach contents. Not much, just a sandwich. The blade used was quite wide and serrated. It tore his body to shreds with each stab. My bet is a bread knife."

Hannah shuddered, trying to push away the images this conjured.

"I already mentioned to Detective Lonnie that the body had been moved three to five hours after death, and stuffed into the trunk then."

"Okay. So you'll send me the report?"

"I'll do it in half an hour."

"Great," Hannah said. "I'll be waiting." She hung up and sighed, then called Matt. He didn't answer his phone. She rolled her eyes and called Violet.

"Hello?"

"Violet, it's Hannah."

"Hey, Hannah."

"I'm calling about the crime scene report," Hannah said. "Do you have it?"

"Sure! I'll send it over."

"Thanks. Say, is Matt there?"

"No, he had to go for a few hours. I don't know where. Do you want me to leave him a message?"

"No need, I just…" Hannah grinned. "Forget it."

"Okay. I'm sending the report as we speak."

"Awesome."

"Oh, and there was a gas station nearby, so we got their CCTV footage. Sending a link. It's still a big file."

"Thanks, Violet," Hannah said, and hung up. A moment later the report popped up in her inbox, as well as a link to the CCTV footage video. She started downloading it, then began reading the report on her monitor.

The steering wheel, door handles, and trunk had been devoid of prints; someone had cleaned up after himself. There were a lot of hairs and fibers, and they'd been sent to the lab. No phone was found anywhere at the crime scene.

There was a page with Violet's sketch of the crime scene. Violet's sketches were incredibly clean and accurate. It was a real gift, turning the chaos and horror of a crime scene into a simple, concise collection of black-and-white geometric shapes. Hannah printed the sketch as well, and added it to the whiteboard.

As sad as it was, the fun part was over. She glanced at Mitchell. He was hardly moving, occasionally nudging the mouse and clicking, his eyes glued to the monitors.

She checked the CCTV footage. It had finished downloading. She double-clicked the file and began viewing the video.

The main subreddit devoted to Abigail Lisman's kidnapping was a tangled mess, and Mitchell took his time processing it. Unlike many others, he did not discount the possibility that someone out there could have found Abigail's kidnapper. People online could be clever and determined when diving into puzzles and mysteries. But one had to ignore the loud majority, who merely parroted what others had already said, or created their own warped version of the case to match their specific agenda.

He was happy to see that the most insane theories were down at the bottom, sometimes disappearing completely. The shared moderation in the Reddit community worked well, at least here. He scanned the bottom threads quickly, and after becoming acquainted with the alien abduction theory, the Yakuza conspiracy, and a clumsily veiled attempt to sell some kind of body lotion, he started from the top.

The most upvoted post was the one that had found the image which showed Abigail and Grace walking down the street together. Then there were some Redditors who either lived in Glenmore Park or came over to investigate the case, posting images, trying to piece together Abigail and Gracie's route. Mitchell read it through, impressed. CrazyKid39 appeared to have traced Abigail and Gracie's route perfectly until they reached the park, just by piecing together the image in which they were seen, a very short statement by the FBI about where Gracie was found, and the Lisman's street name, which the Redditors managed to retrieve.

Then came the finger-pointing. Several images were flagged by different posts as *Potential Suspects*, with the so-called suspects marked by a circle or a crudely drawn arrow. As far as Mitchell could see, all the suspects were flagged due to incredibly flimsy reasons, such as suspicious clothing, strange behavior, and various racist reasons. Since the kidnapping had happened on Saint Patrick's Day, strange behaviors and clothing were rampant. Mitchell counted about a dozen leading suspects, none of which were likely.

RollingPunches appeared twenty-three times in the subreddit, mostly in the comments. He seemed to be one of the more rational, analytical Redditors, and a large number of his comments were dedicated to discounting various suspects, for good reasons. He was very enthusiastic with the Redditors who drove to Glenmore Park to take pictures. Had he decided to join the troops? His last post was over a day before his estimated time of death.

Two of his comments were aimed at a different subreddit called *ProtectOurChildren*. They also appeared in various social networks with the hashtag *#ProtectOurChildren*. Mitchell skimmed the premise. They claimed the Lisman kidnapping would have been avoided if the justice system dealt more harshly with sexual offenders. Chemical castration was lauded as the number one method of dealing with this problem, as well as harsher punishments for any sexual offense. That the Lisman case was almost certainly not related to sexual offenders mattered not at all to the various memes and video clips that began cropping up everywhere.

Once Mitchell's attention was distracted by this group, it was impossible not to notice the others. A different group linked the case to funding of law enforcement agencies. They claimed that the police were focused on revenue from fines instead of crime prevention.

A third group linked it to illegal immigrants.

Gun control, citizen privacy, the targeting of various ethnic groups—Abigail Lisman became a face linking to all those issues and more. Her story and face represented the fear of every parent, and fear is a potent tool for propaganda.

Fear also led many people to search for a reason. Parents wanted to believe this would never happen to them. And they found an outlet: blaming Abigail's parents. Many pointed out the girls had been walking freely in the city at night, as if their mothers didn't care what happened to them. And why were the girls on Instagram in the first place? It was a cesspool of pedophiles and perverts. No girl should be allowed on Instagram before the age of fourteen, or sixteen, or seventeen, or ever. Someone had located an image from the party Naamit and Ron Lisman had been to that night, a picture in which Naamit was holding a bottle of beer. It was circulated with various captions. Mitchell wanted to punch someone.

And then he ran across a conspiracy website collecting proof that Abigail had never been kidnapped at all, that it was a ruse by her parents to catch the media's attention because of their financial difficulties. They demonstrated several similarities to the "balloon boy" hoax from 2009, in which Richard and Mayumi Heene claimed that their son had been inside a helium balloon that had flown away.

By that point, Mitchell was sick of the internet, sick of people, sick of his job. He got up to get himself a cup of coffee. Hannah sat by her computer, watching what seemed to be

CCTV footage, her eyes squinting slightly. A loose strand of hair dropped down her face, and she didn't even seem to notice it. There was something in her intensity that glued him to his place, and he was unable to take his eyes off her. It was the first time he had noticed how green her eyes were. They were nearly olive-colored in the squad room's dim lighting.

She pulled her stare away from the screen. "What?" she said.

"Uh … I'm getting myself some coffee," he answered, flustered. "Do you want some?"

She glanced at the cup on her desk. It was half full. "I forgot my cup," she said, smiling thinly. "It's cold now. Sure, I'd be glad for some more. CCTV footage isn't exactly the most riveting thing to watch."

"Did it get the car?" he asked.

"Yeah, but the driver wore a ski mask, just like Peter said. I'm looking over the rest now, to see if there's anything else we've missed. Anything on the Reddit threads?"

"Not much." Mitchell shook his head. "He seemed to really like the idea of coming to Glenmore Park."

"Yeah, well," Hannah muttered, her eyes returning to the screen. "We all know how that one turned out."

Mitchell went over to the coffee machine, made two cups, handed one to Hannah, and sat back down.

There were several recent mentions in the subreddit of a website called RPM Donations. Though Glen was already dead when the posts were made, Mitchell's interest piqued. He browsed to RPM Donations. At first he didn't really understand how it had to do with the case. It was a website focused mostly on charities for veterans and children's expensive medical operations. Then he found the relevant post. Two days before, RPM had posted about the Abigail Lisman case, explaining that the family couldn't possibly pay the ransom money. It had asked for donations for the ransom.

Mitchell frowned. According to recent updates, money was flowing in. There was apparently a very successful Buzzfeed article listing "The five amazing ways America is trying to save Abigail" that mentioned this charity. It had gone wildly viral, and donations tripled. Some Jewish charities donated money as well.

Mitchell did some browsing, trying to determine if it was a scam. It clearly wasn't. RPM Donations was a well-known website, and was frequently used.

According to the last update, four hours before, they had already collected eighty percent of the ransom money.

"Hey, Hannah," Mitchell said. "I think the Lismans are going to have the ransom to pay the kidnappers."

WEB OF FEAR

Hannah finally called Clint just after eight p.m. He sounded mildly amused by her attempt to try to set up a dinner date which should probably have started an hour before. He said he was exhausted, and already in his motel room, and did not intend to go anywhere. But if she was into take out, he was just about to order some sushi.

Hannah drove over to his motel, feeling irritated with herself for calling so late, for calling at all, and for agreeing to come to his motel room. Then she decided it was all Clint's fault, and that made her feel slightly better.

Glenmore Park had two motels, neither of them incredibly luxurious. Clint was at the Park's Lodge, a U-shaped building with a small, almost unused swimming pool in the center. Hannah climbed the rickety stairs to the second floor and went to room 207, where Clint had told her he was staying.

He opened the door a minute after she knocked. He was dressed casually, in jeans and a gray t-shirt, but the shirt was tight, clinging to his chest, and the jeans looked good on him. Hannah suspected he had dressed up after their conversation, and regretted not doing the same. She wore the same clothes she'd worn to work that day: a faded blue button-down shirt, and black pants on which she had spilled coffee earlier. The pants were black, so the spot probably couldn't be seen, but there was still a faint smell of caffeine surrounding her. Not exactly a seductive odor.

He smiled at her warmly. "Come in," he said.

She walked past him. It was actually a pretty nice room, for a motel. It was brightly lit, with the bed on one side, and the bedsheets clean and straightened. There was a small glass table, about three feet tall, on the other side of the room, with three wooden chairs placed around it. Next to it stood a small desk, with Clint's dark briefcase on it and a gray folder placed neatly on top. There were no clothes on the floor or on the bed, no books littering the desk, nothing to indicate Clint was actually staying there. She didn't even see where he had put his suitcase.

Again she wondered if he'd cleaned up before she got there, or if he was always this clean. When she stayed at a motel, it always looked like a hurricane had struck a clothing shop.

There were two takeout boxes on the table, and two bottles of beer. Clint smiled and sat down, motioning Hannah to join him. She walked over, her eyes catching the gray folder on the desk. Someone had written *A.L 03* on it. It could have been a folder about someone named Al, or about Angeles-Los, but Hannah knew that the A.L stood for Abigail Lisman.

"Are you eating, or should I start alone?" Clint asked, interrupting her thoughts. She sat down across from him, trying to clear her head. She was famished.

"I hope you like what I've ordered," Clint said. "It sounded like a good combination."

She glanced at the box. "It's combination C from Kaito Sushi, right?" she said.

"Yeah," he looked at her in surprise.

"I eat a lot of take out," she said. "There aren't many sushi places in Glenmore Park, and Kaito is the best. Sure, that's good, thanks."

"I assume you don't need a fork," he said.

Hannah smiled thinly. "No, thanks," she said. "I eat with chopsticks."

She demonstrated by taking the chopsticks and grabbing a salmon nigiri from the box. She dipped it in some soy sauce and put it in her mouth. She wondered what was in that folder. New case notes? Were there any updates on the case? New suspects?

"How's it going with the Glen Haney murder?" Clint asked, picking a piece of sushi himself.

Hannah swallowed. "I'm surprised you even heard about it," she said. "Agent Mancuso sounded as if nothing could interest her less."

"That's not true," Clint answered seriously. "She just needs to prioritize. We were all briefed."

"We have a sketch of the man who dropped off the car," Hannah said, and enjoyed the brief look of astonishment on Clint's face. She picked up a small maki, dipping it lightly in the soy.

"Really?"

"Yup. We found a witness."

"That's good! Did you manage to match it?"

"No," Hannah said.

"Send it over. We might have better luck."

"Suddenly you're interested?" Hannah asked.

Clint raised an eyebrow. "Why are you so angry?" he asked.

Hannah picked up another maki piece. As she was about to dip it in the sauce, it fell from the chopsticks' grip, submerging completely in the soy. Hurriedly, she picked it up and stuck the salty thing in her mouth.

"I'm not angry," she lied. "I'm just a bit frustrated to be pushed out of the case like that. And now you're ignoring important leads—"

"We're not ignoring them—"

"Fine," she said sharply. "Prioritizing them. Whatever." Was there any mention of the Glen Haney murder in the folder? She grabbed another nigiri piece, but her movement was too sharp. It split in two, and the rice fell back into the box while the slim strip of fish remained held tightly by the chopsticks.

"And it wasn't our decision to limit your access to the case, Hannah," Clint said softly. "That was a direction from above."

Hannah looked at him doubtfully. Clint had been furious when she'd ignored his instructions in the interrogation room. A day later, their department was politely nudged away from the case. And now she was expected to believe it was a coincidence?

She grabbed another piece, carefully dipped it in the sauce, and brought it to her mouth. It dropped onto her shirt, spattering soy all over her. Great. Now she smelled like a caffeine-dipped salmon nigiri.

"I'll get you a fork," Clint said delicately.

"I don't need a damn fork!" she snapped. She took a napkin and tried to wipe the spot, but she just ended up smearing it more. She could feel the soy soaking through to her skin. Clint stared at her with an expression that made her want to scream. Defiantly, she stood, unbuttoned the shirt, and threw it on the floor behind her. Then, as if he wasn't there at all, she cleaned herself with a napkin.

His face changed as he looked at her, his lips parted. She looked back at him, her eyes narrowing. Still standing, she picked up a maki piece with her fingers, dipped it in the sauce, and put it in her mouth, licking her fingers.

"See?" she whispered. "I don't need a fork." She grabbed the bottle from the table, took a swig, then put it down. She felt Clint's eyes roaming over her sheer black bra, could suddenly feel the mood in the room shifting. Warmth spread from her chest to her stomach, and she licked her lower lip.

Clint stood, and she was once again struck by how much taller than her he was. He walked to her, no more than a couple of steps, and her skin prickled in excitement as he grabbed her, his fingers tightening around her waist. She grasped the back of his head and pulled him toward her, kissing him passionately, the tastes of alcohol and Clint intermingling on her tongue.

They fumbled toward the bed, her breasts crushed against his chest. She slid her fingers into his pants as he struggled to unhook her bra, and they fell back onto the white sheets. She was consumed with need, much hungrier than before. Within moments, they were pulling their clothes off as fast as they possibly could. His hands slid up her thighs.

His skin was warm, so much warmer than hers, and feeling his athletic body pressed against hers filled her with a ravenous desire. She bit him on the shoulder, hard enough to leave a mark, and dug her fingernails hard into his back, letting go of all her pent up anger.

———

They both drowsed off for a bit, still in each other's arms. The tension that built up inside Hannah for the past days had vanished, and she was warm and happy. Finally, Clint untangled himself from her. He asked her if she wanted to shower, and she mumbled she'd go after him. He plodded to the bathroom and closed the door.

She tried to fall asleep, but the sudden craving for a cigarette woke her up. Hannah had quit smoking three years before, but the craving still returned occasionally. She decided to get up and eat the rest of her sushi to fend off the desire. She got up, still naked, and began walking toward the small table. Then she stopped.

Her eyes fell on the gray folder.

She glanced at the bathroom door, listened to the water running, and then walked two steps and opened the folder slightly.

She just wanted a peek. She told herself she owed it to Naamit, who had put her trust in Hannah. But her reflexes took over, and she quickly pored over the pages. There were several transcripts of interviews with Jurgen Adler. Then some summaries about the online activity regarding the case. Some of them mentioned Redditors driving into Glenmore Park every day.

One of the reports mentioned some hacking attempts made on the Glenmore Park PD computer system, and the FBI. Other hackers had targeted a gas station, a local post office, and a couple of clothing shops, to get the CCTV footage from the night of the kidnapping. The hackers were being traced.

Then there was a short page on which her name was mentioned.

It was a report by Agent Clint Ward, detailing her performance in the case investigation, recommending her return to the case.

Someone cleared their throat behind her. She dropped the pages guiltily on the desk and turned around. Clint stood in the bathroom doorway, wearing his shorts. She realized she was still naked, and it made her feel even more embarrassed and exposed, caught red-handed snooping in his stuff.

"Clint, I—"

He gave a small shake of the head, his face hurt. Swallowing her tears, she quickly grabbed her clothes and clumsily put them on, avoiding his eyes. He was silent the entire time, not moving from where he stood. She walked to the motel room door, glanced at him again, then left the room and closed the door behind her.

She resisted the urge to cry all the way home. As far as she was concerned, she didn't deserve to feel sorry for herself.

EIGHTEEN

The kidnapper sat on the couch in her living room, jaw clenched in everlasting anger, thinking about the girl. The television was set to the local news channel, but the sound was muted. She never turned the television off anymore, not even at night when she went to sleep. It made her feel better, knowing there was movement in her house, even if it was only on the television screen. It made her feel as if she was still alive, as if no one had pressed *pause* on her story.

She tried to concentrate, tried to separate her feelings about the past from her plans for the future. Things were changing. There was some sort of charity collecting money for the ransom, and they were apparently about to reach that goal—that impossible goal. That had not been her original plan. But then, she was the one who had decided to put it all out in the open.

Darrel had wanted to send a ransom note made from cut-up newspapers. He hadn't heard that the twenty-first century had arrived. No one cut up newspapers for ransom letters anymore. And if they did, they probably used an app for that. *iRansomLetter*, or something.

Darrel had wanted the ransom letter to be private. But no, she'd wanted to post it on Instagram. She'd wanted the whole city to know what was going on.

She could never have guessed how far the story would blow up. According to a news report she'd seen the day before, donations were being sent even from Japan and Australia.

There was only one internet, that was the thing. Post something online, and you never knew who would read it or where.

There would be no justice here. No vindication for her. No one would pay for the past.

But she could still have a future, if she played her cards right. A future with one and a half million dollars to make her life comfortable. She could still start over, perhaps in a different state or even a different country. Buy a new, better life for herself. Wasn't that a kind of justice?

No, a part of her said. *That's not justice. That's compensation. It's not the same thing.*

She tried to bury that part of her away, tried to concentrate.

The girl had seen her face. That meant … Well, that could mean all sorts of things.

If the girl was returned to her parents, it would be a matter of time before…

But if she wasn't, well then…

She deserved justice.

Could she do it? Kill a child? Perhaps she didn't have to do it herself. She could arrange for it to happen. Would Darrel do it? No, he was too weak. He was actually getting close to the girl. He thought she hadn't noticed the empty pizza cartons he threw away. But she had. She noticed everything.

She could do it. It wasn't really that hard. She had killed a kid just a few days before, hadn't she? She was made of stronger stuff than Darrel.

And then Darrel appeared on her television screen. Well, not him, really, but a sketch—a badly drawn sketch—of her partner in crime.

She turned up the volume, tensing in her chair. The reporter said this man was wanted for questioning by the police and the FBI regarding the murder of Glen Haney.

It took her a moment to realize who Glen Haney was: the kid who had showed up at Darrel's house. The kid she had killed. Damn it! How long before the police figured out whose face was on that sketch? They should move the girl.

But moving the girl had its own risks. Someone could notice. Something could go wrong.

Was it better to just hope the police and FBI wouldn't realize who the sketch matched?

It was a bad sketch.

But they'd figure it out, eventually. And through Darrel they could get to her.

The kid led to her. And Darrel led to her. A trail the police could easily follow.

Things needed to move faster.

She had a future to look forward to. A future with three million dollars to make her life comfortable. And she would have her justice.

Morris Vinson wanted the system to work, he really did. Ideally, they would all live in a country where the police did their job, criminals went to jail, and innocent citizens never got hurt. But this, unfortunately, was not the case. Cops got fat on doughnuts and corruption, the feds had a huge thumb up their ass, and it was up to the public to fix what was broken. Morris was no hero, he'd be the first to admit it; he was just a guy that wanted to do his part for the community.

He didn't like the term "amateur detective." It made him sound … like an amateur. Morris prided himself on being one of the better online investigators out there. In two separate cases, using nothing but his computer, he'd managed to locate criminals—one of them a mugger, the other a drug dealer—and report them to the police. Really, it wasn't so difficult; criminals often boasted about their own law-breaking acts. Morris only needed to be on alert for certain keywords on social media. Simple scripts pointed him in the right direction.

Online criminal investigators often got bad rep, especially after the Boston Marathon Bombing—but what people didn't know was that Redditors had also *pointed out Dzhokar and Tamerlan Tsarnaev*. Sure, they zeroed in on the wrong guy, but didn't the police often do that?

People like Morris could do things the police and the FBI couldn't. They weren't bound to regulations and rules. They were only bound to truth and justice. And they had the power of hundreds of investigators … if they could only make them work together. And Morris was good at that.

When Abigail Lisman's case became known, it was Morris who had opened the main subreddit that was accumulating the intel on the case. He was the one who asked the public to send images of that night. When the image of Abigail and her friend turned up, did anyone call and thank him?

Spoiler alert: They did not.

When people on the subreddit decided to go to Glenmore Park to investigate further, Morris knew he had to be part of it.

They had four agents on scene. That's how they identified themselves. Agents. They were six before, but two had had to go home on Monday because of high school or some shit. That was fine by Morris; this was not a job for kids. The agents he had on the ground were grown men who could handle themselves.

He wasn't formally in charge, of course; the whole point was that they were working individually. Each one had his own leads, his own way of doing things.

Morris, for example, had contacted Yaaasiv42, a guy on Reddit who was also a hacker. He'd asked him to obtain the security camera videos from the gas station and the post office near the scene. Yaaasiv42 told him he wasn't the first to ask him for CCTV feeds from that night, which was surprising. But when he'd asked further questions, the hacker clamped shut. He didn't divulge info about other clients, he said. He named his price, which Morris happily paid, and a day later, he'd sent Morris the footage.

Morris was analyzing the footage when RemiDD posted the first image of "gray hoodie guy." RemiDD had been camping in front of the crime scene, constantly taking pictures of people who went by, hoping that the kidnapper would return to the scene of the crime. Gray hoodie guy went by on Sunday and on Monday.

Their fellow investigators quickly found out gray hoodie guy's identity: Kevin Baker. From that point on, the evidence trail grew incredibly quickly. It turned out he had a van like the one rumored to have been used in the kidnapping. According to a Redditor with access to police records, he had prior convictions. And a picture of him turned up during the night of the kidnapping *only a few hundred feet from the scene.*

It was time for the agents to meet. Morris knew only one of them by face, a lanky pale faced guy named Dan, whose Reddit nickname was Dantor.

Wardenofthenorth turned out to be a short, wide, bearded fellow, completely bald. RemiDD took Morris completely by surprise, as she was actually a woman. He had no problem with that; she looked cool, and he could already imagine meeting her again after this was all over.

But first, it was time to save a little girl's life.

When Mitchell walked into the squad room in the morning, Hannah was already there. He walked over to his computer, bidding her a distracted good morning. She turned her head and he paused.

"Are you okay?" he asked. She looked terrible. Her eyes were swollen; her hair was a mess. Her skin was deathly pale, and for one terrible moment he thought she was about to cry.

"I'm fine," she said, her voice tight. "I just didn't sleep much last night."

"Oh, okay." Mitchell nodded. He could understand. It must be difficult, seeing Abigail's mother every day with nothing new to report and the progress terribly slow. The time since the last Instagram post was growing longer, and some people were beginning to suspect the girl was dead. Hannah was a very intense person even without all that weight on her shoulders. This case was driving her to exhaustion.

He sat down in front of the computer, and pushed the mouse a bit to bring the monitor to life. He read some e-mails, got himself a cup of coffee, then inspected the whiteboard. The latest addition was a frame taken from the CCTV footage the night Haney's body was dropped. It was an image of the car driving down the street, the driver barely visible and wearing a ski mask. These guys definitely knew what they were doing.

"We should do a door-to-door on Cypress Street," he said. "We might find someone else besides Peter Bell who saw the killer."

Hannah nodded. "I also want to go over more of the CCTV footage from that area," she said. "One of them could have our guy after he removed the mask."

He sat down and browsed to the subreddit, interested in seeing how the amateur detectives were progressing.

There were a lot of new posts. Several mentioned someone called "gray hoodie guy." Great. A new suspect.

Mitchell began reading them one by one. He lifted his coffee cup to his lips, and then his hand paused.

There were images of gray hoodie guy walking by the park. Apparently he'd walked by the park two mornings in a row now.

One of the posts gave a name to gray hoodie guy: Kevin Baker.

Another post showed an image of a black van like the one Gracie had described. It said the van belonged to Kevin. There was no actual proof to back this fact up.

A fourth post had a picture taken from the night of the kidnapping. A couple had taken a selfie, hugging and kissing, and in the background was a dark-skinned man wearing a gray hoodie, walking down the street alone, his face blurry. HandsomeBob11 claimed this picture was taken just a few hundred feet from the kidnapping site. He pointed out helpfully that this was the same gray hoodie Kevin had in his possession. He also claimed that the man's face had several basic features which aligned with Kevin's. As far as Mitchell could tell, the only feature both men shared was their skin color.

A fifth post alluded to Kevin's address. Someone had it. It wasn't posted on Reddit, but it was clear that the address had been passed privately between users.

There were a lot of upvotes. A lot of comments. This case, apparently, has gone on long enough. The mob wanted the kidnappers dealt with, and they wanted it now.

Mitchell got up, grabbing his keys and gun from his desk. "Hannah," he said. "We have to go. I think someone is about to get hurt."

Kevin was having a very bad morning. He had woken up with a pounding in his skull. He knew that pounding well, and there was no getting away from it. It was going to develop into a full-blown migraine before the day ended, like it always did.

He took a couple of ibuprofen, swallowing each with several gulps of water. He was brushing his teeth when the phone rang. The caller ID read *ID unknown*, and when he answered, a torrent of curses and threats was hurled at him. He hung up, his heart beating fast.

The phone rang a second time—ID unknown again—and he let it go to voice mail. Whoever it was left him a voice message. He considered calling the police, but doubted they'd do anything about a random abusive call.

He was eating cereal when his phone blipped, showing he had a new text message. He viewed it. It simply said *We found you, you child stealing pervert*.

For a moment he simply stared at the phone, feeling physically ill. He nearly threw up the cereal he had just eaten. He put the rest of the bowl in the sink. Then he began dialing 91 … and paused. The police would probably tell him to come over. And his boss was pissed at him enough already. Best to ignore it.

He considered leaving his phone at home, but who walked around without a phone these days? He shoved it into his backpack, slung it on his back, and walked out of his apartment. The door slammed a little too loudly, making him jump. Everything felt hostile and dangerous. He locked the door behind him, taking several deep breaths.

Down the hall, he pressed the button for the elevator and waited. It took ages to get there. Several times he imagined hearing a noise behind him, and glanced back, seeing nothing. His phone blipped again. He was convinced it was another hateful text. He ignored it, thinking he'd talk to the guys at work, see if they thought he should report this to the police.

There was a group of young people just by the entrance to the building, and he walked by them and turned left to go to work. It took him only a few seconds to realize they were following him.

Kevin was not easily intimidated; he'd had his fair share of bullies at school, and had learned to stand up for himself. But the phone call and the message he'd gotten that morning had rattled him, and he felt slightly panicky. It didn't help that his phone blipped again. The group behind him were walking no more than a dozen feet behind him, saying nothing. It occurred to him that all four of them were white. He risked a quick glance backward.

They were definitely all looking at him, and their eyes were full of hate and anger. He realized his breathing was shallow and fast, his heart rattling in his chest like a drummer in a military parade.

He began running.

He heard them chasing him, shouting to each other. He breathed in deep gulps, the freezing air hurting his lungs. Someone crashed into him and they tumbled down together; his head hit the sidewalk, his vision momentarily clouded. There was a deep sharp pain in his gut as someone kicked him, then another foot hit him in the back. And they were all shouting at him unintelligibly as they kicked him over and over again.

Hannah yelled at Holly the dispatcher as Mitchell swerved the car, turning onto Babel Lane, the tires squealing.

"No, Holly, send one squad car to his home address, the other to the playground on Babel Lane!"

She could hear Holly talking on the radio as she hollered at her. "Three sixty-two, Dispatch."

"Go ahead," a crackling voice answered Holly on the radio. It was Kate, one of the patrol officers.

"Three sixty-two, support needed at 6 Kimball Way."

"Dispatch, this is three sixty-two, copy, on our way."

"And the second patrol to the playing ground," Hannah said again, more calm, as Mitchell slowed down, checking the addresses.

"Detective Shor," Holly sounded pissed off. "The second patrol is currently engaged on the other side of town and I can't—"

"Mitchell!" Hannah pointed ahead.

"I see them," he said grimly, accelerating.

Four people stood in a circle on the sidewalk ahead of them. Though she couldn't see what they were standing over, she could hazard a guess. The way their bodies were hunched, the way their feet were moving, someone was lying on the ground getting the crap beaten out of him.

"Holly, send the patrol to the corner of Babel Lane and Kimball Way, four men are assaulting someone."

"Three sixty-two, Dispatch," she could hear Holly say again. She hung up, pocketing the phone, tensing.

Mitchell didn't bother with parking, and the car bounced over the curb, making Hannah's teeth jolt. The car was still moving when Hannah opened the passenger door and leapt out, shouting, "Police! Everyone freeze and put your hands over your heads!"

Hannah could see a man—probably Kevin Baker—lying on the ground, his hands covering his face. He was curled into the fetal position, and one of the men was kicking him in the back. She didn't hesitate, slamming into the man closest to her and knocking him to the ground. The second person, a woman, got punched in the belly; she groaned in pain, bending over as she tried to catch her breath. By that point, the other two men had stopped kicking Kevin and were staring at Hannah angrily.

"Police!" she heard Mitchell holler. He stood behind the car, his gun trained on the two standing men ... no, not even men. They were almost kids, no more than twenty.

Both of them raised their hands hesitantly.

"What are you pointing that gun at us for?" one of them asked.

Hannah ignored him, kneeling by the man on the ground. His mouth was bleeding, his eyes shut, and he breathed in sharp, pained gulps. But at least he was breathing.

In the distance, Hannah could hear the sirens. The patrol car was coming. "Hey," she said softly. "You're going to be okay."

He didn't move, just stayed in his bent position, lying on the ground, protecting his head with his hands. She laid her hand on his shoulder gently as she pulled her phone from her pocket, called Dispatch and told Holly to get an ambulance to that address.

Hannah kept talking to the man as calmly as she could, trying to make him move, hoping he would open his eyes. She watched Mitchell as he rounded up the four assailants, ordering them to stand against a nearby building, their faces to the wall. They complied, though they kept yelling for things like lawyers, and their parents, pointing out they were just trying to get that guy to tell them what he had done with Abigail.

"I didn't do anything," the man said hoarsely. His voice was low, in pain.

"I know," Hannah told him. "Don't worry, we're not accusing you of anything."

"I didn't take that girl."

"I know," Hannah said again. "These idiots just made a terrible mistake. Your name is Kevin, right?"

He nodded slightly, opening one of his eyes.

"Kevin, we'll get you to a hospital to check you out, okay?"

A patrol car pulled up, and Officers Kate Anthony and Noel Lloyd leapt out of the car. Kate went over to Mitchell and the assailants, while Noel knelt by Hannah.

"What the hell happened?" he asked.

"They thought he was the kidnapper," she said, her voice sharp and angry. "This is getting out of control."

The southern window in Naamit and Ron's living room was the largest window to face the street. Before the kidnapping, there had been a small table by that window, with a potted geranium and a few pictures from their honeymoon. The table had been moved to the corner of the room now. It sat in the darkness, the geranium dried and withered.

Now a chair stood by the window, and Naamit sat on it. She sat on it for hours every day, staring at the street outside. Waiting for Hannah to show up with an update, waiting for one of the FBI agents to come and brief her, waiting for any kind of news.

Secretly—and she didn't tell anyone, hardly admitted it to herself—she was waiting to see Abigail walking down the street, opening the door, running into her arms. She tried to avoid picturing it. The image sometimes felt so real that when it faded, the wound in her heart pounded even more. And even at the best of times, it was quite unbearable.

Debra had visited her earlier, bringing food yet again. She seemed oblivious to the uneaten food in the fridge, adding more on top of it. She would stay with Naamit for an hour or two, trying to distract her, talking about work, about how they were doing without her. Debra was filling in for her, but *only* until this thing was resolved. She reassured Naamit, saying over and over that Abigail was probably just fine.

Naamit couldn't explain to her friend how the word *probably* hurt more than any other. There was nothing worse than not knowing what was happening to her daughter. It was a morbid case of Schrödinger's cat. Abigail was fine, and suffering unbearable torment, and dead.

The afternoon light shone on their front yard. It was a beautiful day, almost cloudless, the sky bright blue. It was still chilly outside, though, and the window pane was cold to the touch.

She hardly heard her phone blip with a new message. She sighed, struggling with the desire to ignore it. Lately it had been blipping and ringing non-stop. At first it had been family members and friends, trying to give her their love. Then, strangers started sending her messages. Sending their support, their condolences, and lately—to her horror—scathing messages and phone calls accusing her of neglecting her daughter, of being a drunkard, of falsifying the kidnapping. It made her sick to her stomach.

But she didn't dare ignore it. The people organizing the ransom donations contacted her as well to update her. They began to discuss the practical matter of transferring the money. They already had enough to pay the ransom, and now the banks and the lawyers were hard at work. She was hazy on the details. Ron was taking care of it, but she still made sure they updated her regarding any problem or issue that might arise.

She picked up the phone and glanced at it. A new e-mail. She clicked it, and for a moment, thought it was another mail sent by the sick individuals who were campaigning against her. Then her heart paused.

"Ron!" she screamed, her head dizzy.

He came running into the living room, his eyes red and unfocused. He'd been sleeping very little, almost as badly as she was. "What?" he asked in alarm. "What happened?"

"It's the kidnappers," she whispered. "They sent me an e-mail." She held out her phone. He snatched it from her fingers and stared at the screen. She moved to stand beside him, and read it for the fourth time

> *From: wegotabigail@guerrillamail.com*
> *To: Naamit Lisman*
> *Subject: Ransom*
>
> *You have the ransom money. Tomorrow, you'll deliver it to us, and get your daughter back. Bring a duffel bag with three million dollars in 100$ bills to the payphone at the corner of Babel Lane and Kimball Way. Be there tomorrow, the 29th of March, 10:00 AM. Do not contact the FBI or the police. If you do, you'll never see your daughter again.*

An image was attached to the e-mail. It was Abigail, holding the *Boston Globe* in her hand. It was difficult to see the details. Was that today's Boston Globe? Naamit had no idea. She hadn't watched the news for the past week, didn't know if the headlines were up to date. She assumed it was, curbing the impulse to check and make sure her daughter was still alive. There were urgent matters to take care of first.

"We need the ransom money," Naamit told Ron. "We need it now. Tell those guys no more lawyers, we need it by tomorrow."

"I'll talk to them," Ron nodded, and she was relieved to see he didn't hesitate, didn't raise objections. He seemed sure he could get it. This was the man she needed right now, someone she could lean on.

"Do you think I should go alone?" she asked. "They contacted me, and—"

"No," Ron said. "I won't let you face them alone. I'll come with you. And we need to talk to Agent Mancuso, see what she thinks we should—"

"No!" she shouted. "We are not calling the FBI or the police! You saw the e-mail. I am not risking Abigail's life."

"But we can't trust those kidnappers blindly," Ron said, raising his voice as well. "They might be lying. They might try to extort more money once they have the ransom. They might … not release Abigail after … I mean … We don't know what we're facing here. We need to talk to Agent—"

"We'll talk to Hannah Shor," Naamit said. "She's the only one I trust. You saw the news. This case is very public.

Who knows what the FBI's motives are? I trust Hannah's motives; she doesn't care about the publicity."

Ron nodded hesitantly. "Okay," he said. "But if Hannah says we need to tell the FBI—"

"No, Ron," Naamit said. "We're involving only Hannah in this. No one else." She dialed Hannah's number.

Hannah answered almost immediately. "Hi, Naamit."

"Hannah? Can you come over? We need to talk to you," Naamit said, wondering if the FBI was listening in on this phone call. "Please."

"I'm on my way," Hannah said immediately, and hung up.

NINETEEN

She walked into the kitchen where Darrel sat, smoking a cigarette, a coffee mug on the table. She could never understand why he smoked inside the house. Didn't he mind the cloying smell of the smoke seeping into everything? His whole home stank like a giant ashtray. Well, all of it but the basement. The basement currently smelled like a public bathroom stall.

He glanced at her, his eyes moving quickly, as they always did when he was nervous. And he had good reason to be. If anything went wrong today, he'd be in jail by nightfall. She was nervous as well.

Not for the first time, she regretted it all: convincing Darrel to do it, kidnapping the girl, posting the updates on

Instagram. Each and every one of her decisions was questionable. Then again, soon she would be in Mexico, with enough money to start a new, comfortable life. Wouldn't that be worth a week of stress?

"Here," she said, giving him the prepaid phone. "Use this if you need to call them, and once you do, remove the battery and—"

"I know the drill," he said sharply. Lately he had been getting more and more irritable at her instructions. "I probably won't need it, anyway. They'll be waiting for me where we told them."

She nodded. Naamit had replied twice to their e-mail, trying to get details, asking where Abigail would be, how and when they would deliver her. They'd ignored both e-mails. Finally she'd written a third reply, stating that she'd be at the location with the ransom money.

"Once I have the money, I'll drive to the replacement car, making sure I'm not followed. I'll transfer the money to my own bag, and call you to say it's done. Then I'll double back here, and you'll join me as soon as you can."

"Good." She nodded again and smiled. He smiled back. He always perked up when she smiled at him. It was sweet, really; he just wanted her approval and appreciation. And probably her body as well. But that would not happen.

She glanced at her own phone to check the time. "We should probably get going," she said. It was a bit early, but she wanted to be out of the house already.

"Yeah." He stood up and walked toward the basement door.

"What the hell are you doing?" she asked sharply.

"I'm just going to talk to Abi … to the kid. Tell her if she behaves, she'll get to see her—"

"I'll take care of that," she said, her voice steely.

"Don't worry, I'm not dumb, I'll put on a mask," he said, glancing at the masks hanging on a nail beside the door. "I just want—"

"Darrel, you have your job, I have mine," she said, tensing. She didn't like this, not at all. He was way too close to the girl, and they couldn't afford any amateurish mistakes. Not today.

He clenched his jaw angrily. "I don't see what the damn problem is. She'll just be calmer when you take her and—"

"The kid doesn't need any more reassurances," she said. She could see his hand tightening into a fist. She had underestimated how attached he'd become to the child. Time to fix it. She took three steps forward, put her hand on his arm. It was probably the first time she'd ever touched him, other than accidentally bumping into each other.

"You don't want to be fresh in her memory today," she said softly. "As soon as they get her back, the FBI will question her. What did you look like? What did you sound like? What did you smell like? Can she describe any of your features? Your eyes?"

He breathed heavily as she stood close to him, closer than ever before.

"She's just a little kid. She probably won't be able to describe you accurately from memory, but if she sees you just hours before returning home?"

"You're right," he said, his voice hoarse.

"Just a few more hours, and we'll be done. With more money than either of us ever imagined."

He nodded, blinking. He turned away from the door.

"I'll see you in a few hours," he said.

"Right." She smiled again.

And he smiled back.

Hannah sat in Naamit's living room, waiting impatiently for Google Maps to load on Ron's laptop. Their internet connection was abysmally slow. Ron paced back and forth, as he had been doing for the past twenty minutes. Naamit sat in front of Hannah, staring at her own lap. She'd burst into tears twice since Hannah had arrived. The stress was clearly too much for her to handle. Hannah hoped she wouldn't do anything stupid during the ransom drop.

"Naamit," she said, "please let me call Agent Ward."

Naamit raised her eyes. "You said you weren't sure if they'd try to ambush the kidnappers or not."

"Yeah … but I'm also not sure if the kidnappers will deliver her. We need to have experienced people involved."

"You're experienced," Naamit said.

"Not with a case like this."

"Is anyone experienced with a case like this?"

Hannah bit her lip, unsure. The publicity surrounding this case was unheard of, as far as she knew. And when she thought of the Redditors, the donated ransom, the strange ransom note … Could anyone really say he had dealt with this kind of case before?

The map finally appeared. "Here we go," she said. Ron and Naamit came over and sat on either side of her. She could hear them both breathing heavily. The tension in the room was wearing her down.

"This is the corner of Babel Lane and Kimball Way, where you should go. It's where Abigail was originally kidnapped. I've gone through that area half a dozen times in the past week, so I know it quite well. They want you waiting by the payphone … here." She pointed at the screen. "That might mean they intend to call that phone with further instructions. It's the only payphone in Glenmore Park, so it's probably not a coincidence that they chose this location. They might tell you to go somewhere else, where there's no surveillance. North of the corner, toward Clayton Road, there's a gas station and a post office. Both have CCTV—"

"What's that?" Naamit interrupted.

"Sorry. It's closed-circuit television. Video cameras pointing outside at the street. When Abigail was kidnapped, the kidnappers made sure not to go through there, to avoid getting caught on film, so I doubt you'll be asked to go that way. It's more likely they'll tell you to go south, toward Joan Avenue. It's all residential that way, and the streets are much quieter. Or they could ask you to—" She stopped, frowning, staring at the map.

"What?" Ron asked.

"Nothing," Hannah said. Something niggled at her, but she couldn't put her finger on it. "They might ask you to cross the playground. Anything is possible. They've been acting very professionally so far; I'd be surprised if they slip up now."

"Do you think we'll need to go far?" Naamit asked.

"I have no idea what you'll be asked to do, but I doubt it," Hannah said. "Especially carrying that." She nodded her head at the big duffel bag on the floor. It was damned heavy. Three million dollars in bills was not easy to carry.

"And then what?" Naamit asked. "When do you think they'll let Abigail go?"

Hannah wondered if Naamit was aware of how many times she had already asked that question. Maybe the real problem was the answer she kept hearing.

"I don't know," Hannah said. "I hope it'll be soon after."

———

Abigail had been in a state of terror ever since that man who came to rescue her had been stabbed to death. Before that happened, she'd wanted to believe chances were in her favor. After all, if the kidnappers didn't intend on returning her, what was the point of wearing those masks? Or taking her picture? Or feeding her?

But when the woman stabbed him with her face unmasked, her eyes cold and distant, Abigail realized two things. The woman had no problem with killing. And now that Abigail knew what the woman looked like, the woman wasn't likely to let her go home.

The kidnappers had tried to clean the large bloodstain off the floor, and they'd managed to remove most of it. But when she looked hard, Abigail could still see the contour of the stain, the slight discoloration in the floor. Some splatters of blood had been left unnoticed on the stairs and on the wall, and Abigail spent hours staring at them, recalling that moment, the man's empty eyes, his mouth opening and closing, making no sound, a small trickle of blood on his cheek. And then that terrible memory of his face going slack, all movement ceasing, when she knew he had died. The woman had gone up the stairs and left the basement, closing and locking the door behind her. Abigail was left, curled in the corner of the room, her eyes shut, refusing to look at the dead body.

The man and woman had finally returned, wearing plastic gloves and rain coats, and took the body with them. Later, they cleaned the floor with cleaning supplies that left a sharp, unpleasant smell lingering in the room—though any smell was preferable to that coppery smell of blood.

Now, when the woman came in to give her food, her eyes burrowed into Abigail. Did the woman believe Abigail didn't remember what she looked like? Abigail prayed that was the case, though she would never forget that cold, emotionless face.

And now the door opened, and the woman stepped in. She was wearing the mask again.

"Get up," the woman said. "We're leaving."

Abigail stood up, shaking. She wanted to ask where, or why, but her lips trembled, her throat clenched in fright. She took a hesitant step toward the woman.

"Come here," the woman said quietly, her voice even and calm. Fearful, Abigail walked closer. The woman, grunting impatiently, strode up to Abigail, grabbing her chin between two vice-like fingers, lifting her face up. Their eyes met, and the woman looked at her for what felt like hours. Finally, she nodded, as if she was satisfied with what she had seen in Abigail's eyes.

Abigail found her voice. "Where—" she started to say, but then the woman clasped the back of her head and pressed a rag to her mouth and nose. Abigail struggled, panicking, her hands clutching at the woman's arms, trying to pull them away, but the woman's fingers just squeezed harder, shoving the rag against her face forcefully, hurting her. Abigail tried to scream, but there was no air, just rancid fumes that made her dizzy and weak, as her muffled screams turned to whimpers and then died out.

———

Ron hefted the bag to his other shoulder. The thing was heavy, more than fifty pounds of hundred-dollar bills. Enough for the kidnappers to start a new life far away, where no one could find them.

He glanced at his wife. Her eyes were sharper than they had been for the past week. She looked around her, constantly glancing over at the payphone as if willing it to ring. She couldn't care less what happened to the kidnappers. She just wanted their daughter back.

For Ron, it was different. He believed someone should pay for the past days that had plunged their family into this constant nightmare. He was also worried that he'd never feel safe, knowing the kidnappers got away. He would constantly feel as if they were still stalking his family, planning a second kidnapping. Knowing it was highly improbable didn't make him feel any different. Hadn't Detective Shor said the kidnapper was someone they knew?

The street was gloomy and gray, with thick dark clouds obscuring the sun. Would it rain soon? They hadn't brought an umbrella. He wondered about the duffel bag. Was it waterproof? There was a lot of money inside it. They had purchased the bag at the nearby Walmart. The previous afternoon had been hectic, talking to the banks and the people who were organizing the donations for the money. They'd drafted some sort of contract, which he had signed after skimming it quickly, hoping he wasn't selling his eternal soul.

He glanced at the time. 10:07. The kidnappers were running late. He wanted to lift the phone from its cradle, check for a tone, but he was worried that they would call at that exact moment.

He looked over at the empty playground. The weather wasn't pleasant enough for parents and nannies to take their kids to the park. The empty swing stood motionless, sad. Abigail and Gracie often sat on this swing, talking.

Had they sat there the night of the kidnapping, waiting for an imaginary boy to show up?

Would he see his daughter today? Hold her in his arms? He pushed the thought away, knowing there wasn't a way to know. He'd been foolish enough to Google kidnapping stories, and had seen enough stories about kidnappers who had killed children instead of returning them. He didn't mention those stories to Naamit.

A lone car drove by. It made him realize how quiet the street was. The kidnappers had chosen well. The only reason to drive by was if you lived here. Babel Lane ran between Clayton Road and Isabelle Avenue, but anyone who wanted to get from one to the other could do so much faster using nearby Treat Boulevard.

"Maybe the phone isn't working," Naamit said with gritted teeth. She was clearly cold, though she didn't say anything. Ron kicked himself for not making her wear a thicker coat. He hadn't taken good enough care of her in the past week. She was falling apart.

"It'll be okay," he said, an empty reassurance that made neither of them feel any better.

Another car drove down the street, nearly passing them by, then suddenly swerved, nearly hitting the sidewalk. The driver's door was flung open, revealing a man wearing a dark ski mask sitting behind the driver's wheel.

"Give me the money, now!" he barked.

Ron didn't move. He wasn't prepared for this sudden appearance, and as always when surprised, he froze. He was a deer, staring at the incoming headlights, unable to budge.

"If you want Abigail, give me the money!" the man said, holding out his hand.

"Ron! Give him the bag!" Naamit screamed at him.

Years of doing what his wife said took hold. As if in a dream, Ron removed the strap of the heavy duffel bag from his shoulder. The bag dropped to the ground with a loud thump, and he dragged it over to the man, who grabbed the strap and swung the bag into the passenger seat.

"Go back home," the man said. "We'll contact you in an hour. If I'm followed in any way, we'll kill her. If not, you'll see your daughter soon." He sounded almost apologetic. He slammed the door. Then, slowly and calmly, the car pulled away, turned around, and drove off. Ron stared after it, dizzy and shocked.

―――

Darrel couldn't believe how flawlessly it had gone. He was sweating profusely when he stopped near the Lismans, and he'd had to overcome the tremor in his voice by talking in a loud, angry tone. He half expected to see a dozen FBI agents leap from the playground, surrounding him. There were numerous places to hide in that area.

But there was no FBI ambush. The couple looked surprised to see him there. They were probably waiting for a call to the payphone, just like his partner had planned. There was no visible tail. He had driven north from Glenmore Park for about twenty minutes, then turned west, toward New Hampshire. Finally, he got off on a silent, remote road and drove along it, stopping after a quarter of a mile. He waited for ten minutes, seeing no one, though he could imagine the police and FBI following his car using satellites, or high zoom binoculars. Perhaps there was a GPS chip in the bag. If that was the case, he had to go on with the plan as fast as possible.

His own car waited at the side of the road, where he had left it earlier. The car he was driving was a used Volvo, bought with cash from a used car salesman in Boston. They had replaced its license plates, just to be safe. He got out, opened his own car, and got his own duffel bag. He opened the ransom bag, leaning back in case it was booby trapped with paint, like he had seen once in a movie.

There was no paint. Just stacks of money. More money than he had ever seen in his life.

Darrel started moving the stacks to his own bag. It took a long time, but he didn't want to just empty one duffel bag into the other. He wanted to make sure he wasn't taking a stray GPS chip with him.

Finally, he was done. He threw the empty duffel bag back into the Volvo, got into his own car, started the engine, and drove away. He began grinning as he removed the latex gloves from his hands. He tossed the mask away as well, knowing he'd never have to wear the damn thing again. He was done.

He glanced over at the duffel bag in the passenger's seat, its zipper still open. Stacks of money winked back at him. His grin widened as he zipped it shut. There was no point risking someone looking through the car's window and noticing the unusual passenger. That's right, he was driving with some guys named Benjamin in his car. Was he over the passenger limit? Well, the car was insured for four passengers other than the driver. But there were thirty thousand Benjamins driving with him. He burst out laughing. That was a good one! Thirty thousand Benjamins! A bit over his passenger limit, wasn't he? He laughed again, tears of relief and happiness springing from his eyes.

He could still see Abigail's mother's eyes as she looked at him, her face begging him to return her daughter. Well, she'd get her daughter back. Finally. The past week had been terrible. Knowing that they were holding back the girl from her parents was hard on them both. He could see the turmoil in his partner's eyes every time they talked about the girl. He saw how she tried to keep her distance.

Of course. She was a woman; she probably felt motherly compassion to the girl. He was relieved they could both finally ease their consciences.

Damn! He was supposed to let his partner know she could set the girl free! He stopped at the side of the road, took the burner phone out and quickly texted. *All good. On my way back.*

The response quickly came back: a thumbs up. They were always careful, never texted each other anything that mentioned the girl, or the ransom. Never talked about it on the phone. Never carried around their own mobile phones when they met. Used burner phones to post those Instagram pictures, each time from a different location, at least thirty miles from Glenmore Park. His partner was the one who insisted on it all. She said they couldn't know what technologies the FBI had, that it was best to be prudent. And she was right. He was glad she was the brains of the operation.

There was a moment of apprehension as he got closer to Glenmore Park. Was that car following him? But no, it turned at the next intersection, to his relief. He had been careful, and the Lisman family would not endanger their daughter's life.

He finally got to his house, and opened the garage door, smiling. It had been hard, coming home for the past week, knowing there was a crying child in his basement. He was relieved she could finally go back home. One day in the far future, he'll send some money her way, a compensation for the terrible week she'd gone through.

He parked the car, hefting the duffel bag on his shoulder. Damn, those thirty thousand Benjamins were heavy. He grinned again at his joke, walking into the house.

She was already waiting for him, to his surprise. She stood in the kitchen, a bottle of champagne on the table. Two full glasses stood on either side. She smiled at him, and he smiled back, reacting to her as always. He loved to see her smile.

"Did you call the parents?" he asked. "Tell them where she is?"

"Of course," she grinned. "Is that the money?"

"That's right! I want you to meet my new friends," he said, unzipping the bag. "They're all named Benjamin."

She didn't laugh. Maybe she didn't get it. She stared into the bag, her grin widening.

He knew how she felt. This was freedom.

"I think we should celebrate," she said, taking one of the glasses and raising it, looking at him.

"Sure!" he said, grabbing the other glass. She sipped from hers and he did the same, just a tiny sip.

"Ugh," he said, feeling the bitterness on his tongue. "I think this champagne has gone bad."

"Really?" She drank another sip. "Tastes fine to me. It's probably just the first sip. Try some more."

"Nah," he said, putting the glass down on the counter. "I wouldn't drink from that. You'll get sick." He inspected the bottle, looking for the expiration date.

"It really tastes fine," she said, stepping up behind him.

"Hey, listen, I know what champagne tastes like, and this champagne is—"

The pain in his back was sharp and terrible. He screamed in agony and turned around. She stood in front of him, her eyes cold and vacant. His abdomen suddenly erupted in pain as well, and he stumbled back, looking down. Blood. So much blood. Where did it all...

Another sharp pain, this time in his chest, and it was her hand on his chest, blood running down her arm, spattering her cheek, just below an emotionless eye. He took another step backward, feeling the pain in his chest becoming worse as he wobbled. It was a knife. When he walked back, it slipped from her fingers, still stuck in his ribcage.

He fumbled at the handle, feeling horror and disbelief. That bitch! She'd tried to kill him! For money! He wrenched the knife from his chest, the pain nearly blinding him, and swung it at her. But she wasn't there anymore. She stared at him with distant eyes from six feet away.

"You bitch," he muttered, stumbling forward, blood bubbling in his mouth. He was going to kill her.

She abruptly moved forward, swinging her hand, and the bottle of champagne smashed against his face, knocking him down.

"Jesus," he mumbled as he rolled to his back. Where was she? His vision got dim; his face was on fire. Where was that knife? He'd been holding it a second ago.

He tried to get up, and something hard hit him on his head again.

TWENTY

People shouted in the hallway, phones rang constantly, cops and detectives ran in and out of the squad room. Hannah tried to concentrate, her head pounding with guilt and self-hatred, trying to figure out how she could help fix this colossal mess.

Naamit and Ron Lisman had gotten home by ten-thirty in the morning, and waited for the call. By eleven, Hannah had joined them, the three of them tense and silent, rushing to any phone that blipped or rang. None of the text messages, e-mails or calls were from the kidnappers. At eleven forty-five, an hour and a half after they had delivered the ransom, Hannah managed to convince them to let her call Agent Mancuso.

The call was short. The result was a huge manhunt, encompassing dozens of FBI agents, the entire Glenmore Park PD, a large portion of the Staties, and some of the Boston PD as well. There were five choppers in the air over various areas. All nearby airports were notified. They assumed that the kidnappers would try to leave the country.

They assumed Abigail Lisman wasn't alive anymore.

Hannah bit her lip, reading through the Glen Haney murder case file again—her only lead to the kidnappers. Any evidence the FBI had regarding the kidnapping case was withheld, especially from her.

She realized she was reading the same paragraph for the third time. In the background she heard Mitchell talking to someone, repeating the same description of the faded blue Volvo that Ron and Naamit had seen.

Finally, she could take it no longer, and called Agent Mancuso. It rang for a very long time and then went to voice mail. She dialed again. This time the agent answered after a few seconds.

"Yeah, Shor, what do you want?"

"Where are we at?" Hannah asked. "Did you send anyone to the junkyard where the kidnappers got rid of their van? Because they'll want to get rid of the Volvo, and—"

"Shor." Agent Mancuso's tone was cold and sharp. "I don't owe you an update. Let me assure you, I know how to do my job. I also knew how to do my job yesterday, when the Lismans called you and told you the kidnappers had contacted them. If you had told them to call us—"

"I did tell them—"

"If you had *persuaded* them to call us, we would have arrested the kidnappers by now, and maybe we'd have Abigail Lisman as well. Hell, Hannah, you should have called us yourself! Who cares what the mother told you? She isn't an experienced officer of the law, is she? You are—or at least you're supposed to be. I don't know what the hell I was thinking. I should have told them to take you off the case as soon as I heard you knew the mother personally. And I definitely should have done that after the interview with that asshole, Jurgen. You're a disaster, Shor."

Hannah bit her lip. "I did what I thought—"

"I don't care. Tell it to your damn captain, who persuaded me to give you a chance. Listen, Shor, I tell it like it is. So here's what I think: if you had called us yesterday, Abigail Lisman would still be alive."

The line went dead.

Hannah gently placed the phone in its cradle. The noise was overpowering, and a feeling of claustrophobia suddenly assaulted her. She stood up and stumbled out of the room, intent on going outside, but halfway to the exit a wave of nausea hit her and she bolted toward the bathroom. She got to the stall just in time, and threw up the little food she had in her stomach. She stayed on her knees, coughing and spitting, her head pounding.

If you had called us yesterday, Abigail Lisman would still be alive.

An uncontrollable sob emerged from her lips. She closed the toilet lid, sat on it and cried into her hands, trying to remain silent. She couldn't face coworker sympathy right now.

After crying for several minutes, she breathed deeply, forced herself to calm down. Her head was now clearer. The kidnappers had disappeared with the ransom, and Abigail hadn't returned. The FBI assumed Abigail was dead, and they dealt with kidnapping cases all the time. They knew what they were talking about. There was no going around the fact that she was probably gone. The only thing that remained was catching the kidnappers. Getting justice.

That word had never felt emptier. Hannah didn't care about justice. All she wanted was to return Abigail to Naamit and Ron and…

Why had the kidnappers kept Abigail alive for so long? The Lismans would have paid the ransom even if they hadn't received that last image of Abigail holding the newspaper. It made no sense, unless they had intended on setting her free. And the ransom delivery had gone flawlessly, so why hadn't they done it? Had they had second thoughts?

Had they decided to keep Abigail as a hostage?

No, the FBI clearly believed she was dead, and—

Hannah paused and tried to think from a different perspective.

Suppose she was the FBI agent in charge of the most publicized kidnapping case in recent years. And suppose she was notified that the parents had been contacted by the kidnappers, and had told only one detective, who didn't inform anyone. The ransom was paid, the kidnappers were gone, the child was still missing.

She'd be furious. And she'd want to assume the worst: the detective screwed up, and it was her fault the child was dead.

But was Abigail really dead? Probably. But as far as Hannah was concerned, she couldn't be. If Abigail was dead, Hannah was useless. She didn't care about catching the kidnappers. Didn't care about anything, really. But if Abigail was alive…

If Abigail was alive, she might be living on borrowed time. They'd kept her as a hostage, a bargaining chip in case they got caught on their way out of the country. Or they just weren't sure how to return her, and didn't want to take any unnecessary risks. Once they got away they would either set her free, or get rid of her.

In that case, it was up to the police and the FBI to catch the kidnappers before that happened. It was up to Hannah to do the best she could to return Abigail to her parents. She *had* to assume Abigail was still alive.

She got up and strode back to the squad room. She made herself a cup of coffee and sat at her desk, looking at the Haney case file. This was stupid. She couldn't just act as if nothing had happened. She had a new lead: the ransom drop at the payphone. There was a faded blue Volvo. She could try to get a list of all blue Volvos in the area, and the people they were registered to. She wished Matt was there to give her some info. There could be a unique tire mark on the pavement, or maybe the car got scratched when it abruptly stopped, leaving fragments of its paint behind. But if there was anything there, the FBI agents were checking it out.

Okay, forget the forensics of the ransom delivery. What else? Her mind zoomed out, trying to see the bigger picture. Who were the suspects? Someone close to the parents, hating them, a low level administrator…

Her heartbeat quickened. What about Debra? Had they ever thoroughly checked her? They'd done background checks on everyone, but had they ever looked closer? A low level administrator, close to Naamit. Did she have reason to hate her?

Three reasons at least. Naamit had been promoted to management, and not her. She'd had a miscarriage, while Naamit had a beautiful daughter. Debra's husband had left her, while Naamit was happily married.

How had she not seen it before? It was right in front of her, it was…

No. She was forcing the puzzle piece to fit. Sometimes you could connect the pieces together, and they almost seemed to match, even though you had to push a bit too hard. But it was the wrong piece. Debra had an alibi for the night of the kidnapping. Naamit had been at an office party. She had specifically mentioned that all her coworkers were there. Hannah would call Naamit and verify it with her, but she could already feel in her gut that Debra was innocent. No, it was someone else. She mentally went over the people they'd encountered in the investigation. No one seemed to meet the profile.

She sighed, tried to shift gears again—turn the case around, look for another angle, another fresh perspective. She could go door-to-door, ask anyone who lived nearby if they had seen the car. Someone might have gotten its license plate. She could try and get the CCTV footage from the gas station and the post office. It might be problematic without a warrant, but she could try.

It was worth a shot. She opened a map of the street on her computer, trying to decide where to start. The post office and the gas station were the only two businesses in the area. She'll start with them. Then she'd go door to door in a hundred feet parameter...

She frowned. There was that niggling feeling again, at the back of her mind. Something about the street map bothered her. She concentrated, trying to fish out the pesky detail, as if it was a tiny thorn wedged deeply under her skin.

The gas station and the post office were the only two businesses in the area. She recalled the report in Clint's briefcase. The CCTV footage of various businesses in Glenmore Park had been hacked. A gas station, a post office, two clothing shops...

There were no clothing shops near the kidnapping scene. Why had their footage been hacked?

She chewed her lip, trying to figure it out. She searched online for clothing shops in Glenmore Park, and scanned the list. Most were at the Glenmore Park Mall, some on Clayton Road, but nowhere near the area of the kidnapping, two were on the other side of town. It made no sense.

She got up, and went down to the lobby. Officer McLure was manning the reception desk, and he nodded at her.

"McLure," she said, "do you have a cigarette?"

He frowned. "Didn't you quit, Detective?"

She nodded. "Three years. But today is a bad day."

He fished a crumpled box from his pocket and tossed it to her. "The lighter is inside," he said.

"Thanks," she said. He looked as if he was about to say something, then shrugged and leaned back in his chair, remaining silent.

Hannah stepped out of the station and walked around the corner of the building. She put a cigarette in her mouth and lit it, tasting the familiar taste of nicotine, smoke, and impending lung cancer. It felt good.

She smoked the cigarette slowly, staring at the parking lot. The Redditors could have thought that the clothing shops might have cameras pointing at the road. Who knew what those weirdos thought. Hell, they could be just looking for footage of a changing booth with a hot customer inside…

The cigarette dropped from her mouth. She cursed, stepped on it, and picked up the stub. Then she rushed into the station, tossing the box back to McLure, who caught it without even raising his head. She stormed into the squad room yet again, sat at her desk, and browsed to Abigail's Instagram. There they were, the three famous photos posted by the kidnappers. The second image was a full body shot of Abigail standing up.

Then she browsed to the subreddit, and clicked the top post, which was still the famous picture of Abigail and Gracie on the street together.

She looked from one to the other.

It was almost impossible to tell—the color was the same, and the picture on the street was fuzzy and unfocused. But Abigail was wearing different pants.

The kidnappers had bought her new pants.

———

Mitchell was pretty sure this lead would go nowhere. Sure, once he looked at the pictures, he saw the pants looked a bit different, but to drop everything and go check out the CCTV footage of clothing shops from a week before sounded like a stretch. Especially since they didn't have enough for a warrant.

But Hannah had that spark in her eye. He could see the enthusiasm and hope in her face, and he couldn't bring himself to tell her it was a lost cause. Neither could Bernard, and the three of them divided the clothing shops in Glenmore Park between them.

The first one was a very quick visit. They didn't have any black pants for girls, nor had they had any a week before.

If all five of his assigned clothing shops had ended that quickly, he would have been back at the police station in time for the evening take out. But the second clothing shop did have black pants for girls. He asked for the CCTV footage of a week before. A long argument regarding customer privacy followed. It ended only when Mitchell told the manager that he knew a reporter who would be glad to publish a story about that store, and how the manager had prevented the return of little Abigail Lisman. The manager grumbled, then checked his books and said that the pants in question hadn't been sold at all during the week after Saint Patrick's Day.

Mitchell was now at the third shop. He approached the counter, where a teenager employee stood, folding a few shirts. When she noticed him, her mouth stretched into a smile so fake it could have been plastic, and she asked in an annoying sing song voice, "Can I help you?"

"I would like to talk to the manager," Mitchell said.

"The manager is busy," she said, in the same voice. He wondered if this was what she always sounded like. Perhaps that was how they talked on her planet. "Is there something I can help you with?"

He showed her his badge. "Detective Lonnie," he said. "I'm investigating Abigail Lisman's kidnapping. I need to see your security footage."

The plastic smile disappeared. "I'll call the manager," she said in a normal human voice.

"Thank you."

She went to the back of the store. Mitchell leaned against the counter and looked around him. A small blonde girl in a pink dress, about six or seven years old, came out of the changing booth and approached a sour-faced woman.

"What do you think, Mommy?" she asked.

The woman glanced at her. "It makes you look a bit fat, Kimmy," she said. "Let's keep looking."

Mitchell curbed his desire to arrest the woman on the spot and drag her to the station. "I think you look fantastic," he said aloud. "Like a princess."

The girl looked at him and giggled shyly. He smiled at her. Her mother glanced at him, her eyes widening as she took in his looks. She smiled as well. "It's her birthday," she said. "We're buying her a new dress."

"Well, she's a beautiful girl," Mitchell said. He had half a dozen acidic sentences to follow that one. *I bet she takes after her father.* Or *pink really looks good on your granddaughter*. But the girl looked so happy, and he decided to let it slide.

"Can I help you?" A thirtyish woman with short black hair and a cute face approached him with the other employee.

"I'm Detective Lonnie from the Glenmore Park PD. I'm investigating the Abigail Lisman kidnapping case. I'm looking for a man or a woman who bought black pants for a twelve-year-old girl, about a week ago, probably on the 18th of March, right after Saint Patrick's Day. I hoped I could take a look in your CCTV footage."

"We only keep the footage from the last seventy-two hours," the manager said.

"Oh," Mitchell said. "Can you check the books, see if—"

"What kind of pants?" the employee asked.

Mitchell fished in his pocket for his phone, and browsed to Abigail Lisman's Instagram page. He showed her the photos.

"Oh," the employee said. "Those! Yeah, we sell them here. Let me think…" She frowned, clenching her jaw as if the process of thinking required unimaginable effort.

"They might have been bought by this man," he said, flipping to the sketch image.

She looked at it. "Yes!" she said. "I remember him! Val, you remember? I told you about the guy who looked totally hung over, that came to buy clothing for his niece but he didn't know her size, and he was so confused by all the options that he nearly left, but I told him…" She slowly stopped talking as she realized Mitchell and the manager were staring at her.

"When was that?" Mitchell asked.

"Just after Saint Patrick's Day," she said in a meek voice. "He's the kidnapper? He didn't look like a kidnapper. I didn't know. I'm so sorry—"

"Casey," Val said, in what Mitchell thought was an incredibly patient voice. "At what time? And do you remember if he paid in cash or—"

"He paid with a credit card," Casey said quickly. "I remember. It was a credit card."

It took them less than ten minutes to find the transaction in their records. His name was Darrel Simmons.

———

Hannah's heart beat wildly as she took the Kevlar vest out of her trunk and put it on. Her car was parked near a patrol car and several FBI vehicles. There was a group of eight FBI SWAT agents in full gear preparing to charge Darrel Simmons's house. They weren't taking any chances.

Hannah and Mitchell, along with the other two cops, were assigned to watch the perimeter—or, as Mitchell put it, the "stay out of the way" positions. The only reason they were even there was because Hannah and Mitchell had given them the address. Neither Agent Mancuso nor Clint really acknowledged their presence.

The garage door was closed, and the house was dark. The SWAT members had night vision goggles on, though Clint and Mancuso didn't bother with them. Hannah guessed they would follow after the SWAT team stormed the house.

True to her prediction, the SWAT team took positions around the house with Mancuso and Clint hanging back. The SWAT member closest to the door kicked it open, and the man next to him threw something inside. A moment later, there was a sharp flash and a loud bang, and the team charged inside. From her "stay out of the way" position, Hannah could still hear them yelling as they stormed from room to room.

Finally, someone shouted that it was clear. Mancuso and Clint ran after the SWAT team. Hannah followed, Mitchell joining her. As they got to the house, the lights turned on inside. Hannah ran through the front door, stopping instantly as the familiar coppery scent of blood filled her nostrils. She exchanged looks with Mitchell as they inched toward the light. Even before they entered the room, Hannah could see the brown smudges on the floor. For one terrible moment she imagined herself telling Naamit her daughter had been found dead in the kidnapper's house.

But it wasn't Abigail. On the kitchen floor, amidst a large pool of dried blood, lay the body of Darrel Simmons. He was lying on his stomach, head turned to the side, face twisted in pain.

"The house is clean," one of the agents reported to Mancuso. "There's nobody else here. We found a small bed and a latrine bucket in the basement."

Hannah shut her eyes. The other kidnapper had disappeared, and had taken Abigail with him.

TWENTY-ONE

Hannah was aware of movement around her, the murmuring of the crime scene investigators, FBI agents talking silently with each other or on the phone, the chatter of the police radio in a patrol car outside, sharp and concise. She stared at the single unbroken champagne flute on the kitchen table, a reddish-brown trickle of dried blood on its side. She felt sick.

The info had been there the day before. They could have been here sooner. They'd have found Abigail, returned her to her parents.

Now they had a dead body, and no sign of Abigail.

Mitchell had gone down to the basement with one of the agents, to examine the room where Abigail had been trapped for the past week. Hannah couldn't bring herself to do so.

Annie knelt by the body, taking its temperature. Not far from her, Matt carefully scraped blood from the floor into a small jar. The jurisdiction issue of the crime scene was unclear. It was a murder scene in Glenmore Park, so the case belonged to the police department. But it was directly related to the kidnapping of Abigail Lisman, which meant it was in the FBI's hands.

No one was arguing just yet, though Hannah could see the dark clouds of discontent in the near future. But for now, the FBI were happy to use Matt and Violet as crime scene investigators, since they were available. There was no question about Annie being the official person to pronounce that the dead body was indeed, a dead body.

Annie stood up and cleared her throat. She looked hesitantly around her, as if unsure who to address. Hannah met her gaze, and shook her head slightly. Annie nodded, then glanced at Agent Mancuso.

"Um … Agent?"

Agent Mancuso walked over, carefully avoiding the large blood stain that surrounded most of the body. "Yes. Doctor Turner, right?"

"Uh … sure. You can call me Annie."

It was clear that Mancuso was not in the mood to do so. "Okay, Doctor, what are your findings?"

"Rigor mortis is in progress," Annie said. "According to that, and the temperature of the body, the deceased has been dead between five and six hours. There are almost no signs of lividity and the body is very pale, indicating the deceased has bled to death." She paused, and both of them, as well as Hannah, glanced at the huge blood stain on the floor. "I believe the main source of the bleeding is the slash on the throat. There are also two visible stab wounds, one in his back and one in his chest. There are multiple scratches on his face, caused by what seems to be a broken object with sharp edges…" Annie pointedly glanced over to the smashed champagne bottle on the floor. "And another wound on the back of his head, possibly from the same object."

"Was there a struggle?" Mancuso asked.

"I wouldn't think a very significant one. Struggles often accelerate rigor mortis, and this isn't the case. But, of course, I'll be able to tell you more once I do a full autopsy. And Matt would probably be able to determine more from the blood spatter. I…" she hesitated.

"Go on," Mancuso said.

"It's a bit premature, but I would guess after being stabbed at least once he fell to the floor, and was hit on the head with the … with a hard object," Annie said, careful not to mention the bottle. It wasn't her job to make that connection. "At that point he would have been completely incapacitated, perhaps even unconscious. Then his attacker may have stabbed him in the back. And then he pulled his head up, using his hair, and slashed his throat."

"Thank you, Doctor Turner," Mancuso said, frowning. She turned to Matt. "Mr. Lowery, right?"

Matt straightened. "That's right."

"How long until you and your team finish with this crime scene?"

Matt glanced at the rest of his "team." Violet was in the corner of the room, her brow furrowed as she sketched the scene. "I'd say five to six hours," Matt said. "We need to go through the basement as well."

"I see," Mancuso said, frowning. "Any initial assessment you want to share?"

"We have two champagne glasses, one broken and one intact, and a broken bottle," Matt said. "And a lot of blood."

"Really," Mancuso said dryly. She was clearly unimpressed.

"There's also something missing," Matt said.

Hannah tensed, looking at Matt intently.

"What do you mean, missing?"

"Well…" he walked over to one of the blood spatters on the floor. "You see this spatter here?"

Hannah looked at the spatter he indicated. There was a series of spots on the floor, their trajectory pointing away from the body. They ended in a smear.

"Yes," Mancuso said.

"And see that spatter here?" He pointed at a smaller spatter, a foot away.

"Yes."

"It's the same spatter," Matt said. "There was a large object here. Some of the blood hit it as it splashed. Then, later, the object was removed, accounting for the clean spot and the smear."

"I see," Mancuso said. Her tone warmed up. Apparently, Mancuso had no problem with the way everyone here conducted their work, except for Hannah. "Could it be a duffel bag?"

Matt shrugged. "Sure. Size fits."

Mancuso turned her head and exchanged meaningful looks with Clint.

"Well," a familiar voice said behind Hannah. "This is a damn mess."

"Captain Bailey," Mancuso said, her tone raised in surprise. "What brings you here?"

"I heard there was a murder in my city," Bailey said, carefully walking into the room, sliding a pair of gloves onto his hands. "And I understand that you want to work on the case together with my detectives."

"This murder is a part of the Abigail Lisman kidnapping case," Mancuso said sharply. "And it is in the hands of the—"

"Perhaps we should talk about it outside," Bailey suggested. "I'm an old bureaucrat, and the sight of so much blood makes me dizzy."

Mancuso blinked, then nodded curtly. "Very well," she said. "Let's step outside."

They both brushed past Hannah on their way. She looked at them walking out, then turned her eyes to meet Clint's. He quickly looked away. She returned her stare to the single champagne flute on the table.

———

It was cold outside, and the night wind froze Fred Bailey's ears. He could handle cold quite well—pretty much a must if you worked as a cop in the Glenmore Park PD—but his ears always hurt when it was windy. Couldn't be helped. There were certain things that a police captain could wear, and earmuffs were not on the list.

Mancuso didn't seem to mind the cold at all. She was a stony one, especially when angry. In the many years they'd worked together, he'd never seen her display a sign of weakness. But he thought he could see the turmoil in her eyes. There wasn't just anger there, there was pain as well. Maybe he just saw what he felt.

"I want us to work together on this case," he said.

"Like hell," she answered angrily. "This is our case, and you know it, Bailey."

"Who cares whose case is this?" he said, his tone soft, though loud enough to be heard over the wind. "It's everyone's case. You don't care about the publicity. You've never cared about that. That's your boss's problem, not yours. You just want to find the girl."

"That's right," Mancuso snapped. "And I can't let your detectives mess with my investigation, calling their own shots, with no one to rein them in when needed."

That one stung, and Fred made sure his face remained completely neutral. "My detectives are the best detectives in the state," he said. "Sure, they can occasionally be a bit … difficult—"

"You call that difficult? If Shor had told us about the phone call—"

"If Detective Shor had told you about the phone call you might have caught the kidnappers, sure. Or Abigail Lisman might have been killed."

"She's probably dead anyway."

"Maybe," Fred said. "No signs of recent violence in the basement. She was taken away alive."

"We would have caught them!"

"Or not!" he snapped, losing his temper. "*Would, would.* What the hell is wrong with you? This is where we're at now.

There's a kid missing, a dead kidnapper, and the clock is ticking. Do you really want to talk about something that might have happened?"

Mancuso glared at him, clenching her fists.

"Would you have done differently?" he asked, lowering his voice. "In her position, would you have reported the call despite the mother's request? Endangering the mother's child?"

"Yes."

"Bullshit. I know you better than that. You would have done exactly the same. And it might have been the right call."

Mancuso shook her head and said nothing.

"What's going on, Christine?" he asked.

She stared at the house, her mouth twisted in a bitter grimace. "We have more than a hundred and fifty agents, professionals, and consultants working on this case," she said. "I've been managing it for the past week. I'm almost never home. The only time I see my daughter, she's already sleeping. All my men are working double shifts. And still, we didn't notice that she was wearing different pants. Never followed that lead. If we'd noticed this a day earlier..." She stopped talking, clenching her jaw. A sudden gust of wind caught her hair, messing it up. She didn't seem to notice.

"Plenty of guilt to go around," Fred said. "You know, my father used to say guilt is like ice cream. Everyone wants a bite—"

"—unless it's mint flavored." Mancuso said.

Fred blinked in surprise. "How did you know?"

"My Mom used to say that all the time."

"Seriously?"

"Yeah. I have no idea what it means, though."

"Yeah," Fred said. "Neither do I."

They stood in silence. Damn, his ears hurt. Perhaps black earmuffs were acceptable after all. Dignified, even. He wasn't getting any younger.

"Detective Shor is the one who noticed the pants," he said carefully.

"I know," Mancuso said.

"She has her moments, you know. She can be damn hard to work with sometimes, but she's probably the most brilliant detective in my squad."

Mancuso nodded. Bailey decided to wait.

"Fine," she said eventually. "But Fred, I want her to report to you. No more bullshit. And if any of us tells her to do something, I want her to act as if it's the divine word of God."

"Of course," Fred grinned, mentally filtering the last sentence.

Far away, thunder rumbled ominously.

"All right," Mancuso said. "Let's go inside. I'm freezing."

They began walking toward the front door.

"Do you think I could wear earmuffs?" he asked.

"No."

"Not even if they're black?"

"Absolutely not, Bailey, and we shall never mention this again."

Hannah watched Violet take crime scene photos, feeling envious. There was something about Violet, a certain feeling of wholeness. She always seemed calm, always did her job with perfection, didn't seem to mind that people treated Matt like her boss even though he wasn't.

Hannah wondered if Violet ever lay in bed for hours, unable to fall asleep because her mind couldn't turn off. Did she ever punish herself for days and weeks about a decision she'd made? Did she ever feel as if she was being stretched, about to break, like three-hour-old bubble gum?

Matt came out of the basement and approached Hannah.

"There are dry blood stains on one of the walls in the basement," he said, "as well as the bottom stairs. And the floor looks like there was a large stain on it, and someone cleaned it. It's possible to see the outline where they cleaned. The stain pattern on the wall indicates that it was probably a stabbing."

Hannah froze in fear. "Could it be Abigail?" she whispered.

Matt looked at her thoughtfully. "Maybe," he said. "If she was stabbed several days ago."

"How many days?"

He shrugged. "I need to run some tests," he said. "Blood dries very quickly."

Hannah's brain spun. "Hang on," she said. "You said there was blood on the stairs."

"Yes," Matt said. "The stabbing occurred on the stairs to the basement."

"And then the victim tumbled down the stairs to the floor?"

"That's the most likely explanation, but I'll need to—"

"It's Glen Haney's blood," Hannah said. "That's where he was killed. It matches the findings on the body."

"I'll run a DNA test," Matt said.

"It's him," Hannah said, with a certainty she was desperate to feel.

Captain Bailey and Agent Mancuso walked back inside. Bailey approached Hannah. "Detective Shor," he said, "you'll be investigating this case with Detective Lonnie."

Hannah's eyes widened in surprise. She glanced at Mancuso, saw her and Clint speaking with each other in hushed tones. There were black pouches under Mancuso's eyes. She stood as if it took all her effort not to crumple on the floor like a used rag. Hannah knew how she felt.

"You'll be working with the FBI. Agent Ward is assigned to the case as well. I want to be filled in about everything you find out."

"Yes, sir," she replied dutifully

"Hannah…" he said.

"Yes?"

"This wasn't your fault. Now find that girl, please."

"Yes, sir."

"I'm going home," he said. "There are enough agents, investigators, and detectives here to fill a stadium. You don't need me."

She nodded at him. "Thank you, sir."

He left. She chewed her lip, then approached Clint. Mancuso had left as well, and Clint was now talking on the phone. She waited patiently for him to finish the call. Finally, he hung up and looked at her.

"Hey," she said.

"Hey yourself," he answered, his face passive and unsmiling.

She sighed. "I'm … sorry?"

"Are you asking me if you're sorry? How would I know that?"

"No! I'm telling you I'm sorry," Hannah said. "I screwed up. I shouldn't have looked in your files. And I should have told you when Naamit received that e-mail—"

He shook his head. "There's no way to know what would have happened if you did," he said. "I understand why you didn't." His voice was still tight. His past warmth was gone. Hannah wondered if it would ever return.

"Thanks," she said.

They looked at each other for a moment, and Hannah understood that they'd never be in each other's arms again. She had broken his trust, and even as easygoing as Clint was, this wasn't something he could just forget.

"They found the Volvo that Simmons was driving this morning," Clint finally said, his voice slightly softer, though the formality stayed. "They just informed me."

"Yeah?" Hannah blinked, trying to sharpen her dulled wits.

"Yes. In New Hampshire, at the side of the road. With the duffel bag the Lismans used to deliver the ransom. Empty of course."

"He switched cars and bags," Hannah said.

"Yeah, like the kidnapping. They don't keep using a vehicle once they committed a crime while driving it. Our people are going over the car and the scene, see if he left any trace."

"Even if he did, we know he was the one driving it," Hannah said. "I doubt anything would lead to his accomplice."

"True. I was also told he has a criminal record. Burglary. He was released six months ago, after two years in prison."

"Anything else in his file?"

"Minor misdemeanors. Nothing serious. He had a fence he used to work with, so we're sending an agent to talk to the guy, see if he knows anything. Darrel could have been working with someone from his past. We're contacting the patrol officer who caught him as well, an Officer … Finley?"

"Kevin Finley," Hannah nodded. She doubted Kevin would have anything useful to say. He was not exactly the sharpest tool in the shed. Or the nicest, for that matter.

"Right. We're also already in the middle of a door-to-door, to see if anyone saw anything. There are several CCTV cameras around here—one of them might give us something useful, though I doubt it. Those guys were very careful, and you could pretty much drive all the way from here to the highway without being caught on video."

"What do you think happened?"

"Well … The kidnappers met here to celebrate." Clint nodded at the champagne flute on the table. "I guess they fought about something. A disagreement about the ransom money? One grabbed a knife, stabbed Darrel, broke the champagne bottle on his head, then finished the job. Grabbed the money and took off."

"What about Abigail?"

"Took her with him. Probably as a hostage. If he'd wanted to finish her off, he could have done it here, left her with Darrel's body."

"Maybe they moved her earlier," Hannah suggested.

"Yeah."

"Detective," Matt called. Both of them turned their heads toward him. He was frowning at something near the door to the basement. They walked over. There was a small nail in the wall.

"What is it?" Hannah asked.

"Check out the fibers on the nail," Matt said.

Hannah looked closely. A bunch of black fibers were twirled around it.

"Simmons probably used to hang his coat here," she suggested.

"There's a coat rack by the door," Clint said.

"And it's a weird place for it," Matt said. "Didn't the other kid ... Gracie, say the kidnappers had ski masks?"

"That's right," Hannah said.

"I think they hung them here," Matt said.

"Why here?" Clint frowned. "Why not in a drawer somewhere or—"

"Because they wanted to put them on whenever they went down to the basement," Hannah said, suddenly excited. "They didn't want Abigail to see their faces."

"So they probably did intend to set her free," Clint said. "There's no mask here."

"Whoever took Abigail took the mask as well," Hannah said. "He might still intend to let her go."

"Did he leave the house wearing a mask, carrying a child?" Clint asked. "They wouldn't have made it three blocks before being arrested."

"There's a sharp smell of something chemical in the basement," Matt said. "The girl was possibly knocked out before they got into the car."

"And if the car was in the garage, no one would see them getting into it," Hannah said. "He probably put her in the trunk."

"Okay," Clint said. "Let's keep looking."

Driven by renewed enthusiasm, Hannah began slowly investigating each room, careful not to move anything that hadn't been processed yet. She found several empty pizza boxes in the garbage outside, and made sure those were bagged as evidence as well. She returned to the kitchen and stood in the entrance, trying to get a feel for what had happened.

The body was gone, taken to the morgue. The entire room was littered with evidence tags, and Matt was carefully placing shards of glass into an evidence bag. Violet was dusting the champagne glass on the table.

Something felt … missing. Darrel had been a big man. If there had been a heated argument, he wouldn't have gone without a fight. But despite the large stain on the floor and the broken bottle, the kitchen looked too clean for a struggle. There was a drying rack by the sink, full of glasses and plates, completely untouched. The champagne glass on the table stood undisturbed. No … This was quick.

Violet frowned, looking at the champagne glass. Hannah approached her.

"What is it?" she asked.

"Smell this," Violet said, motioning to the glass.

Hannah sniffed. "Smells like champagne," she said.

Violet shook her head. "There's something else…" She looked around the room. "Anyone here with a good sense of smell?"

One of the FBI agents turned his head. "Me," he said. His nose was actually kind of small, almost button-like, and Hannah doubted there was a sharp sense of smell accompanying it.

"Can you smell this glass?" Violet asked.

"Sure," he said and approached.

"I have a good sense of smell," Hannah mentioned as he sniffed. "I didn't smell anything."

"Yeah, there's a weird smell here," the agent said, raising his head. "Something like … almonds?"

Violet nodded. "Cyanide smells like almonds," she told Hannah. "Not everyone can smell it, even if you have a wicked sense of smell. It's a genetic thing. I think there's poison in this champagne glass."

Hannah looked at her in surprise. "So … one of them tried to poison the other?"

"I guess so."

Clint walked over, overhearing the discussion. "Are you sure about this?" he asked.

She shrugged. "We'll get it to your lab and test it," she said. "But the smell's there for sure."

"So one of them tried to kill the other even before the stabbing," Clint said.

"The taste would be quite bitter," Violet said. "Also, Cyanide is weakened when you put it in a sugary alcoholic drink. It reacts with the sugar, and creates a different compound called Amyg … Amyg … Matt! What do you call the thing that cyanide and sugar makes?"

"Amygdalin," Matt said, joining them.

"Right," Violet said. "So I'm guessing he drank a bit, noticed the weird taste, and put the thing down. And it wasn't strong enough to affect him. Most people don't know that cyanide isn't effective in sugared alcohol."

"And then they fought," Clint said.

"No," Hannah said with certainty. "And then the other kidnapper stabbed him in the back, taking him down. He thought the poison might fail. This entire thing was planned."

Her phone rang. Bernard's name appeared on the display and she felt a pang of longing. Her partnership with Bernard was never loaded, never complicated. She answered the call.

"Hey," she said.

"Hey," he said. "Darrel Simmons has a criminal record."

"Yeah," she said. "I know, the FBI told me."

"Okay," Bernard said. "So I just called the city jail. Apparently he shared his cell for the last two years of his incarceration with a man named Gustav Bowler."

"Is Gustav out?" Hannah asked.

"No, he's still inside. He's in for three more years."

"Okay. Thanks, Bernard. Anything else?"

"No. How's it going there?"

"It's getting complicated. I'll fill you in later."

She hung up. "Simmons had a cellmate for the past two years named Gustav Bowler," she told Clint.

He nodded. "We'll send someone to talk to him."

"I'll go," Hannah said. "Want to join?"

Clint shook his head. "I need to update Mancuso about this development, and get this champagne tested ASAP," he said. Hannah thought he just wanted to avoid her. "If our other kidnapper bought the cyanide, we might be able to trace him that way."

"Okay," Hannah said. "I'll let you know if I find anything."

———

Gustav Bowler was a short, wide man, with a head as flat as a shelf. Atop the shelf lay stubbly blond hair, through which his pink scalp was easily visible. He watched Hannah and Mitchell as they sat in front of him, his eyes giving away nothing but slight boredom.

"Mr. Bowler, you were cellmates with Darrel Simmons for two years," Hannah said.

"Two years?" he asked, his voice relaxed and sleepy. "If you say so. Time does fly when you're having fun."

"Did he talk to you often?"

"Yeah. He was a good guy. A good cellmate. Didn't get violent, or angry. Never tried anything funny, even though I could sometimes hear him masturbate at night. Didn't snore either, unlike the asshole who currently shares my cell. He snores like a chainsaw."

"Mr. Bowler, did Simmons ever—"

"He did fart though. Said the prison food gave him gas. Quite frankly, it gives everyone gas. Prison yard sometimes sounds like a tuba concert."

"Mr. Bowler, did Sim—"

"I can hold it in, but it probably isn't so healthy. I don't think Darrel could hold it in. Our cell smelled like a sewer gone bad."

"Did Simmons ever talk to you about—"

"I think if anyone had ever lit a match in our cell after dinner, the whole prison would have blown up." Gustav burst out laughing. "Can you imagine that? Death by fart fire?"

Hannah massaged her temple. She was well aware of the obsession men had with flatulence. All her Dad's jokes included someone farting. He used to tell them at dinner, and her mother had never failed to remind him they were eating. Still, she was not here to talk about digestion problems.

"Darrel Simmons is dead," she said abruptly.

Gustav's laugh died. "Really?" he asked.

"Yes. I wanted to know if—"

"Oh, man. How did he die? Was he in pain? Does his mother know? Did you contact his mother? Oh, man…" A tear ran down Gustav's cheek, and his meaty lips quivered.

"I'm sorry," Hannah said. "I can see you were very close. We could really use your help catching his killer. Did he ever—"

"Oh, shit, I'm sorry. Did you say killer?" Gustav buried his face in his hands, his shoulders shuddering.

Hannah glanced at Mitchell. He nodded and cleared his throat.

"Hey man," he said softly. "Hey, Gustav. Here." He pulled a Kleenex packet out of his pocket and handed it over to the crying man.

After a second, Gustav removed his hands from his face and took one. He blew his nose into it, then took another one to wipe his eyes.

"I'm sorry," he said, his voice still quavering. "It's just … we spent two years together here, you know? He once stopped two bastards who were about to … assault me in the shower. We talked, you know. A place like this, you need a friend."

Mitchell put his hand on Gustav's arm and squeezed lightly. Gustav raised his eyes to look at Mitchell. His breath shuddered as Mitchell said, "I totally understand. I once had a very good friend. I get what you're going through."

"Yeah, I mean … We were very close, you know?" Gustav whispered.

"Yeah," Mitchell answered.

Hannah watched in disbelief as Gustav's face slowly relaxed. Jacob had once told her Mitchell could get anyone in pain to open up to him, but she'd never seen it for herself.

"Detective Shor and I are looking for Darrel's killer," Mitchell said.

"Oh man. How did the bastard kill him? Was he in pain?"

"No, it was very quick," Mitchell said, his eyes soft and truthful.

Hannah thought about Simmons in the pool of blood. *Quick, my ass.*

"Did you call his mother?"

"The police are notifying her," Mitchell said. "But we need to catch the person who did this."

"Yeah, sure. You get that bastard!"

"Did Darrel ever tell you what he planned on doing once he got out?"

"Well, he told me after he got out," Gustav said.

Hannah could see Mitchell tense up. "He visited you?" Mitchell asked.

"Yeah, I told you. We were really good friends. Came here six weeks ago. Told me he had something really huge. That he was planning something big with his boss. Said it was gonna change his life. Told me he'd leave me some money to come and join him once I'm out, like in that movie *The Shawshank Redemption*, you know? Except I look way better than Morgan Freeman, that's what he said." Gustav smiled, new tears springing from his eyes. "How we laughed at that joke. He was such a funny guy."

"Do you know who his boss was?"

"No, he never said."

"Do you know where he worked?"

"I forget. It started with an *M*, I think Something like *Mush Tools* or *Moche Tools*…"

"Koche Toolworks?" Hannah said sharply.

"Yeah, that's it! Funny, doesn't start with an *M* now that I think about it."

Hannah was already standing up. "Thank you, Mr. Bowler," she said. "You've been very helpful."

TWENTY-TWO

Lance Koche sat in the interrogation room, trying to look tough, his lawyer by his side. Hannah could sense he wasn't as calm as he wanted them to believe. A guy like Koche, you talked to him in his office, and he thought that he was untouchable. Protected in his seat of power, like a king.

But come to his home, arrest him, drag him to the station? The king realizes he has lost his throne. And when a king loses his throne, he often loses his head soon after. She watched him through the one-way glass, his eyes constantly shifting, his left foot jerking nervously as his lawyer talked to him in a hushed tone.

"Shall we?" Clint asked. He stood by her side, his eyes intent on the glass.

"Yeah," Hannah said. "Let's go." She glanced at Mitchell. "Five minutes," she said. He nodded.

She walked into the interrogation room, Clint following behind her. She sat down in front of Koche. His lawyer didn't bluster, didn't demand his immediate release, didn't claim they were holding his client illegally. This usually meant she was dealing with a professional. It made sense. When it came to lawyers, the richer you were, the better they were.

"Gentlemen," Hannah said. "Mr. Koche has already met us. I'm Detective Shor. This is Agent Ward from the FBI."

"And I'm Gideon Bates," the lawyer said. "I'm representing Mr. Koche, of course."

"Mr. Koche," Hannah said. "Where is Abigail Lisman?"

"I don't know," he said, stony-faced.

"I think you do," Hannah said. "After all, you are the one who had her kidnapped."

"I think we're done here," Bates said.

"We're not, Mr. Bates. Your client kidnapped a twelve-year-old girl from her mother, and I intend to find her," Hannah said.

"I can see that's what you think, which is why I say we're done. My client kidnapped no one, and I'm not going to sit here, letting you twist what my client has to say to match your mistaken theory."

"If your client kidnapped no one, and can prove it, he can go home tonight and sleep in his own bed," Clint said. "But if you terminate this interview, he'll go to federal prison to await his trial."

"It's difficult to prove a negative, Agent Ward," Bates said. "My client is innocent. What proof do you have that he kidnapped the girl?"

"We have enough," Clint said.

"Well, I think that isn't sufficient," Bates said.

"Tell me what you have," Koche interrupted. "I'll answer your questions."

"Well, we have the private detective you hired to investigate your biological daughter," Hannah said.

"You had that before."

"We know Darrel Simmons was one of the kidnappers," Hannah said. "Do you know him, Mr. Koche?"

Koche frowned. "Darrel Simmons?" he asked. "The porter?"

"So you do know him."

"Of course I do. I employed him for a few weeks. He's one of the kidnappers?"

"That's right," Hannah said carefully. She had made a foolish mistake, and said *was* when she talked about Darrel Simmons. But now that Koche was talking about him in present tense, she wondered if Koche hadn't been informed about Simmons' death. She was certain the person who murdered Simmons wasn't Koche, but a third accomplice. Perhaps Koche had been double-crossed as well.

"Darrel Simmons hasn't worked for me for the past month," Koche said. "This is … very unsettling. Are you sure he's involved?"

"Our turn to ask questions," Clint said. "When did you hire Darrel Simmons?"

"I'm not sure," Koche said, frowning. "Two months ago, I think."

"Interesting, that you chose to hire a man with a criminal background," Clint said. "Do you believe in second chances, Mr. Koche?"

"I wasn't aware he had a criminal background," Koche said. "I don't hire criminals."

"You don't run a background check on your future employees?"

"Of course I do."

"Well, Simmons just got out of jail six months ago."

Koche's lips tightened, and he said nothing.

"Is your business in difficulty, Mr. Koche?" Clint asked

"What has that got to do with anything?"

"Let me answer that for you. It is. You owe a lot of money to a lot of people."

"How do you know that?" Koche asked, his face reddening.

"I'm with the FBI," Clint said. "It's my job to know. I'd even say you were about to go bankrupt. Maybe the idea of a sudden duffel bag full of money began to sound attractive."

"Don't say anything," Bates said. "They're just fishing."

"I am not about to go bankrupt," Koche said. "We're resizing. I sold my entire inventory of disc sanders and jackhammers to a competitor last month. I don't need to kidnap a child to get some emergency funds."

"We can offer you a deal right now if you give us Abigail Lisman's location," Hannah said point blank.

"I can't do that; I don't know where she is. I had nothing to do with her kidnapping."

"Perhaps you were frustrated," Hannah said. "Felt like all those years with your daughter had been stolen? Decided to give Naamit Lisman a taste of her own medicine and take her daughter, earn some money to save your business on the side?"

"That's ridiculous! I never wanted a child, and if I had known the woman was pregnant I would have insisted that she get an abortion! Besides, what money? Naamit Lisman doesn't have a dime to her name. Why would I ask her for ransom?"

"That's why you did it on Instagram," Clint said, leaning forward. "You knew someone would pay the ransom."

"Enough!" Bates said sharply. "My client—"

The door to the interrogation room opened, and Bates stopped talking. Mitchell walked in with several sheets of paper in his hand and gave them to Hannah. He leaned down and whispered in her ear. "There you go. Like we saw before, he has four warehouses and a small cabin by the beach. We haven't found anything else yet."

His warm breath tickled her ear. He was incredibly close, and she tried to ignore his smell as she lowered her face to the pages, hoping that no one noticed the sudden flush in her cheeks. Mitchell left the room.

"Detective Lonnie just informed me that we have the addresses of your warehouses, as well as that nice cabin you own," she said. "Our people are on their way to search them as we speak."

Bates spoke up. "You need a search warrant to—"

"We have one," she said. "Judge Roth was very sympathetic. And I'm sure that if you have anything else in your papers, we'll find it, Mr. Koche. Tell us now where Abigail is, and we'll cut a deal."

There was a moment of silence, and Koche's eyes shifted downward, his jaw clenching.

"I have nothing to add," he finally said.

The thumping on Jurgen Adler's door woke him up with a start. He blinked in his bed, confused, existential questions like "Who am I," "Where am I," and "What is that noise" running through his mind. The first two questions were easily answered; the third took longer.

Once he realized that it was the noise of a fist thumping on a door—and even worse, his own door, not one of the neighbors'—he considered going back to sleep. He'd had some unpleasant encounters with the landlady lately, and he suspected this might be one of those. If not her, it could be the FBI again. He had just been released two days ago. He wasn't keen to get into federal custody again.

Eventually he got up and opened the door, mostly because he didn't want the neighbors to wake up from the noise. His right-side neighbor was a young, single mother of two, and had once told Jurgen she slept about ten minutes every night.

Detective Hannah Shor stood at his doorstep. She looked terrible. She was wet, her hair matted on her head in a tangled mess, her face pale. Her coat was completely drenched. For the first time, he noticed the sound of rain outside. It was pouring.

"Hannah," he said. Then, after a moment of contemplation, added, "What time is it?"

"It's half past two," Hannah said.

"Oh. What are you doing here?"

"Looking for Abigail Lisman."

"I didn't kidnap her, Hannah."

"I know you didn't, you idiot," she said irritably. "Koche did. I need you to help me figure out how, and where he's holding her."

Jurgen's brain struggled to understand what the hell was going on. "Koche? You mean Lance Koche?"

"Yeah." She looked at him. "Aren't you going to invite me in?"

"Uh … sure. Come in. I'll make a shitload of coffee."

"Good. I need it," Hannah said, stepping inside. Jurgen closed the door. She took off her coat. Her clothes underneath were mostly dry, though her pants seemed soggy at the bottom.

"It's almost colder in here than outside," Hannah said, staring at him. He wore his cotton pajamas. "Aren't you cold?"

"I don't get cold," Jurgen said. "Not easily, at least. Must be my Norwegian half."

He walked to the kitchen and began preparing coffee. "So why do you think Lance Koche kidnapped Abigail?"

"That's where the evidence led me," she said, sitting on one of the three chairs in the kitchen. "He had you following her. A man named Darrel Simmons was involved in the kidnapping. He also worked for Koche. And he told a friend he was planning a big job with his employer. We know Koche is on the verge of bankruptcy, so he needs some extra money. And we suspect he wanted to get back at Naamit Lisman for keeping Abigail a secret from him all those years."

"I see," Jurgen said, filling two gargantuan mugs. He put one in front of Hannah and sat down. "Did you catch Darrel Simmons?"

"He's dead."

"Oh," Jurgen said, and sipped from his mug.

"Did you know him?"

"No. I didn't know too many people at Koche Toolworks."

"Anyway, Abigail was trapped in his house for a whole week. We got there today, Simmons was dead, and Abigail was gone."

"You think Koche killed him?"

"No," Hannah shook her head. "Not directly, at least. There's a third person involved."

Jurgen nodded, thoughtful. He looked at Hannah, who seemed less hostile than usual, a bit subdued. Mostly, when he met people from the Glenmore Park PD, he got dirty looks. He was the rotten apple in the barrel, the one who had made them all look bad. Bernard was even worse than most. The man had big eyes that must have belonged to a puppy in a previous life. Whenever they met, his eyes would fill up with hurt and disappointment, the eyes of a man who had been lied to by his best friend.

Well, such was life. But now Hannah just looked exhausted, and lost. It made him want to hug her, to tell her everything would be okay.

"So…" he said.

"Yeah?"

"What do you want from me?" he asked delicately. Hannah did not want his hug. Probably.

"I want you to turn on your detective brain, and figure out who Koche worked with," Hannah said. "Or tell me where he's keeping Abigail!"

"How?"

"Damn it, Jurgen! You worked for the man; you delivered those images of Abigail to him. Think! What was he interested in? Who did he talk to? Did you ever see him conferring with someone about something that wasn't related to power tools? Did he have any shady contacts? Bernard said you were a brilliant detective!"

"He didn't say that," Jurgen said, wishing he could believe her.

"Well … he said you would have been a brilliant detective, if you hadn't been so greedy and immoral."

"Ah. That sounds more like him."

"I think..." Hannah's voice choked. "I think the third kidnapper took Abigail as a hostage. That he isn't sure if he's going to keep her alive, and he wants to see if things go badly for him. Once he figures out he's safe, he'll kill her. I don't believe we have much time."

She got up and paced the small kitchen. "We're digging into Koche's papers and files. But there are hundreds of thousands of e-mails, the bookkeeping of that company is staggering. There are more than thirty FBI agents going through it all, and they still haven't covered more than five percent. It's taking too long!"

"His warehouses!" Jurgen suddenly said. "He has a lot of warehouses; he might be keeping her in one of them!"

"We checked all his warehouses. Nothing there but stacks of power tools. We also checked his beach cabin. No one has been there for months."

She grabbed the huge mug and took a large gulp. Jurgen began to worry. She didn't look like she should be drinking coffee. How long could a person stay awake before having a nervous breakdown? He remembered reading the statistics somewhere.

"What else do you have on him?" he asked.

She eyed him, frowning. "Stuff. I can't tell you everything."

"Because I'm dirty?"

"No. Because you're a civilian, and the FBI is already very unhappy with me, and—"

"Okay, okay," he said, irritated. "What can you tell me?"

She thought for a moment. "Koche Toolworks has sixty-seven employees. Used to be more, but there was a round of layoffs recently. The company's in debt, and Koche sold some of his inventory to pay part of it. He still has inventory worth two-point-eight million dollars, but his debt is over five million, so it won't be enough to pay it—"

"It will be, if he has the ransom money," Jurgen said.

"Right. That's what we thought. Though that would mean he would have to obtain the entire ransom amount."

"Maybe he has," Jurgen suggested. "That might be why Simmons is dead. The other kidnapper could be dead as well."

"Yeah." Hannah nodded. She chewed her lip. "We know this job was planned for some months. Simmons told his friend about it six weeks ago."

"Are you sure he was talking about the same job?" Jurgen asked. "He might have been talking about a different one."

"He said it was one big job, and he was planning it with his employer." Hannah shrugged. "Anyway, Koche asked you to start following Abigail about two months ago, right?"

"Right."

"Well, that's it. There's a reference in his e-mail account about the lawsuit of an employee, over illegal termination. We checked into that; the employee is clean, has an alibi, and it isn't likely that he'd be Koche's accomplice. Koche got quite angry in that e-mail, though. All caps, a lot of threats, so it should probably be investigated further."

"All that in his business e-mail account?" Jurgen lifted an eyebrow. "Or his private account?"

"What?"

"Which e-mail account? I mean, it's a business lawsuit so I assume—"

"We only know of one e-mail account," Hannah said, her eyes widening.

"He has two," Jurgen said. "I found that out because I sent the pictures to the business account at first. Then he told me to send them to his private Gmail account. He said his personal assistant goes over his business e-mails, and he preferred to keep this private."

"Shit!" Hannah said. "I need to tell Agent Ward. They can probably find a way to enter his private account from his computer!"

"Well..." Jurgen hesitated. "I know how to log in to his private account."

There was a moment of silence. Uncomfortable, Jurgen took another sip from his mug.

"How do you know that?" Hannah asked.

"When we met, I stood behind him as he accessed his account to see the images I sent him. I saw him type his password."

"It wasn't hidden?"

"It was. I was looking at his fingers."

Hannah blinked. "And you could figure it out just by looking at his fingers?"

"I have a very good memory," Jurgen said. "And sharp eyesight."

"And why did you look at his fingers when he typed?"

Jurgen grinned. "What did Bernard call me again? Greedy and immoral?"

Hannah smiled as well. "Okay, then," she said.

―――

Abigail's arms hurt. The rope was chafing her wrists, and her shoulders ached from the unnatural angle forced on her for the past day. She had woken in a dark vast space, her hands tied behind her back, her legs tied as well. She was leaning against a cold metal wall, and could hear the rain outside, spattering on the wall. It filled the entire space with a dull rumble.

The room was almost empty, dust covering every inch of the floor. The only thing in the room was an old-looking green car. There were no windows in the room; the dim light came from a neon lamp in the ceiling. Her kidnapper, the woman, paced the room, muttering to herself.

She wore no mask.

Time crawled by, each second feeling like a week. Abigail was nauseous at first, an after-effect of whatever it was the woman had used to knock her out. But over time the nausea passed, then returned, this time a result of her hunger and thirst. Her mouth was parched, her tongue swollen, her throat dry. At one point, the woman opened the trunk of the car and rummaged inside, pulling out a plastic-wrapped sandwich. Abigail's hopes were dashed as the woman tore off the wrapper and began to eat it.

"Please," she said, in a half-whisper. "Can I have some?"

The woman ignored her. Abigail repeated the request, and the woman glanced at her, her eyes cold and acidic. She had looked like that on the day she killed that boy. Abigail quickly lowered her head.

She shifted a bit, trying to find a position that would remove the tension from her shoulders. She suspected that if she laid down it would be slightly better, but she wasn't sure she'd be able to sit back up. For some reason, the thought scared her. Sitting up, even tied as she was, felt slightly safer than laying down on the floor.

The woman dug through her small handbag, and pulled out a small plastic water bottle. Abigail yearned for that bottle more than anything she'd ever wanted. She imagined the cold water running over her dry tongue, down her throat, taking away the terrible thirst that engulfed her.

"Please," she croaked, her voice alien to her ears. "I need some water."

The woman sipped from the bottle and screwed on the cap.

"Please!" Abigail half-sobbed. She didn't care if the woman hit her. She just wanted to drink.

The woman's head turned sharply. The same cold eyes looked at her, and Abigail could see something else in them: hate.

She walked over, her high heels tapping on the floor, the sound echoing in the empty space. She knelt by Abigail, and grabbed her chin like she had done before, forcing Abigail's face up.

"The child has its father's eyes," the woman said, her voice shrill, each syllable spat out like a piece of inedible gristle. "Twisted with lies and manipulation. I will not be deceived again! Not me, I've learned my lesson." She barked a small laugh that froze Abigail's heart. It didn't sound like the laughter of a woman. It sounded like the laughter of the hyenas in the *Lion King*. "I have what I need. I don't need this child anymore. It's time to finish what I started."

She rose and walked briskly to the green car. She pulled a set of keys from her pocket, and opened the trunk, then bent inside. When she rose, she held an object in her hand. For a moment Abigail didn't understand what she was seeing. The woman was cast in shadows, and the item in her hand looked like a large strawberry popsicle.

But then the woman moved, the object came into light, and Abigail felt all her muscles tense. It was a knife, its blade covered in dried blood. The woman walked slowly over to Abigail, her eyes glazing over, becoming detached.

The child, the woman had called her. Abigail's heart rattled in her chest as she tried to squirm away, feeling panic suffuse her. The woman talked about her like an object, something that could be discarded at will.

"My name is Abigail Lisman," she said, trying to overcome the shaking in her voice. "My mother's name is Naamit." She was about to mention her father, then realized it was smarter not to. "I have a friend named Gracie. We like watching cartoons together … Please!"

The woman's steps slowed, though she still approached Abigail, her eyes staring into the distance.

"I won second place in gymnastics last year. I have a small teddy bear my grandmother bought me when I was a year old. I still sleep with it, but I don't tell anyone."

The woman halted, her eyes focusing, the distant gaze gone.

"I love pop music and reading, and I love going to the beach more than anything. I'm twelve years old. For my birthday, I got a—"

"Shut up!" the woman barked. Her eyes were wide, angry. She looked at Abigail, her mouth twisted in a grimace of fury, then turned back, tossed the knife into the trunk, and shut it.

Picking up her water bottle and unscrewing the cap, she walked over to Abigail. With an abrupt motion, she brought the bottle to Abigail's lips, and Abigail could feel the edge of it cutting her gums, could taste the coppery taste of blood in her mouth. The woman tilted the bottle, and water poured into Abigail's mouth. She couldn't drink fast enough and she coughed and sputtered, water pouring down her chin on her shirt.

Finally, the woman pulled the bottle away. "You're still useful to me, child," she said, her voice trembling, halting. "I might need you as a hostage. But I promise you this." She suddenly smiled, a terrible, manic smile. "Your father will never see you again." She rose and walked to the car. She opened the door, sat inside, and shut it.

Abigail breathed hard, shaking. She was cold. Her drenched shirt clung to her skin, freezing her. She whimpered, dropping to the floor, as a fit of sobs overtook her.

TWENTY-THREE

Hannah woke up disoriented, and took a moment to get her bearings. She was in Jurgen's living room, lying on his couch, covered with a small blanket. She blinked several times, trying to figure out what had happened.

Lance Koche's e-mail account had been disappointing. He obviously almost never used it, preferring to use his business e-mail account instead. He had received five hundred and twelve e-mails in the past three years, and most of them were marked unread. There was a medical test result that turned out fine, some e-mails regarding a newsletter subscription, several receipts for books, some purchases of flowers, a necklace, a watch, and a television. There was a series of e-mails in which Koche discussed a private lawsuit with his lawyer—something to do with libel, but it was eventually settled out of court.

All of Jurgen's e-mails with Abigail's photos were there as well, except for the first one, sent to the business account. Jurgen and Hannah went over the e-mails twice. When she began nodding off, Jurgen had suggested she rest her eyes for ten minutes on the couch.

Jurgen still sat in front of the computer. "Good morning," he said without glancing back.

"What time is it?" she muttered.

"Just after seven."

"Damn it!" Hannah said, frustrated. "I didn't mean to sleep like that! Why didn't you wake me up?"

"I think you needed a few hours of sleep," Jurgen said. "How are you feeling now? Fresh?"

"I feel terrible," she muttered. "I'm going to make myself a cup of coffee."

"Make me one as well," he said distractedly.

She plodded to the kitchen and made two mugs of coffee, without bothering to wash them from the night before. She glanced outside the kitchen window. It didn't look like morning. The sky was completely hidden by the dark storm clouds, and a torrent of rain was washing the streets of Glenmore Park. She returned to the living room and handed one mug to Jurgen.

"There's something weird about the ransom," he said, sipping from his mug.

"Yeah?" Hannah said.

"You think that Koche knew the ransom letter would go viral, that people would donate the ransom money."

"That's right," Hannah said, suppressing a yawn.

"It's kind of a stretch. But suppose he really did know that. Why ask for three million? His debt was five million, right? He couldn't cover his debt with three million."

"Well, yeah," Hannah said. "But he could cover the debt with the ransom money and the rest of his inventory."

"But then he'd be bankrupt," Jurgen pointed out. "That doesn't sound like a good plan for a man like Koche. I mean … he'd end up with nothing."

"Maybe he planned to split with the money," Hannah said, shrugging.

Jurgen shook his head. "He doesn't seem like the kind of man to run away. You know what I think? Let's suppose Koche didn't conspire to kidnap Abigail."

"Okay," Hannah said. She wasn't about to argue. All the evidence indicated that Koche was guilty, but examining cases from different angles often proved useful.

"Suppose someone knew that Koche's business was already struggling. He could raise almost three million dollars for the ransom by selling his inventory, but then his business would be doomed."

"So you're saying someone kidnapped Abigail to ruin Koche?"

"We have several glaring suspects," Jurgen pointed at the screen. "This guy, with the libel suit. Your angry employee. A desperate competitor."

"The FBI profiler thought the kidnapper hated Abigail's parents," Hannah said slowly. "But no one knew that Abigail is Koche's daughter. No, that doesn't make any sense."

"He might have told someone!"

"I doubt it."

"We should at least check if—"

"We will," she snapped, "but your theory doesn't hold water."

He glanced backward at her. "You know, it isn't my job to figure this out. This is a police problem. I'm not on the force anymore; you guys kicked me out—"

"It was your own damn fault."

"Okay, listen—"

"The paternity test," Hannah interrupted him again. "The one that Naamit sent him. It isn't in this account."

Jurgen shrugged. "She could have just handed it to him."

"No, she sent it by e-mail," Hannah said. "Koche told us. She must have sent it to his business account."

"Yeah, okay."

"Someone could have read his e-mails in the office," Hannah said. "Maybe his computer was unlocked, and someone opened his mailbox and saw the paternity test."

"That's possible," Jurgen said. "The IT guy? I mean, he wouldn't even need to creep into the office. He could probably access all of Koche's e-mails from the server or something."

"Right," Hannah frowned. "But he didn't have a problem with Koche. Your theory requires a motive."

"Money is a good motive," Jurgen said.

"So now it's just about money? No, if someone else did it, he could have kidnapped just some random rich kid. Why go after Koche's biological daughter, whom he never even acknowledged? It doesn't make sense."

"So suppose someone who hated him in the company accessed his e-mail," Jurgen said.

"Yeah." Hannah chewed her lip. "But this doesn't match the fact that Darrel Simmons told his friend he was planning something big with his boss—"

"His employer," Jurgen said.

"What?"

"Earlier, you told me Simmons said that he was planning something big with his *employer*."

Hannah frowned. "He said … boss. Not employer."

"Uh-huh."

"The boss is the one who gives the instructions," Hannah said slowly. "Not necessarily the one in charge. Koche doesn't strike me as the kind of the man who tells his porters what to do."

Jurgen nodded slowly. "So who was Simmons's boss?" he asked. "Who told him what to do?"

Hannah thought. She could feel it, the puzzle disassembling in her brain, reassembling to create a completely different picture. It was like an optical illusion, where all of a sudden you realized the drawing you were looking at could be interpreted differently. It wasn't a middle aged man at all, it was a young woman.

Megan, Koche's assistant.

Jurgen had said she went over all of Koche's business e-mails. That was part of her *job*. Koche had bought a necklace and flowers using his private account. He had used that account because he wanted to surprise his *girlfriend*, the one who went over his business e-mails. And then, a year ago, the flower e-mails stopped. Koche had broken off the affair.

What had Koche said to them a few days before? *It wasn't the first time a woman tried to get me with this trick. They say they're on the pill, then suddenly, it turns out they're pregnant, and I'm supposed to pay the bills*. She'd thought he was talking about Naamit. But no, he was talking about someone else who turned out to be pregnant. Megan. And he didn't want her child. And later, she found out he'd had a child with another woman.

"Megan, his personal assistant," Hannah said, her words fast, her heart beating quickly. "She saw the paternity test. And your first e-mail. She knew Koche had taken an interest in his biological daughter. She had access to *everything*. She knew how much money it would take to destroy Koche's business completely. And she was probably the person who managed the porters. She was Simmons's boss…" She thought for a moment. Koche claimed he never hired anyone with a criminal record. "She was planning this when she hired Simmons. She knew about his criminal record, probably thought he would be able to help her pull it off. That was what Simmons was talking about. He was planning a big job with Megan, his boss. They were planning to kidnap Koche's biological daughter! And … holy crap, this matches Zoe's profile of the kidnapper!"

"Who's Zoe?"

"The FBI forensic psychologist," she said distractedly, thinking. Horror began to seep into her mind. "Simmons must have thought they were going to return Abigail. But that might never have been Megan's intention. Maybe she wanted to ruin Koche's business and his life, killing his daughter. That's why she killed Simmons."

"So you think she killed Abigail?" Jurgen asked, his voice soft.

"Maybe." Her voice trembled. "Or not. We never found a body. She would have left Abigail dead with Simmons, right?"

Jurgen shrugged, his face blank.

"She might intend to use her as a hostage," Hannah said. "Or to make a spectacle of Abigail's death. I don't think she's dead yet. I think Koche would have known if she was. I think Megan would have let him know."

Jurgen nodded, and Hannah could imagine what he thought. He thought that Hannah didn't really believe Abigail was alive, she was just hoping for it. And he was right.

———

Mitchell was doing what he did best: sitting in front of a computer, sifting through information. He was in Koche Toolworks, with Agent Mancuso, Agent Ward, and several other FBI agents, and he felt very out of place. He mentally cursed Hannah yet again for not showing up. When she was there, they were the Glenmore Park PD team, participating in a joint investigation. When she wasn't there he was "sore thumb Lonnie," the only one who wasn't an FBI agent.

He was reading all the e-mails Lance Koche had sent or received that included any reference to Darrel Simmons. There weren't many. In fact, so far it was hard to prove the two men even knew each other beyond the fact that Simmons worked at Koche Toolworks. Koche didn't have a lot to do with his porters. He let one of his underlings do that job.

He sighed and leaned back. Perhaps his time would be better spent looking again for any address which might be used to hide Abigail Lisman. The night before, he had made a list of hundreds of addresses mentioned in Koche's e-mails. He opened the spreadsheet and started going over them.

He heard Agent Mancuso answer her phone. "Hello? Yes, Detective?"

He lost interest in the spreadsheet, listening to the phone call.

"No, she isn't here. No one is. I assume Koche's lawyers told his employees to—"

She stopped talking. Mitchell turned around and looked at her. She frowned, listening intently to the other side of the call.

"I see," she finally said. "I'll send a team over to her house. Get over here as soon as you can." She hung up. "That was

Detective Shor. Koche's personal assistant might be our missing kidnapper. Her name is Megan—"

"Shaffer," Agent Ward said. "Megan Shaffer. I have her address right here." He checked something on his computer. The room had gone completely silent, everyone tense, waiting. "32 Old Quarry Road, apartment 13," he finally said.

Mancuso nodded and pursed her lips. After thinking for a moment she said, "Okay. Detective Shor gave me good reasons for her suspicions. It's not definite, but I don't want to blow this in case she's right. Agents Constantine, Fuller, Manning, and Ward, we're going to Megan Shaffer's apartment. I'll have SWAT rendezvous with us there."

Several agents leaped from their chairs. Mitchell grabbed his keys and gun, and stood up as well. Mancuso was already on the phone, talking to someone, asking for a SWAT team. She strode out of the room, the other agents in her wake. Mitchell was about to follow when he noticed that Agent Ward was still sitting down, frowning at his computer.

"What is it?" Mitchell asked.

"It's an apartment building," Ward said. "There was a garage in Simmons house, and we think they used it to get her in and out of their vehicle. But Megan would have to take her out of the car right on the street to get her into her apartment."

"They might have underground parking," Mitchell suggested.

"It would still be the building's public parking," Ward said. "She's been very careful so far. Would she really carry the kid up to her apartment in a building, where she could meet any of her neighbors on the way?"

"Maybe Abigail isn't with her," Mitchell said. "She might be…" He didn't finish the sentence.

Ward nodded. "Could be," he said. "But in that case, there's no reason to hurry. Four agents and a SWAT team are on their way to Megan Shaffer's home. They'll get her. But let's assume Abigail is alive. It's an assumption that makes me happy."

"You're just like Hannah," Mitchell said.

Agent Ward paused, then nodded slowly. "Thanks, I think," he said. "So … where would Megan take her?"

"We should check her computer," Mitchell suggested.

"That's a good idea. I'll call the IT guy, see if he can give me her password."

Clint went over to the desk outside Koche's office, where Megan usually worked, his phone to his ear. Mitchell listened distractedly to the agent talking on the phone. Finally, he called Hannah.

"Yeah?" Hannah said.

"Why do you think Megan is the kidnapper?"

"I'll tell you when I get there, Mitchell. But she didn't do it with Lance Koche. She did it to get back at him. I think they had an affair."

"Yeah, okay," he said, and hung up. If Hannah was right, Lance Koche wasn't the one who had called the shots. All their work going over his property, checking his warehouses…

He paused, then he sat in front of the computer. Koche had told them he sold some of his inventory to pay for his debt. Would that mean he didn't need the storage space? He checked his list of addresses. There—two warehouses that Koche used to rent, and had cleared out a month before, terminating the contract. Mitchell found the owner in Koche's contacts and called him.

"Billy Fallow, Storage Solutions," the man answered almost immediately.

"Hello," Mitchell said. "My name is Detective Lonnie, from the Glenmore Park PD. Lance Koche used to rent two warehouses from you, right?"

"That's right," Billy said, his voice suspicious. "But he doesn't anymore. Bastard terminated the contract. Refused to pay the fine, told me there are rats in my warehouses. Threatened to sue. Damn asshole, there are no rats—"

"Mr. Fallow, is anyone else renting those warehouses right now?"

"No offense, Detective, but that's private information. If you get a warrant—"

"I'm investigating the Abigail Lisman kidnapping, and every minute counts," Mitchell said. "You don't have to give me their names. Just answer one question. Is one of those warehouses rented by Megan Shaffer?"

"Yeah, that's right," the man said, sounding surprised. "Contacted me two days after Koche emptied the place. Said she heard I had an available warehouse. There aren't many warehouses in Glenmore Park, Detective. She was lucky to find—"

"Thank you for your help," Mitchell said and hung up. "Ward!" he shouted. "I know where she is!"

———

Hannah washed her face in Jurgen's bathroom, trying to remove the cobwebs of sleep from her face. She put some water on her hair and attempted to give it a reasonable shape, failing spectacularly. That would teach her to sleep on someone's couch.

The hell with it. She needed to be with Mancuso and the rest. She came out of the bathroom and looked for her handbag.

"Where are you going?" Jurgen asked.

"I don't know yet," she said. "Mancuso told me to get to Koche Toolworks."

"Wouldn't you rather go to Megan's house?" Jurgen asked.

"I'd rather do what I'm told for once," Hannah said shortly. "Thanks for all your help."

"Can I come with you?"

"Absolutely not." She opened the front door. "I really appreciate everything," she said. "You're not such a bad—"

Her phone rang. Mitchell. She answered. "Yeah?"

"Hannah?" he shouted. He sounded as if he was riding in a car. "I'm with Agent Ward. I don't think Megan is in her apartment. She rented a warehouse a month ago. Down on Marsh Creek Road! We're all on our way, but it'll take us some time, it's on the other goddamn side of the city—"

"Marsh Creek Road?" she said, surprised. "I'm just five minutes away."

"What? Where are you?"

"I'm at Jurgen Adler's house."

"You're what? Why?"

"Never mind! I'm going there now!"

"Hannah, listen!" Mitchell half yelled. "This could be a hostage situation. Don't do anything stupid! Wait for the SWAT team!"

Said the man who cornered a serial killer with a hostage, Hannah thought. "I'll just look around," she said, leaving the apartment and running down the stairs. "I won't go inside unless Abigail is in immediate danger."

"Hann ... Don't ... Megan..." The reception was breaking up in the stairway. She reached the exit and froze.

A storm raged outside. The street had completely morphed, the water pouring down, flooding the road. The wind bent the treetops, pushing the torrent of rain sideways.

"Oh, hell!" Hannah muttered. Last night she had found a parking spot a few blocks away, no more than a five-minute walk from the building. But now it would be a twenty-minute swim against the wind.

"Where are we going?" Jurgen asked, materializing beside her.

"You're not going anywhere," Hannah said angrily, bracing herself for the struggle toward her car.

"This is my car right here," Jurgen said, pointing at the blue Ford Fiesta parked directly in front of them. Hannah recognized it from a previous encounter.

"Okay," she said. "But I'm driving. Give me the keys."

"No one drives Sharon but me," Jurgen said.

"Sharon? Seriously? Jurgen, I've seen you drive."

"Take it or leave it."

She hesitated for a moment. "Fine!" she finally said. "Come on."

Jurgen pointed the remote at the car and unlocked it. Although it took no more than three steps to get to the car, both of them were soaking wet by the time they were inside.

"Where to?"

"There's a storage facility on Marsh Creek Road," she said.

"I know it," he said. He started the car, and the engine revved as he navigated the car out of the parking spot.

The road was mostly empty. The few cars on it drove slowly as the rain spattered against them. This was Glenmore Park, and the residents were used to snow and rain, but people still preferred to stay at home when the weather could be described as "the wrath of God."

Jurgen drove fast, his car screeching as he passed a small van. Hannah curbed the desire to tell him to slow down. She wanted to get to the storage facility as fast as possible

"So, do you want to barge inside, save the girl from Megan?" Jurgen asked.

"No," Hannah said. "It's too dangerous. This is not the time to be a hero. We'll get there, make sure she's there, and wait for SWAT. They can disable Megan and secure Abigail without anyone getting hurt."

Jurgen nodded. Hannah stared grimly ahead. It was hard to see even three feet in any direction. The darkness of the rain surrounded them, swallowing the car's lights whole. The water on the road was deep in many places, and Hannah prayed they wouldn't get stuck. Damn the weather! Couldn't this storm have happened a day or two later?

Two red lights appeared in front of them: tail lights. In front of them was a white Buick, and like all the other cars on the road, it crawled slowly ahead. Jurgen sharply swerved the steering wheel to pass, and Sharon moved into the other lane. He hit the gas, the car's engine screaming in anger as they overtook the Buick.

And then, out of the darkness, a pair of bright yellow lights—headlights—appeared. Close. Too close.

"Jurgen!" Hannah screamed, her voice swallowed by the roar of the engine as Jurgen floored the pedal. He swiveled the steering wheel, their car veering sharply back to their own lane, the Buick behind them honking furiously—and the beam of Sharon's headlights hit the windshield of the opposite car for a second as it breezed by.

Hannah stared in front of her, shocked, her mind processing what she had just seen. "Turn the car around!" she screamed at Jurgen.

"What? Why?"

"That was Megan! She was driving in that damn car! She's getting away!"

TWENTY-FOUR

Abigail screamed her throat hoarse, half in terror, half in desperation. This time, the woman hadn't bothered with knocking her out. She'd just dumped her, still tied up, in the trunk of the car, then shut it. The darkness was suffocating. Could she run out of air? It felt as if she could. She breathed heavily, feeling the vibration of the car.

A few minutes after she was shut in the trunk, the engine hummed into life and the car began to move. Then, almost immediately after, a terrible roar filled her ears and she began screaming again, twisting, kicking around her with her tied legs.

It was rain, she finally realized. They were outside, and it was raining on the trunk.

Exhausted, she lay still, feeling the bumps in the road as they jarred her bones. She ached all over. She was tired; she wanted it all to be over. She half regretted stopping the woman the night before. She was going to die anyway. What was the point of prolonging it?

She closed her eyes and thought of her parents. On rainy evenings, her mother would sometimes get a board game, like Monopoly or Scrabble, and the three of them would play together. Sometimes her dad made popcorn. She could almost smell the aroma of the warm popcorn as her dad placed the bowl on the table, always warning her to avoid the uncooked kernels.

She'd never see them again. She wanted to cry, wanted to sob, wanted to mourn herself. But she was too tired to do even that.

Something was hurting her leg. She could feel it, a sharp object, jostled out of its place by one of the road bumps, now wedged against her ankle. Another bump and she screamed in pain. The thing had cut into her.

The knife. The bloody knife the woman had threatened her with yesterday. She had thrown it into the trunk. Abigail twisted around, trying to grab the sharp object, but she only managed to cut her leg again. It felt deep, and her head was dizzy with pain.

Switching strategies, she tried to kick the blade away. She could try to get it closer to her hands—or at least further from her bleeding legs.

The roar of the rain mingled with the hum of the engine and the keen whistle of the wind as she kicked again and again. She missed twice, her every movement clumsy and cumbersome. Her third kick hit the mark. She felt the contact, heard the thing clattering somewhere, but she didn't know where. She had lost it.

She twisted very carefully, afraid that a sudden movement would impale her on the sharp blade. Slowly she moved like a snake in the small confines of the trunk, trying to feel with her entire body for the knife.

Her stomach hit it first—the knife's handle, by the touch, to her immense relief. It was a slow process, but she managed to turn around, her fingers clumsily grabbing the handle.

The blade was sharp, but it was difficult to cut the rope tying her wrists. She cut herself twice more, the second time nearly dropping the knife. Then, all of a sudden, she could feel the bite of the rope ease. She was loose!

She whimpered again, this time in relief, as she clenched and unclenched her fists, feeling the blood flow into her hands.

Once she was done, cutting the ropes on her ankles was easy.

She stopped to think. She was untied. She had a knife. Now what?

The rain intensified, the noise on the car's roof deafening. Hannah found it almost impossible to hear anything above the torrent. She was yelling at Mitchell on the phone.

"No!" she screamed. "We're not going to the warehouse! We're following Megan's car, damn it!"

At least, she prayed it was Megan's car. They were definitely following a dim set of taillights, the only ones they had spotted after they had turned around. The car they were tailing was driving very fast considering the weather, which made Hannah suspect they were chasing the right one. Of course, it could also be a dumb college student with a death wish. Jurgen's face was a frozen mask of concentration as he followed the car. In this rain, the taillights could disappear at any moment.

"Is Abigail in the car?" Mitchell yelled back.

"I don't know!" Hannah shouted. "I only saw Megan in the driver's seat. Abigail could be in the back seat, or she could be in the trunk!"

"I'll talk to Mancuso, she'll send some agents to the warehouse, check if anyone's there!" Mitchell said. "Can you describe the car?"

Damn it. The best she could come up with was *it's wet*. "I couldn't see it very clearly. The color's dark! Black, or dark green, I'm not sure, and—"

"It's a dark green Honda Civic," Jurgen said, his fists clenching the wheel tightly. "License plate ends with the digits three nine two."

Hannah glanced at him in amazement. She had been with the man for less than twelve hours, and he had already displayed a frustrating amount of talent. She repeated the description for Mitchell.

"Okay, where are you?" Mitchell asked. He had to repeat the question three times until Hannah understood.

"She's driving up Sycamore Pass Road!" Hannah shouted. "We just passed Johnson's Bend." Johnson's Bend was named after the Johnson family, who had lost control of their car on the bend, flipped three times, and crashed into a tree, killing them all. It represented the edge of the urban part of Glenmore Park. Beyond it there was a large reservation area that spanned the rest of the way, until it ended at Route 128.

"So she's driving north." Mitchell said.

"I think so."

"Okay! I'll talk to Mancuso, give you an update as soon as possible!" he yelled and hung up.

Sycamore Pass Road was completely empty except for their car and the car they were following. It was a route best avoided in bad weather, since large tree branches often littered the road; sometimes, in bad storms, whole trees fell and blocked the way. But it was the fastest way to get to the highway.

"Where do you think she's going?" Jurgen asked.

"I don't know," Hannah said darkly. "I think she's mostly just trying to get as far as possible."

"How will we stop her?" Jurgen asked. "I mean, if she has Abigail—"

"I don't know."

"We can't force her off the road if—"

"Damn it, Jurgen, I don't know! But we're not going to lose—look out!"

A huge branch hit their hood, then flew off. Jurgen swerved, momentarily losing control of the car, then he straightened, his fingers white with effort.

"Jesus!" he said. "This damn road! We need to get the hell away from it."

"That's what's going to happen," Hannah said darkly. "She's getting on 128. Keep your eyes on her."

She had a feeling Megan had noticed them. The woman was about to try and lose them amidst the traffic on the highway. And Hannah did not intend to let that happen.

"We're trying to catch up with Detective Shor!" Mitchell yelled into the phone. "She's on the suspect's tail on 128!"

"Where are you, Mitchell?" Mancuso asked.

"Just getting on Sycamore Pass Road from Clayton Road!" Mitchell shouted. "Mancuso, you need to blockade 128. We can't let her escape!"

"I'll handle it, Detective," Mancuso said. "Is Detective Shor driving on her own?"

"What's that? I can't hear you!" Mitchell shouted. He had heard her just fine, but this was a discussion he wasn't about to get into.

"I said—"

"Agent Mancuso, you're breaking up! I will call again once we're on 128. Just get that goddamn blockade ready!" he hung up.

Agent Ward's Chevy hummed like a jet plane, and Mitchell suspected it had a similar engine. The car hurtled down the road at breakneck speed. Mitchell's heart hammered in terror. Could Ward even see anything beyond the bridge of his nose in this weather?

"Ward, slow down, we're getting to Johnson's Bend!" He shouted.

"What?"

"Slow do—Shit!"

They reached the bend too fast. Ward turned the wheel as hard as he could, hitting the brakes, and the car swerved out of control, running into the opposite lane. Oncoming headlights were getting closer frighteningly fast, as the car skidded, screeching ... then suddenly veered back to its own lane, the headlights in the opposite lane blowing past them.

Mitchell heard a loud screaming, and realized it was coming from his own throat. He stopped and took a deep breath, looking down. A surprising item was lying on the floor, by his feet. It was a lacy white bra.

"Ward," he said in a shaky voice, "please don't do that again."

"Okay," Ward said, his voice tense. "I'm ... sorry."

"There's a bra on the floor," Mitchell said.

"Oh."

There was a moment of silence.

"It must have been under the seat, and the sharp turn ... dislodged it," Ward said.

"Right."

Another moment of silence followed as Ward carefully accelerated again. "It's not mine," he finally said.

"Whose is it? Your girlfriend's?"

"No. I don't have a girlfriend. It belongs to an acquaintance."

"Oh," Mitchell said, and grinned. "I wish I had acquaintances like that."

Ward glanced at him, his face unreadable. "Yeah," he finally said. "She's something else."

―――

Megan realized that she had been gritting her teeth for the past twenty minutes, ever since she had noticed she was being followed. The car on her tail kept pace with her as she accelerated, zigzagging between the cars on 128. Perhaps she should be trying to camouflage herself in the traffic, but whenever she decided to slow down, she would notice the headlights of the car following her getting closer, and her foot would step on the gas pedal.

When had she stopped following the plan? When had she started making abrupt decisions, obeying her instincts instead of her brain?

Was it when she had killed that boy that broke into Darrel's home, letting the child see her face? Or when Lance had shoved his hand under her skirt after the police showed up, trying to get her to cheer him up for old times' sake?

Or maybe the breaking point was when she had decided to kill her partner.

Whatever the moment was, she hardly knew what she was doing anymore. The plan had been to wait a week after the kidnapping and then leave Glenmore Park for a long vacation out of the States, probably in Mexico. She'd still thought she was going to Mexico the night before. But then she'd turned north when she realized she was being followed. No good reason behind it, just something in her mind that whispered she should.

She should have killed the child. She shouldn't have killed Darrel. She should never have kidnapped the child. She should never have slept with Lance.

Shoulda, woulda, coulda.

She had three million dollars in a duffel bag in the back seat, a kidnapped child in the trunk, and she was headed north on a very stormy day, being tailed by at least one car. What would Megan the planner tell her to do?

Megan the planner would say that she should assume whoever was following her was in contact with the FBI. Which meant blockades. And helicopters. Except, as long as this God-sent storm was blowing, no helicopters for the FBI.

Fine. Blockades on major roads. Like 128.

Megan the planner would tell her to get off the highway, and to turn west as soon as possible. Then go south, road-tripping down to Mexico.

Megan the planner would tell her the child is a useful hostage right now. It was the only reason her tail was keeping its distance. But once she lost her tail, she should lose the child. The child was a liability.

Should she kill the child, or set her free?

Megan the planner couldn't care less.

Megan the impulsive angel of vengeance grinned.

She got closer to an exit sign. *Exit 56*, it read. *Scotland Rd Newbury.*

Megan the impulsive angel of vengeance got in the leftmost lane. The car chasing her did the same.

And then she abruptly twisted the steering wheel, crossing the two lanes, the car thumping as it got off the road, missing the exit by a few feet, driving on mud and grass. For a moment she thought she might skid, or get stuck. But she didn't.

———

"She's getting off!" Hannah screamed. "Follow her!"

Jurgen veered, then saw the headlights in the rearview mirror. He screamed, and twisted the wheel back, the car squealing as it went back to the leftmost lane. There was a sickening crunch as the oncoming car's side mirror crashed into their own side mirror.

"No, damn it!" Hannah shouted at him. "She's getting away!"

There was nothing he could do about it. They breezed past the exit. Hannah screeched at him, cursing, her face twisted in a mask of disappointment and rage. Jurgen slowed the car, taking a deep breath. There was one chance, only one chance.

They had missed Exit 56, the exit to Scotland Road.

But they hadn't missed the entrance where Scotland Road merged onto Highway 128.

As it neared, he checked the rearview mirror. Two oncoming cars. Too close? Maybe. But they only had one shot at this. Ignoring Hannah's yelling, he took a deep breath, then hit the brakes, turning the wheel.

The car skidded out of control, spinning, the world spinning with it, the trees filling their view as they turned and turned.

His foot pressed the gas pedal, and Sharon, God bless her, hummed in response and jolted forward, driving down the entrance to 128, going the wrong way. Jurgen prayed to all the gods he knew that no cars would be driving up the entrance to the highway.

Fortunately, he knew a lot of gods. The road was empty. They reached Scotland Road, and Jurgen moved into the correct lane. He realized he wasn't breathing, and exhaled loudly. Megan's taillights were dim in the distance … but visible.

"What was it that you said about my driving?" he asked.

Hannah said nothing. She was clearly shocked by his awesomeness. Also, she looked as if she was about to faint. He decided to let her recuperate as he accelerated.

Abigail finally managed to locate a … thing. Feeling it with her fingers, it appeared to be a small handle.

It would open the trunk; she was sure of it.

She curbed her desire to pull the thing immediately. Once she opened the trunk, the woman would know she was free. She would stop the car, get out and kill her. Abigail had seen the look in the woman's eyes, knew she wouldn't hesitate. It was worth considering.

What were her other options?

She could do nothing. Wait. Stab the woman when she opened the trunk.

But who knew when that would happen? Who knew where they were driving to? What if the woman was joining a gang of kidnappers? Abigail would not be able to fight them off. No, that wasn't a good option.

She touched the other side of the trunk. It was soft, leathery. The back seat. She could cut the seat, crawl through there. Put her knife to the woman's throat. Make her stop the car. Except … It would take time to cut the seat. It would be clumsy to crawl through. And she was weak from her day without food or sleep, from having her limbs tied up. That, too, would end badly.

Option three. Pull the handle. The trunk would pop open. The car was going fast; she could feel it. She would jump out and roll onto the road. Even in the unlikely event that the road was empty and no car hit her, she'd most certainly die. Bad option. Very bad option.

And those were her only three options. She was about to die. She nearly burst into tears again.

But at least if she jumped out of the car, there was a chance someone would find her body. Her mom would know what had happened to her. And the woman who had kidnapped her would lose.

She pulled the handle.

Nothing happened.

She nearly burst out laughing. Well. That option was gone. So what was it? Cut though the seat, or wait and see what happens.

She pulled the handle again, with all her strength,

And the trunk lid popped open, the rain drenching her body.

"Mitchell!" Hannah shouted into her phone. "Where are you?"

"We're driving up 128!" Mitchell shouted. "The FBI barricaded the road just before the bridge! She'll be trapped, Hannah. She'll have to stop!"

"We're not on 128 anymore!" Hannah yelled back. "The bitch got off on Scotland Road!"

There was a moment of silence. "Damn it!" Mitchell finally said.

"Yeah."

"Okay, listen…" Another pause. "Okay, I've got the map here. You're driving toward Newburyport, right?"

"Right!"

"Okay, We'll get off at the next exit, and get to the Newburyport bridge before she does. We'll create our own damn blockade. She has nowhere to go, Hannah, I swear. We'll stop her on the bridge."

"What if she has Abigail?"

"We have to stop her, Hannah. We'll see where that gets us!"

"Okay," Hannah hung up. "Mitchell says there's a bridge up ahead," she told Jurgen. "They'll block it. She'll have nowhere to go."

"Unless she drives into Newburyport," Jurgen said.

"Yeah, well … that's all we've got."

"Where are all the damn FBI agents?" Jurgen exploded. "Why aren't they here?"

Hannah shook her head. "They're not as good as we are," she said, grinning at him.

"Yeah, yeah, tell that to—Oh, shit!"

Hannah looked ahead to see what had startled him, and her mouth gaped. The trunk of Megan's car had opened. It was hard to see, but a small head seemed to be peering out of it.

"That's her!" Hannah screamed, half in panic, half in joy. "She's alive!"

"Not for long, if she jumps," Jurgen said, his jaw clenched. "We're going over seventy. The fall will crush every bone in her body."

"We're out of time," Hannah muttered, her mind whirling with possibilities. "Get us closer!"

"What are you going to do?"

She ignored him and hunched down in her seat. Then, before he could say anything, she kicked upward.

The windshield cracked.

"What the hell are you—"

She kicked again, and some pieces broke free. Rain drops started hitting her in her face.

"Hannah, stop that!"

She kicked a third time. A huge part of the windshield broke away, tumbling off the car. The rain drenched them both.

"Damn it, Hannah!" Jurgen screamed at her.

"Get us closer!" Hannah shouted at him. "If she jumps on our car, she'll be fine! We're both driving at the same speed!"

"You're insane!"

She took out her gun and started smashing what was left of the windshield. Pieces scattered everywhere.

They were out of options. They were out of time.

The rain poured on Abigail as she looked around her. She was on an empty road, in the middle of nowhere, surrounded by trees. The car was driving terribly fast, even faster than she had thought. And another car was following it, getting closer.

If she jumped, she would die for sure.

The car she was in suddenly swerved left and then right. The woman had noticed the trunk was open. Was she trying to knock Abigail out? Abigail hunched down, her heart hammering. She screamed for help, though she knew no one could possibly hear her.

And then there were lights around her. Street lights! They were driving through a town! She could see houses.

The streets were empty, except for an occasional car driving by. The vehicle she was riding in was still hurtling way too fast.

The car behind them was now very close. To her shock, she could see their front windshield was missing. The driver, an Asian man, was steering with his eyes half shut against the violent rain that hit his face. By his side sat a small, pale woman, her wet hair whipping in the wind. She shouted something at Abigail, but the words were impossible to hear. What did the woman want? What had happened to their window?

"Help me!" Abigail screamed.

The woman motioned with her arms—motioned at herself, as if saying *come here*.

It was insane. The woman was crazy. Did she think Abigail could fly?

The car grew closer; it was now only six feet away. Five feet. Four feet.

They went under a bridge, then another one. Abigail could hear the *whoosh* sound as they did, and the air vibrated around her. She was petrified with fear.

Three feet.

The woman yelled something again. Over and over.

Abigail.

She was calling Abigail's name. And motioning for her to come, to fly over to their car. Abigail shook her head, feeling her heart plummet in her chest. Surely the woman didn't want her to…

She could feel the road tilting. They were going up. Up a bridge. Above a river. She could see the water below, as the wind hit them, creating torrential waves, small boats rising and falling.

"Abigail!" the woman screamed. "Jump!"

Abigail stood up, hesitating, the car's tremors vibrating through her feet.

―――

Megan was out of options. The road was blocked ahead; they had managed to outmaneuver her. In the rearview mirror, she saw the open trunk and knew that, beyond it, her pursuers were close.

She could only think of Lance Koche. How he had told her coldly that she had to get an abortion, that he would pay for it. How he had terminated their affair, but still occasionally copped a feel, as if to emphasize that he could. How excited he had been by the prospect of a daughter from another woman, a daughter he had never known.

The bastard. She hadn't managed to ruin him and his business, but she could still destroy the prospect of fatherhood he'd thought he had.

It was time to end it. It was time to end it all.

―――

Abigail tensed, steadying herself, and the car veered right, hitting the edge of the bridge, the metal screeching. She fell back into the trunk. The car behind crashed into them, the trunk's metal frame bending and tearing noisily. She was sure she was about to die.

And then the noise stopped and their vehicle was on the road again, away from the edge.

The kidnapper had tried to drive them off the bridge. She wanted to kill them both.

She would try again. There was no more time.

She stood up, thought *on the count of three. One…*

And then she jumped.

Hannah could see the blockade that Mitchell and Clint had created at the end of the bridge. Their car blocked two lanes. Another car, probably commandeered for this purpose, blocked the other lanes.

Megan could see the blockade, too.

When she suddenly hit the bridge's edge, Hannah died inside. She saw Abigail lose her footing, knew there was no way she could stop this from happening, that the car was about to fly off the bridge.

The bridge's safety wall somehow held. Megan's car veered to the left, moving away from the edge. Hannah screamed—she didn't even know what, or why. Megan was trying to kill herself, and take Abigail with her in the process. A final attempt at revenge against a man who had hurt her.

And then Abigail stood again and Hannah yelled at her to jump. *Jump*!

And Abigail jumped.

Their car was driving slightly faster than Megan's as Abigail landed on their hood, rolling toward the broken windshield. Hannah heard the *thump* as Abigail's head hit the edge of the windshield, and the rest of her body fell into the car. And then Abigail was in her arms, her head lolling, and Hannah was crying her name, crying for Jurgen to stop, crying for something to happen.

She never saw Megan's car clearing the edge of the bridge. She just heard it, the sound of metal crushing and tearing, of Jurgen cursing. All Hannah could look at was Abigail's lifeless face in her hands. Her eyes were closed, her skin cold.

The car stopped.

"Abigail? Abigail!" Hannah shouted.

The rain drenched her as she put her hand on the girl's chest.

And when she felt it heave, and Abigail's eyelids fluttered, Hannah felt grateful for the rain that drenched her, and masked her tears.

TWENTY-FIVE

The bartender put the tequila shot in front of Hannah, then gave her a small plate with a slice of lemon and some salt. Hannah ignored the lemon and the salt, and downed the tequila in one quick gulp. She grimaced, unused to the taste. She usually stuck to beer, but tonight she needed more.

"One more," she said to the bartender.

He looked at her, raising an eyebrow. "Yeah, you seemed to really enjoy the last one," he said, placing another shot glass on the bar. Hannah looked at the liquid as he poured.

"Maybe it's an acquired taste," she said.

He nodded. "It is, but not this stuff. You want to acquire a taste, going for the cheapest bottle is not the right way to do it."

She tilted her head, drinking the sharp-tasting liquid. "Okay, then," she said. "Give me whatever you think is the right sort of tequila."

The bartender glanced at Bernard, who sat by her side. "It's fine," Bernard said. "I'm driving her home."

The bartender muttered to himself, turning around.

"So," Bernard said. "I couldn't help but notice that you switched partners three times in the last month."

"How's that?" Hannah asked, playing with the empty shot glass.

"First there was Agent Ward," Bernard said, raising one finger. "A fed. I get it. The feds get invited to all the cool parties."

"He wasn't really my partner," Hannah mumbled, feeling the strands of regret that were still linked to Clint in her mind.

"Then, Mitchell Lonnie," Bernard said, raising a second finger. "I guess the mopey eyes got to you? Because I know that, aside from that, I'm way more handsome." He grinned at her.

Hannah smiled back, hoping her slight blush couldn't be seen in the dim lighting of the bar.

"And then, none other than my previous partner, Jurgen Adler," Bernard said, raising a third finger. "That one hurt. A stab in the back."

"He wasn't my partner, for God's sake," Hannah said angrily. "He just had some important info. He was a witness in the case."

"And now you're back with me," Bernard said, ignoring her. "You know what that tells me?"

"What?"

Bernard quirked an eyebrow. "That they all pale in comparison to my superior detective skills, and my exceptional hair."

Hannah burst out laughing. "You're full of shit."

"She can laugh!" Bernard said in mock surprise. "I thought you'd forgotten how."

The grim mood that had enveloped Hannah for the past week returned. She frowned.

"Hannah, I'll lay it out simple. You saved the girl, got her back to her grateful parents, and the kidnappers will never hurt anyone again. Case closed, lets party."

"Uh-huh. A girl and her family traumatized, three dead people. I really did well there."

"Give yourself a break."

"She nearly died at least twice, Bernard," Hannah said. "I could have figured it out faster, if I wasn't so wrapped up in my…" she hesitated. "Stuff."

Bernard shook his head. "You can't just abandon your life whenever a case pops up."

"Did you see the headlines about the case?"

Bernard nodded. "Apparently you single-handedly saved Abigail Lisman." He grinned. "That's amazing!"

"Yeah, and that's not the only drivel they had out there. Did you see how they portrayed Megan Shaffer? They said she had been used by Darrel Simmons, who was the criminal mastermind behind it all. Made her sound like a poor, weak woman, who killed herself in the end in regret and fear."

"Yeah, well…" Bernard shrugged. "Why do you care?"

Hannah didn't answer. She didn't know why it bugged her so much, but it did. She drank the third tequila shot the bartender handed her. If it tasted better, she didn't have the palate to discern it.

"I also saw a small quote from Lance Koche," Bernard said. "He was shocked or something."

"That bastard," Hannah said. "It all started because of the affair he had with his assistant. You know what's crazy? Megan Shaffer kidnapped Abigail to hurt him, make him go bankrupt by paying the ransom … but he never did! He would have let the kid die. I mean … even though Megan hated him, she still believed he was a better man than he really was."

"Crazy," Bernard said, nodding in agreement. "You know what else is crazy? The way you obsess about a case after it's done. To quote the *Glenmore Park Gazette*, you cracked the case. It's done, Hannah. You did good. Learn to enjoy life's little victories. You know what I'll do? I'll buy you a cake. With whipped cream. We'll throw a little Hannah-cracked-the-case party. I'll invite the entire squad."

"I'll kill you if you do that," Hannah said evenly. She wasn't entirely sure if Bernard was kidding or serious.

"I'm not worried. We've already established you can't really partner with anyone else but me," Bernard said.

They sat in silence for a few minutes. Hannah thought about Abigail, Naamit, and Ron. About their future.

"Anything else?" the bartender asked.

"Just the tab, please," Hannah told him. She looked at Bernard. "I'll try, okay?"

He smiled at her. "That's all I can really ask," he said.

———

As Abigail walked into her room for the first time since the kidnapping, she was struck by immense relief, all of her muscles becoming rubbery at once. She managed to stumble to her own bed, and lay down gingerly. Her head still hurt, even though a week had passed since the night of the storm, when she hit it. She had spent the whole week in the hospital.

She was relieved to be with her parents again, but staying at the hospital had stretched her nerves beyond the breaking point, and she'd found herself crying uncontrollably more than once. Everyone thought they understood. She'd been through so much. And she had a concussion. Crying was understandable.

They understood nothing. She'd tried to explain it only once, to her mother, but she could immediately see the confusion in her mother's eyes.

After a whole week alone in a dimly lit basement, everything was just too much. Too many doctors and nurses and psychologists. Too many detectives and FBI agents asking her questions. Too many friends and relatives visiting constantly, bringing her gifts. Too much light.

She couldn't even begin to handle her so-called "fame." Gracie told her that *everyone in the world* knew who she was. Though she thought it was an exaggeration, she had seen herself on too many news channels to remain ignorant. Her mom tried to shield her from it, but it was impossible. Seven different hospital patients and two nurses asked to take a selfie with her. Reporters tried to talk to her several times.

Once she was given a new phone, she logged into her Instagram account, saw the famous ransom pictures and the thousands of comments, and logged out. They had to give her a mild sedative to help her fall asleep that night.

All she wanted was to curl up in her bed, her mother by her side, caressing her hair.

And now, finally, they'd released her to go home. She lay on the bed, staring at the ceiling.

"Abby, do you want something to drink? Or eat?" her mother asked, standing in the doorway. She had that tone; Abigail had learned to spot it lately. She was worried, but tried not to let it show.

"No thanks," she answered, "I'm not hungry." She'd been losing weight, something else her parents were worried about. Part of it was the concussion—it made her nauseous, and if she ate too much she threw up. Part of it was just the mess in her head.

Her mother came in and kissed her on the forehead. Then she walked out, half tiptoeing, as if the noise of her footsteps was too much for Abigail's fragile state.

Her phone blipped. She glanced at the screen. It was a message from Gracie.

Back home yet?

She typed in *yup, just got here*

Everyone at school are asking about you

She stared at the screen, tensing up. Was this how it would be now? She'd go to school, and people would constantly talk to her about the kidnapping, ask her about it, ask if she was okay, whisper behind her back?

Couldn't it all just ... go away?

Yeah. Tell them I'm good, she typed.

You know how I told you about Samantha's new pants? The ones she wears all the time?

Yeah

Guess who came to school today with the SAME pants

I don't know. Kyla?

No. Mrs. Huber!!!

Abigail giggled. *OMG* she typed. She realized it was the first time she laughed since she had escaped. It felt ... good.

She took a deep breath, then logged into her Instagram account. Her face—grim, eyes puffy—stared at her. And the nasty caption, ending with the hashtag #WeGotAbigail.

She selected the image and deleted it. Then she deleted the others.

Those images would never be gone. They were everywhere, in news articles, blogs, shared on Instagram, Facebook, Twitter ... But she didn't need them in her own account.

After a moment's hesitation, she positioned herself in front of the window of her bedroom, lifted her phone, and snapped several photos.

She looked at them in the gallery. Far from the best selfies she'd ever taken, but one of them was good enough.

She uploaded the image. She hesitated for a minute, started writing a caption, deleted it, tried writing something else, deleted that too. She finally just wrote #AbigailIsHome, and hit *Share*.

INTERESTED in reading additional Glenmore Park books? Great! You can try:

Spider's Web - *Detective Mitchell Lonnie is pursuing The Deadly Messenger, a psychotic serial killer. But when his sister gets involved, the stakes rise very high.* Get it on Amazon at:

WWW.AMAZON.COM/DP/B01G7AB5MI

Deadly Web - *One Night, Two Dead Victims. Killers Don't Patiently Wait Their Turn Before Committing Murder.* Get it on Amazon at:

WWW.AMAZON.COM/DP/B01G4AL7V0

You can subscribe to Mike Omer's mailing list to receive a notification when future Glenmore Park books will be released at:

STRANGEREALM.COM/MAILINGLIST/

ABOUT THE AUTHOR

Mike Omer is the author of the Glenmore Park Mystery Series. He has been in the past a journalist, a game developer and the CEO of the company Loadingames. He is married to a woman who diligently forces him to live his dream, and the father of an angel, a pixie and a gremlin. He has two voracious hounds that *wag their tail quite menacingly* at anyone who comes near his home.

Mike loves to write about true people who are perpetrators or victims of crimes. He also likes writing funny stuff. He mixes these two loves quite passionately into his mystery books.

You can contact Mike by sending him an e-mail to

MIKE@STRANGEREALM.COM

ACKNOWLEDGMENTS

This book, like all my other books, couldn't have been written without my wife Liora. She knows when to cheer me on, and when to tell me that "I just need to rewrite the first half." She never hesitates, even when I stomp my foot and shout that it isn't fair. She's the strongest supporter anyone could wish for, and I can't believe my luck.

Thanks to Christine Mancuso for giving me thoughtful, invaluable chapter by chapter comments, which helped me get this book just right.

Thanks to Richard Stockford who answered all of my questions with the patience and diligence of a saint.

Thanks to Tammi Labrecque for editing this novel. This would have been unreadable without her. As always, she outdid herself.

Thanks to all of the authors in Author's Corner, for the endless support, sharing their knowledge, their wisdom, their jokes and their stickers. It's the only place that I visit every day.

Thanks to my parents for both their invaluable advice and their endless support.

Printed in Great Britain
by Amazon